"Embarrassment burns a lot of calories."

Sara followed that statement with another spoonful of ice cream. "I'm thinking of writing a diet book."

"I don't think your diet will catch on," Janey said.

"It's not the most pleasant way to lose weight."

Janey shook her head. "It's just that most women can't stick to a diet for six days. You've been embarrassing yourself over Max for what, six years now?"

Sara dropped her spoon into the carton and sat back in her chair. Having the last half decade of her life boiled down to that one basic truth made her feel like throwing up.

"I'm sorry, Sara. I didn't mean to hurt your feelings. But it's only a matter of time before someone's seriously injured or you're completely bankrupt or both."

"Yeah, a short time," Sara agreed. "I almost wish I could stop loving Max. The only problem is how do I do it?"

Dear Reader,

I've always believed that humor is an essential part of love and marriage. After eighteen years, three kids and numerous pets, there've been times when my choice was to either laugh or scream. You know what I'm talking about, right? The kids give each other haircuts or the new puppy chews a hole in the living-room carpet and everyone else finds it hilarious, so you just have to laugh along with them.

Sara Lewis is having a lot of those moments lately, except she doesn't need dogs or kids to be accident-prone. All she needs is Max Devlin. One look at him and she can't remember she has feet, let alone what to do with them. Before she knows it, she's involved in some sort of accident, and Max is laughing along with the whole town. Worse yet, everyone in the small, eccentric community of Erskine, Montana, knows she's in love with him—everyone but Max!

When she confesses the truth, Max discovers just what she's been going through—because suddenly he's having accidents of his own. Can he overcome the messy divorce in his past and open his heart again before Sara leaves town for good—not only for his and Sara's sake, but for the good of his eight-year-old son?

I hope you love Sara, Max and Joey, and their story, as much as I enjoyed bringing it to life. And look for the story of Sara's best friend, Janey Walters, coming in September 2005.

Penny McCusker

MAD ABOUT MAX

Penny McCusker

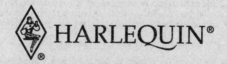

HARLEQUIN®

TORONTO • NEW YORK • LONDON
AMSTERDAM • PARIS • SYDNEY • HAMBURG
STOCKHOLM • ATHENS • TOKYO • MILAN • MADRID
PRAGUE • WARSAW • BUDAPEST • AUCKLAND

ISBN 0-373-75067-6

MAD ABOUT MAX

Copyright © 2005 by Penny McCusker.

This edition published by arrangement with Harlequin Books S.A.

® and TM are trademarks of the publisher. Trademarks indicated with
® are registered in the United States Patent and Trademark Office, the
Canadian Trade Marks Office and in other countries.

www.eHarlequin.com

Printed in U.S.A.

For Mom and Dad; it started fifty-five years ago.
Nine kids, seventeen grandkids and eight
great-grandkids later it's still going strong.
That's love. And maybe a little insanity.

Chapter One

"Please tell me that wasn't superglue."

Sara Lewis tore her gaze away from the gorgeous—and worried—blue eyes of Max Devlin, looking up to where her hands were flattened against the wall over his head. Even when she saw the damning evidence squished between her right palm and her third-grade class's mangled Open House banner, she refused to admit it, even to herself.

If she admitted she was holding a drained tube of superglue in her hand, she might begin to wonder if there'd been any stray drops. And where they might have landed. That sort of speculation would only lead her to conclusions she'd be better off not drawing, conclusions like there was no way a stray drop could have landed on the floor. Not with her body plastered to Max's. No, that kind of speculation would lead her right smack-dab into trouble.

As if she could have gotten into any more trouble.

She'd been standing on a chair, putting up the banner her third-grade class had created to welcome their parents to Erskine Elementary's Open House. But her hands had jerked when she heard Max's voice out in the hallway, and she'd torn it clear in half. She'd grabbed the tube of glue off her desk to save the irreplaceable strip of laboriously scrawled greetings and brilliant artwork, and jumped back on her chair, only to find Max already there. He'd grabbed one end of the banner, then dived for the other as it fluttered away. Now he was spread-eagled against the wall, clutching both ends of the banner, trapped by Sara and her chair.

She'd pulled the ragged ends of the banner together, but just as she'd started to glue them, Max had turned around and nearly knocked her over. "Hold still," she'd said sharply, not quite allowing herself to notice that he was facing her now, that perfect male body against hers, that heart-stopping face only inches away. Instead, she'd asked him to hold the banner in place while she applied the glue. The rest was history. Or in her case infamy.

"Uh, Sara…" Max was trying to slide out from between her and the wall, but she met his eyes again and shook her head.

"Just a little longer, Max. I want to make sure the glue is dry."

What she really needed was a moment to figure out how badly she'd humiliated herself this time. Experimentally, she stuck her backside out. Sure enough, the front of her red pleather skirt tented dead center, stuck fast to the lowermost pearl button on Max's shirt—the button that was just above his belt buckle, which was right above his—

Sara slammed her hips back against his belly, an automatic reaction intended to halt the dangerous direction of her thoughts and hide the proof of her latest misadventure. It was like throwing fuel on the fire her imagination had started.

Max's breath whooshed out, hot and moist against the inner slopes of her breasts. She didn't waste time wondering how she could feel his breath right through her heavy angora sweater. It made perfect sense, considering that his face was buried between her breasts, his mouth right at the bottom of her breastbone.

Too bad the sweater wasn't a V-neck, Sara caught herself

thinking, a low, cleavage-baring V-neck. Her front-clasp bra would have posed no problem to a talented man like Max Devlin, and his mouth was there anyway. Blood rushed into her face, then drained away to throb deep and low, just about where his belt buckle was digging into her—

"Sara!"

She snapped back to reality, noting the exasperation in his voice, even muffled as it was by the regrettably turtle-necked sweater. Reluctantly, she arched away from him. The man had to breathe, after all.

"There's a perfectly reasonable explanation for this," she said in a perfectly reasonable tone of voice. In fact, that tone amazed her, considering that she was pressed against a man she'd been secretly in love with for the better part of six years.

"There always is, Sara," Max said, exasperation giving way to amusement. "There was a perfectly reasonable explanation for how Mrs. Tilford's cat wound up on top of the church bell tower."

Sara grimaced.

"There was a perfectly reasonable explanation for why Jenny Hastings went into the Crimp 'N Cut a blonde and came out a redhead. Barn-red."

Sara cringed.

"And there was a perfectly reasonable explanation for the new stained-glass window in the town hall looking more like an advertisement for a brothel than a reenactment of Erskine's founding father rescuing the Indian maidens."

She huffed out a breath, indignant. "I only broke the one pane."

"Yeah, the pane between the grateful, kneeling maidens and the very happy Jim 'Mountain Man' Erskine."

"The talk would die down if the mayor let me get the pane

fixed instead of just shoving the rest of them together so it looked like the Indian maidens were, well, really grateful."

"People are coming from miles around to see it," Max reminded her. "He'd lose the vote of every businessman in town if he ruined the best moneymaker they've ever had."

Sara huffed out another breath. It was a little hypocritical for the people of Erskine, Montana, to pick on her for something they were capitalizing on, especially when she did have a perfectly good reason for why it had happened, why bad luck seemed to follow her around like a black cloud. Except she couldn't tell anyone what that reason was, especially not Max. Because he was the reason.

One look at him and all she could think about was how it would feel to have his mouth on hers, his hands on her body, the long, solid length of him pressing her down into a soft mattress or a haystack or against a wall... Sara glanced away from the white-painted cement block just inches from her face, but she couldn't hide from the truth.

She loved a man who'd closed off his heart, a man who tossed up a barrier whenever a woman got too close to him. Except for her, Sara thought. He seemed perfectly content with her friendship, and she was too afraid of losing it to ask him for anything more, so she did her best to hide her feelings and, while she was concentrating on that, something embarrassing always happened.

But that wasn't really the point, Sara reminded herself. The point was that she was superglued to Max Devlin.

"I'm sorry, Max."

She didn't have to elaborate. He looked down to where her skirt and his button were getting up close and personal, then at her face again. His expression, raised eyebrows and half smile, said it all.

"At least the superglue isn't dripping anymore."

"Sara, Sara, Sara," he said with a chuckle that resonated through her ribs and did serious damage to her heart. "What am I going to do with you?"

She could have told him, if her breath hadn't backed up in her lungs, if the thought of what she wanted him to do to her didn't have all the blood draining out of her brain so she couldn't even put words to the images that haunted her nights and dazzled her days. She would have told him, if she'd had the courage.

"Unstick me," she said, then found herself almost wishing she was talking about more than her skirt.

Six years was a long time to love a man who only considered her a friend, a long time to love that man's son as if he were her own. A long time to dream… Without Max there would be a huge hole in her life, but Sara wanted more than a friend. She wanted a man to sit down to dinner with each night, a man to share her joys and sorrows, a man to give her children of her own. The longer she held out for the impossible, the longer she would be ignoring the possible.

She stared down into Max's laughing eyes and accepted that she was just too stubborn to believe anything was impossible.

"Is the banner all right?" Max asked.

Sarah took one last rewardingly deep breath and glanced up. Somehow she'd managed to repair the off-center tear so well, even she could barely see the seam from less than a foot away. "Move your hands," she said.

Max dropped his arms, rolling his shoulders and whistling out a breath.

Sara eased her hands off the banner, first one, then the other, keeping them within easy slapping distance, just in case. The paper sagged a bit in the middle, then settled. She let out her pent-up breath. "It's holding."

"I'm sure glad to hear that."

She let her arms drop, forgetting that she was standing on a child's classroom chair. Max caught her around the hips just as she lost her footing on the slippery wooden seat.

Sara froze. Not just her body—her heart stopped, she quit breathing and time, as she knew it, ground to a halt. Her eyelids fluttered down, her gaze accidentally colliding with Max's, eyes as blue as the flame of a Bunsen burner. He flexed his fingers, and every nerve in her body shrieked back to life. Her heart lurched into an unsteady rhythm, the blood pounding where his fingers bracketed her hips. Purely out of self-defense, she braced her hands on his shoulders and tried to climb down from the chair. Away from him.

The wash of cool air on her thighs stopped her. Of course, she thought, closing her eyes and heaving out a shaky breath, she was still joined to Max by the bonds of holy superglue. She longed to get naked with him, but not in her classroom, mere moments before twenty-five third-graders and their parents were due to arrive for Open House. She had to get out of this embarrassing situation before someone saw her. If that meant giving Max a close-up of her shockingly unteacherlike black satin panties, so be it.

Max wasn't as anxious to put her modesty on the line as she was. "Uh, I think you should stay where you are," he said, his hands tightening on her hips, his wary eyes on the way her hemline rose when she tried again to step down from the chair.

"Half the town is going to walk in that door in a few minutes." Or a few seconds, Sara corrected, as the sound of voices and footsteps drifted in from the hallway, reminding her that her clock was at least five minutes slow.

Peep show and Max's hands be damned, she jumped down from the chair and leaned to the right, grabbing the scissors off her desk. Max's mouth dropped open, but Sara didn't give him time to react to seeing a lethal weapon in the hand of someone who couldn't walk straight half the time. She snipped, and in a show of grace and balance the likes of which no ballet dancer could have duplicated and no one in Erskine would have believed her capable, she raced to the peg across the room, grabbed her art apron off the hook and slipped it over her head, tying it and turning just as sixty pounds of eight-year-old launched himself into her arms.

"Hi, Sara—I mean, Miss Lewis," Joey said, his arms tight about her waist.

Sara's heart melted, all her self-consciousness draining away. "Hi yourself, Mr. Devlin." She hugged Joey back, then let him go, her smile coming more easily and sincerely as she welcomed the students and parents streaming into the classroom. This was where she belonged, where she felt competent and confident, no matter what.

She didn't look at Max again, didn't have to assure herself that he'd found a way to cover that damning swatch of red pleather sticking to his shirt button. If anyone saw it and figured out why she was wearing a paint-blotched apron, he'd be just as embarrassed as she would.

"Hey, Sara—" Joey tugged on her sleeve, too, just in case his exuberant words didn't get her attention.

"Hey, Joey." She ruffled his sandy-brown hair, so much like his father's. Max Devlin had it all in the looks department— sun-bleached hair that made her hands itch to brush it from his brow, sparkling blue eyes and a smile that always made her breath catch. His son was going to be just as big a heartbreaker when he grew up.

"Dad let me sleep over at Jason Hartfield's last night."

"Good for you." And for Max, Sara thought as she hunkered down. Joey was the only family Max had; he rarely let the boy out of his sight for anything other than school. She was glad he'd realized that Joey was old enough to go farther afield than the old bunkhouse she rented on their ranch. And that he'd been wise enough to let him go. "Did you have a good time?"

"The best. We went hiking and had a bonfire and stayed up late watching scary movies and eating popcorn. It was almost ten o'clock before Mrs. Hartfield made us turn off the light."

"Ten o'clock. Wow," Sara said, suitably impressed. "And I'll bet you were still up at five in the morning to help Jason with his chores 'cause that's the kind of friend you are."

He blushed, his grubby tennis shoe tracing the ribbons of color wound through the dark blue background of the new carpeting. "It was no big deal," he mumbled. "Hey, did Dad tell you he gave me a colt of my own? He says I'm old enough now."

He was growing too fast, Sara thought, her heart aching with love and pride, and a slight pang at how quickly time was passing. Not long ago he'd been a toddler she'd sung lullabies to, then a preschooler with such an appetite for knowledge that she'd had to teach him to read so she wouldn't spend every spare minute reading to him. She'd battled back the same tears of pride and joy on his first day of school, and every milestone since, that she was experiencing now.

If there'd been any justice in the world Joey would have belonged to her instead of a woman who wanted fame and fortune badly enough to trade in a good man and a wonderful son for minor roles in B movies. But life didn't work that way, and Sara counted herself lucky just for the blessings she'd been given.

Joey tugged on her sleeve, waiting until she focused on him again. "I named my colt Spielberg, Sara. He's six months old and Dad's going to help me raise him. I get to feed him and brush him—Dad says that's so he'll get used to me and start depending on me. And when Spielberg is two, Dad's going to help me saddle-break him."

"What a lucky kid you are." Sara smiled and nudged him with her elbow, eight-year-old style, so he wouldn't get embarrassed again. "If you want, I'll lend you my video camera and you can document the whole thing."

Joey's eyes widened. His fondest wish was to become a movie director—which explained the colt's name. "Would you really do that?"

"Absolutely. The camera just sits around most of the time, and I know you'll take good care of it."

"If he doesn't, I'll ground him for life," Max said as he came to stand beside his son. He put one hand on Joey's shoulder and reached the other out to her.

Sara took it, let him help her to her feet, then hung on to him when she wobbled unsteadily.

"You okay?" Max asked.

"My foot's asleep," she lied, letting go of his hand even though she had the perfect excuse to keep holding it. Most of the adults in the room were watching avidly, and she wasn't about to give them any more entertainment than she had to. "Joey was just telling me about Spielberg—the horse, not the director."

"Yeah," Max chuckled. "I guess he caught the movie bug from his mom. You sure you want to hang that name on him, pal?"

"Yep," Joey said matter-of-factly, then changed the subject between one breath and the next. "Hey, Sara—"

"Miss Lewis," Max corrected, his deep voice sending shivers down Sara's spine.

"Sorry, S—Miss Lewis. Dad and me're going to the church hall for ice cream after the Open House. Are you coming, too?"

"Um…" Sara usually avoided the town dances, ice-cream socials and potluck dinners, afraid she'd do something clumsy and wind up ruining everyone's time. She glanced at Max and knew that he knew what she was thinking. His sympathy made her want to cry, though it felt more like frustration than gratitude. "I don't think so, Joey."

"But everyone in town will be there, Sara. You can drive over with Dad and me in the pickup."

"Sara has her own car," Max pointed out.

"That would be dumb when we're all going to the same place," Joey said.

Max shrugged and gave Sara a resigned smile. "I think Joey wants you to come have ice cream with us."

Not as much as she did. The three of them in the cab of Max's pickup, headed to a town gathering, was like a picture of heaven to her. Like they were a real family... "I'll think about it," Sara said, knowing she'd already given it way too much thought for her own good. That dream was so big a part of her life that she was very careful not to indulge herself too much, in case she stepped over the line between fantasy and reality.

"Okay," Joey said, his face lighting up when he spied the Hartfields coming in the door. "Jason's here," he said, all but dancing with excitement, then catapulting across the room to greet his friend before Max had time to do more than nod.

Sara glanced over at Max, whatever she'd been about to say incinerated when she caught him staring at her apron—right about the place where that little diamond-shaped hole in her skirt would be. Which reminded her... She let her gaze drift up, casually, to where the matching bit of red pleather was, or should have been.

"I tucked it down below my waistband," Max said by way of explanation. "The shirt is so tight on the back of my neck I feel like it's trying to saw its way through my spine, but what's a little paralysis compared to a lady's honor?"

Sara risked a glance at his face. He was smiling, his eyes sparkling like the sun on water.

She looked away before she did something stupid, like tell him just how desperately she loved him. "Thank you," she managed to choke out.

"No problem," Max said with the same kind of offhanded shrug his son used so often. "You getting a cold?"

Sara cleared her throat and kept her eyes off him so it wouldn't tighten up again. "I guess I must be."

"You should go home early, fix yourself a whiskey, lemon and honey and tuck yourself into bed with a hot-water bottle."

"That sounds like just the cure."

"Dad!"

"Gotta go, Sara. You take care of yourself."

"Mmm-hmm," Sara mumbled, looking up in time to see Max saunter off toward his son. And he knew just how to saunter, she thought as she watched his long, strong legs carry him and his jeans-clad backside away from her.

"You should tuck yourself into bed with something hot all right, but if I were you, I'd try the doctor rather than his cure."

"Janey!" Sara glanced around, worried that someone had overheard her best friend—her only friend, aside from Max— and the one person she could confide in *about* Max. Without Janey Walters's friendship, unquestioning support and wicked sense of humor, Sara knew she'd have gone off the deep end years ago.

"Relax," Janey said. "I'm not about to let anyone hear me talking like that. I have a reputation to uphold in this town."

"So do I," Sara said glumly.

"Aw, poor Sara." Janey stuck out her bottom lip in sympathy, and put her arm around Sara's shoulders. "People just pick on you because you're an outsider. One of them city gals," she added in an overdone drawl.

"I've been here almost six years," Sara muttered. "When do I get to be one of you folk?"

"When pigs fly," Janey said matter-of-factly. "Either you grow up around here or you marry someone from around here—then you get accepted by default. It's tradition."

Sara felt even more dejected by that. "I can't change the past, and it doesn't look like I have much hope for the future, either."

"Don't take it so hard. Everyone knows you're the best thing to hit this town since government ranching subsidies. Wondering what you'll do next is more entertaining than anything on TV, and more lucrative, too."

"Thanks," Sara said on a heavy exhalation. "I'd managed to forget about the pool."

Mike Shasta, owner of the Ersk Inn, had run the betting pools in town longer than anyone could remember. There were the normal sports, and things like who was going to have the prize bull at the county fair that year. Of course pretty much everyone voted for themselves in that one, and few of the ranchers had time to sit around watching sports, especially during the summer, so the baseball pool had never been what Mike called successful. Hockey came in the winter, so it typically did the best of all the sports pools.

But never as well as the Sara Lewis pool.

The Sara Lewis pool was a big white sheet of poster board that hung on the wall of the Ersk Inn, with dates across the top and times down the side, forming squares for each sixty-minute interval. People paid five dollars to put their name in a square, hoping they'd be lucky enough to choose the occurrence of her next accident. As technology went, it wasn't exactly state of the art, but that poster board did the job. As a matter of fact, it got a lot of attention, Sara had heard. As if making a fool of herself every few weeks wasn't enough, practically the whole town spent a good portion of their leisure time hoping she'd do it again and keeping a sharp eye out to make sure they didn't miss it when she did. If anyone but Max had known why she was wearing a paint-stained art apron at Open House…

It didn't bear thinking about. Much as she loved Janey and trusted her silence, Sara wouldn't even tell her best friend that she'd accidentally superglued herself to Max. Of all the things she'd done, this was the most humiliating yet.

All she had to do, Sara told herself, was get through the rest of the evening with no one the wiser. It couldn't be all that hard, and as the evening progressed, it seemed as if she might just pull it off. No one asked about her apron, and the scavenger hunt she and the children had set up was a big success, every parent ending up with a prize all the more precious for having been made by their own child's hands. Sara stayed away from Max, which meant that she kept her composure.

And missed the moment when he let the cat out of the bag.

A school event was no different from any other social occasion in town. The women gathered in one corner to trade recipes and organize the next potluck. The men gathered in another to discuss the price of beef and swap fish stories. Aside from Joey, if there was anything in the world Max liked more than his ranch, it was fishing. And if there was one thing universal to great fishing stories, it was exaggeration.

Max apparently lifted his arms to lend credence to his latest one-that-got-away tale, and the red pleather-decorated button popped right out of the waistband of his pants.

It was the sudden hush from that corner of the room that first caught Sara's attention. She glanced over in time to hear The Question.

"Hey, Max, what's that on your button?"

Sara really didn't blame Max. It was an accident, and if there was anything she understood it was accidents. Just like she understood when he fumbled for an answer, his gaze automatically shooting to her.

That stereotype about big, dumb cowboys was just that— a stereotype. As if it had been choreographed, the circle of men turned and looked at her, back at Max's traitorous button, then back at her, this time their eyes dropping inevitably to her skirt—or what could be seen of it behind her apron. Her big, concealing apron.

The room erupted in shouts, questions about who had the winning square and laughter. Parents and students from the surrounding classes crowded in, attracted by the pandemonium, until the room was overflowing. Sara found herself at the front of the room, standing right beneath that troublesome banner as the whole embarrassing story came out.

After one glance at Max, his only assistance to shrug apologetically, Sara let everyone laugh and tease her good-naturedly, smiling and going along with the jokes. She caught sight of Jenny Hastings, her hair cropped boyishly short except for the tiniest fringe of barn-red. If Jenny could withstand the fallout of one of Sara's episodes, Sara could surely take it—within reason.

She let the ribbing go on for a full fifteen minutes, then held up her hands, her sudden willingness to talk bringing an instant hush to the room. "All that matters is that we saved the banner," she said, looking up at the item in question—just at the moment it decided to come loose.

The superglued center seam parted with a quiet whoosh, the two sides of the banner floating down right over her head. As if that wasn't enough, the tacks she'd used to hold up the corners suddenly popped out, wreathing Sara in ten feet of white paper that smelled like crayon and felt like the weight of the world settling on her shoulders.

She slumped back against the blackboard, listening as

everyone filed out of the room. Even when Max offered to help her, she sent him on his way. As accidents went, having a paper banner over her head wasn't so bad. At least it hid her tears.

Chapter Two

"Hi, Dad!"

Max shouldered the fifty-pound sack of grain he'd been about to load into the back of his pickup and turned toward the entrance of the feed store to see Joey running in his direction. Sara stood in the open doorway, one hand on the jamb, the other lifted to shade her eyes from the bright sunshine so she could see into the dim interior.

Joey was halfway across the cavernous space when he veered off suddenly, like a heat-seeking missile. Only in Joey's case, it was kittens that drew him, a whole carton of them with FREE written on the side in big, bold letters.

Just what he needed, Max thought as he bumped the sack up and off his shoulder, letting it fall onto the pile in the back of the pickup. Joey already had a hamster, three goldfish, a parakeet and two dogs, and those were the indoor pets. But even if he'd known about the kittens when he asked Sara to drop Joey off after school, Max still would've done it. It would be worth adding to the menagerie if he succeeded in dragging her out of her self-imposed isolation. And dragging, he figured, was exactly what it would take, considering that she was going to leave without even saying hello to him or goodbye to Joey.

"Sara, wait," he called before she could do more than turn around.

For a minute it seemed she was going to pretend she hadn't heard him. Then she turned back, stepped through the doorway and stood there, seeming about as relaxed as a sinner at the Pearly Gates.

Max supposed he should feel sorry for her, but he wasn't really in a sympathetic mood. Impatient was more like it, with enough confusion thrown in to remind him that Sara was a woman and when a woman was involved in any sort of relationship, a man never completely understood what was going on. He knew Sara well enough to have a pretty good idea, though.

After one of her accidents, she usually kept a low profile, staying away from the more public places and the more vocal residents of Erskine. That had never included him before, but then, neither had one of her accidents.

She must still be embarrassed by what had happened two weeks ago, and no wonder. It couldn't have been pleasant for Sara to have her hips pressed to his—to find herself stuck to a man she considered a brother. And being a woman, she just naturally couldn't let it go and forget it like he could. At least not until they got the awkward first meeting over with.

"I've barely seen you in two weeks," Max called out. "Come over and talk to me while I finish loading up."

But instead of reaching for the next sack, he leaned against the side of his pickup, hooked his thumbs in his front pockets and watched Sara walk across the feed store. He couldn't resist. Even with her normally bubbly personality weighted down by embarrassment, she exuded so much energy that a person's eyes were naturally drawn to her.

Copper-colored curls bounced around her shoulders with every step. Her dark, lively eyes sparkled, and the corners of her mouth were lifted in the slight smile that rarely left her face. She wasn't beautiful by the standards set for magazines or movie screens, but she had more charm and personality than any actress or model. And she was a lot more entertaining. Just watching her was a spectator sport, even on a day where the most interesting thing she did was choose what to wear.

Today it was a flame-bright orange sweater, black tights dotted with jack-o'-lanterns—in honor of the big day coming at the end of the week—and a black skirt that flared and floated around her slender thighs and hips with every jaunty step.

Max got a sudden, strong flash of the way those hips had felt between his palms two weeks ago, the resilient feel of her flesh where his fingers had gripped her, the warmth of all that tight, fake red leather. And then there'd been that hole she'd snipped in her skirt. He could have sworn he saw black lace through that hole.

He dropped that memory like a mental hot potato. Thinking about Sara and black lace at the same time was just wrong.

She belonged to the white-cotton set, that asexual group of females in every man's life who baked cookies, stepped in to baby-sit at a moment's notice and knew how to heal any injury with a Band-Aid and a kiss. Aside from Joey, Sara was the closest thing to a family Max had, and if there'd been a time, once, when he might have seen her in a different light, a more romantic light, he'd deep-sixed the thought before it could even begin to take hold.

He had a dismal record when it came to love and marriage—all the men in his family did. His grandmother had died young, leaving his grandfather alone to raise a young son and run a ranch. His father and mother had called it quits before they'd been married ten years, and his own marriage had lasted substantially less time. Instead of heeding the lessons he'd learned by example, Max had been young and foolish enough to try the "love conquers all" route. The only thing love conquered, he'd learned, was any man by the name of Devlin.

At least, Joey didn't have to be shuttled from household to household, like he'd been. Julia, his ex-wife, hadn't asked for anything from their marriage but her freedom. She'd wanted Hollywood, she had the looks for it, and Lord knows she'd done a damned good job *acting* like a wife and mother during their few years together.

No, that wasn't entirely fair. They'd wanted different things, he and Julia, and she'd loved him once, enough to give him a son. For that alone he would never regret his marriage. And regardless of the terms of their divorce, she did her best by Joey, visiting when she could, occasionally calling him on the phone and having him out to stay with her in the summer, no matter what she had to do to swing it. Usually, though, it was just father and son. The same as it had always been in his family.

A man with that kind of sorry history had no right getting involved with any woman, let alone the settling kind like Sara. She deserved someone who could come to her fresh and loving, and give her the home and family she deserved.

It was just a matter of time before some lucky guy whisked her off to the altar and out of his life. When that day came, Max would be the first to congratulate her and wish her well. When that day came…

Frowning, he tore his eyes off her and bent to lift another sack of grain. But he knew when she stopped behind him, even before he caught a faint whiff of her perfume. "Where are you off to—" he paused to launch the sack off his shoulder and into the truck "—in such a hurry that you can't even say hi to a friend?"

"Groceries," she said. "It was either the diner or the market, and at least at the market I can stock up so I won't have to eat out. Or shop again for a while."

Anything to stay out of town until the hubbub blew over, Max interpreted, and had to hide his grin before he turned to face her. It was good to hear her sounding like her old self again. "You could always go out on the range and catch yourself a steer."

She shook her head, the corners of her mouth curving up into a reluctant grin. "As long as they stay out of town, they're safe from me."

"Now that's not strictly true, Sara. Remember the time old man Winston's cows got out and wandered into the road? It's a good thing I was fixing his fence when you happened by. If you hadn't seen me waving my red flag of a shirt and shouting like a lunatic, you would've driven head-on into the middle of them."

"Lucky for me you were there, Max, and that you happened to have your shirt off at the time so you could use it to catch my attention."

"It was lucky, all right. You didn't get hurt, and the cows started giving milk again after about a week or so."

"If you're trying to cheer me up, you can stop now."

Max laughed, finally understanding her sarcasm. "I'm almost done here," he said. "If you wait a few minutes, the human stomach and I will go to the market with you. We must be out of something the way Joey eats."

Sara's smile dimmed. "Thanks, Max, but I think…it might be better if I go alone. I mean, after the glue and all, you know…" She looked at the floor, her even white teeth worrying at her bottom lip before she met his eyes again. "I wouldn't want anyone getting the wrong idea. About you and me."

"I think we can risk being seen together in public without anyone getting the wrong idea."

"Yeah," Sara said on a heavy sigh, the thought of braving the teasing of her friends and neighbors obviously pulling her mood down again.

Max could have kicked himself for bringing it up after he'd worked so hard to make her smile, but he didn't have to rack his brain for a way to cheer her up again. Joey did it for him. He ran up just then, two mixed-breed kittens clinging precariously to his jacket by their needle-sharp claws and mewing pitifully. "Mr. Landry says I can have them both."

As grateful as he was for the return of Sara's company, Max wasn't about to reward his son with a pair of kittens. "They're not even weaned yet, Joey."

"They must be, Dad. The mom cat is gone and there's a dog in there with them."

"I know. Mr. Landry told me... I'm afraid the kittens' mother died, son. It just so happened that Mr. Landry's dog had weaned a litter of pups not long before, so he brought her in to see if she'd adopt the kittens and she did. It happens sometimes."

Joey thought for a second, then shrugged as if it were an everyday occurrence for a dog to adopt a bunch of newborn kittens. Of course in his world, Max reflected sadly, mothers went away and life carried on.

"Can I have them when they're weaned?" Joey asked, his one-track mind barely making a detour.

"Who's going to take care of them all day while you're at school?"

"Sara will let me bring them to school, won't you, Sara? They can be..." Joey's face scrunched up, but in the end he puffed out his breath in defeat. "What's it called when they belong to the whole class?"

"Mascots?" Sara supplied.

"That's it! They can be mascots to the third grade. We can all take turns bringing them home on the weekends."

"I doubt Mrs. Erskine-Lippert will agree to that," Sara said.

Joey snorted. "Ooh, the principal. I heard Mr. Jamison, the sixth-grade teacher, call her Mrs. Irksome. I was gonna look it up in the dictionary, but I figured it meant, you know, trouble. And I couldn't spell it," he added as an afterthought.

"You shouldn't repeat things like that," Max admonished. He managed to hide his smile, but his eyes, when he lifted them to meet Sara's, were shining with amusement.

She couldn't help smiling back, her sadness lifting as she watched father and son bicker good-naturedly over the kittens. She might not have Max's love, let alone his ring on her finger, and she might not have a paper labeling her Joey's mother, but she still got moments like this, precious pearls strung between the humdrum, lonely hours that made up the greater part of her life. And who, she asked herself, could ask for more than that?

"I'll make you a deal," Max said to his son, resorting to bribery when reason didn't work. "If you leave the kittens here, I'll take you to the diner and you can have anything you want."

Joey stopped in midobjection. "Anything I want?"

"Yep, and we'll take Sara with us and feed her some pie— just as soon as I'm finished." He had to yell the last part because Joey was already running across the feed store to return the kittens to their cardboard home. "And then we'll take you to the market afterward," Max said to Sara.

"It's nice of you to invite me, but—"

"No buts. It's been two weeks since…you know," he finished, bending to heft another sack and muscle it into the truck bed. "You can't hide away forever."

No, she couldn't hide away forever, and even if she could, Sara thought, the people of Erskine would still be waiting to rub her nose in what had happened at the Open House. It wasn't just that, however; she didn't think she could bear to spend the next few hours with Max. For two weeks she'd been trying to forget those few seconds she'd spent plastered against him. Her memory was just too darned vivid; all she had to do was close her eyes and she was back there again, fighting a real battle with spontaneous combustion.

Watching him work only fanned the flames. He bent, lifted, twisted and dropped each sack, the slide and bunch of muscle beneath worn denim and plaid making her heart pound and her breath shorten until her head began to spin. She couldn't have taken a steady step if her life depended on it; going to the diner with him would be sheer foolishness. Worse than tempting fate, she would be daring fate to make a fool of her again.

"Really, Max, I'd rather just go home and open a can of soup," she said, her voice growing stronger when she pulled her gaze off his backside. "I have a lot of papers to grade tonight, anyway."

"What papers?" Joey asked as he rejoined them. "You let us grade each other's papers today."

"And I still have to check them over," she said to Joey, tweaking the hair that was growing past his collar. "Maybe your dad should take you to get a haircut, instead, and I'll bake you a whole pie of your own this weekend. Cherry."

Cherry pie was one of the basic food groups to Joey, but he didn't even waver. "Nope. Dad promised me the diner and he never goes back on a promise."

"Well, then, you guys have a good time, and maybe I'll see you later at the ranch."

"Nope, Sara, I promised you the diner and I never go back on a promise." Max bent to lift the last sack of feed and heave it into the truck.

The combination of all those muscles flexing and the sexy little grunt he uttered completely stalled Sara's thought processes. If Jack the Ripper had popped in and asked her to take a walk, she'd have wandered into the closest alley with him, no questions asked, so it was no wonder she said okay to Max.

She watched, dazed, as he pulled an old, faded bandanna from his back pocket and wiped his face, but it wasn't until he yelled out to Mrs. Landry that he was leaving his truck in the feed store for a while that she snapped out of her haze and realized what she'd done.

Max gestured for her to precede him, and Sara had no choice. He figured he was helping her get over her latest humiliation, and she didn't have the courage to tell him otherwise. Maybe if she didn't look at him she'd be okay.

The street side of the feed store was a huge door that rolled aside to let vehicles in to be loaded. In the middle of the large door was a smaller pedestrian door. Max opened it, warning Sara to step over the lip at the bottom. And just to make sure she didn't trip, he cupped her left elbow.

She tripped.

How could she stay upright with his fingers wrapped around her arm, shooting heat and need into her bloodstream in such a quick and overwhelming burst that she forgot she even *had* feet, let alone what she was supposed to do with them?

Max's fingers tightened around her arm, hard enough to bruise, but Sara stumbled forward anyway, right into the flow of pedestrian traffic on the crowded sidewalk of the town's main street. Her right arm shot out for balance, knocking a bag of groceries from old Mrs. Barnett's arms. The sack hit the sidewalk, but Sara barely noticed the brown paper bottom burst open, disgorging an assortment of cans and boxes, along with a spreading puddle of white.

Max and Joey stooped to help the elderly woman salvage what she could of her groceries. Sara went after the half-dozen oranges that had tumbled out of the bag and headed for freedom, oblivious to the potential for disaster. She managed to scoop up five of them and place them in the shallow pocket formed when she lifted the hem of her sweater. The sixth orange insisted on giving her trouble, rolling and bumping down the sidewalk between the feet of unsuspecting pedestrians as though it had a will of its own and no concept of the laws of physics.

Sara ducked and weaved like a quarterback dodging linemen, cradling her sweaterload of oranges more carefully than any football, her goal an even half-dozen rather than seven points. But every time she reached down to grab that last orange, the obnoxious little fruit managed to skip away at the last instant.

Frustrated, she elbowed her way in front of Mr. Fellowes, the undertaker, and planted her foot sideways in front of the orange. It rolled to a nice, obedient stop less than a finger's width from her arch, as if it were planning to stop there anyway. Sara bent to pick it up, and Mr. Fellowes ran smack dab into her backside.

They both went sprawling, the oranges flew out of Sara's sweater, bounding off the boardwalk and down the curb. Right into the path of the delivery boy from Yee's combination Chinese Laundry and Restaurant. He hit the brakes, too late to prevent the front tire of his bicycle from squishing a navel orange into aromatic, slippery pulp. The bike skidded, the delivery boy jumping off just before it slammed into the curb and lurched sideways.

The sack of Chinese food made a graceful arc as it flew out of the bicycle's basket, the plastic bag flapping cheerfully before it plopped down on the sidewalk, right at Sara's feet. The bundle of laundry in the rear basket slipped its paper and string constrictions, pelting her with some unfortunate man's clothing.

And to top it all off, she'd drawn a crowd.

But then how could she not? she asked herself, as she pulled a pair of white boxers from her shoulder and dropped them at her feet. She stood in the midst of chaos, a bag of Chinese food, an undertaker, a delivery boy and his bicycle at her feet. A circle of white shirts and underwear surrounded her, with oranges supplying just the right splash of color here and there. All that was missing was a tent and a couple more rings.

The stunned silence was broken, finally, by Mr. Fellowes's groan. Max eased his way through the circle of onlookers and helped the old man to his feet.

"I am so sorry, Mr. Fellowes," Sara said, rushing to take his other arm and hold on to him until he recovered his balance. She didn't look at Max. She couldn't.

"Don't give it another thought, my dear," the undertaker said. "It was more my fault than yours. After all, I collided with you."

Because she'd stopped dead in front of him. But Sara kept that to herself. Why give her friends and neighbors yet another reason to ridicule her?

Mr. Fellowes patted her hand, absently peering around him.

"Is something wrong? Aside from the obvious," Sara added, sending the snickering crowd her best glare, the one that always silenced her third-grade class. It didn't surprise her that it worked on the people of Erskine.

"I'm fine," Mr. Fellowes said. "Only…you haven't seen my eyeglasses, have you? I'm afraid I lost them when I bumped into you."

"I'm sure they're around here somewhere." Sara took a step back and heard a sickening crunch. "Um…I think I found them."

On the bright side, it was deathly quiet again. Except for the person at the back of the growing crowd who yelled, "I won!"

All Sara could think was that she'd lost. Again.

"SO WHAT DID YOU DO THEN?" Janey Walters asked, picking at the sweet-and-sour pork and cashew chicken still left on her plate.

"I did what I always do," Sara said glumly. She'd assured Mr. Fellowes and Mrs. Barnett that she'd make reparation, and given Yee's delivery boy all the cash she had on her. He'd insisted she take the sack of Chinese food, the little white containers mostly intact despite their foray into the world of flight. In the interests of escape, she'd accepted it without argument and hightailed it to Janey's big Victorian house on the edge of town. "Max tried to talk me into going to the diner with him and Joey, but…" She raised one shoulder and let it fall again, her eyes on her plate of untouched Chinese food.

"The teasing didn't use to bother you so much," Janey observed.

"It's not really the teasing, it's just…" Sara sighed. "I don't really know what it is, Janey. I couldn't face the town, and I definitely couldn't face Max."

"Why not? Isn't this partly his fault?"

"He can't help how he feels."

"Yes, he can. If he could see past the end of his nose—"

Sara shoved her plate away and bent forward, banging her head lightly on the tabletop.

Janey bit back the rest of what she'd been about to say. She felt as if she were swallowing a pincushion, but what kind of friend would she be if she vented her own anger and frustration when Sara was in no condition to hear it? "At least we got dinner out of it," she said, instead.

Sara straightened, managing a half smile. "Cold, slightly bruised Chinese food?"

Janey shrugged. "Nothing a microwave couldn't fix. And it beats leftovers, which is what was on the menu since I was dining solo tonight." Jessie, her nine-year-old daughter, was across the street having dinner with Mrs. Halliwell. Jessie didn't have any grandparents, Mrs. Halliwell didn't have any grandchildren, and it gave Janey a night off, so everybody got something out of the arrangement.

She pushed back from the table and went to the fridge, returning with a half gallon of ice cream and a bottle of chocolate syrup. "And since you brought the main course, the least I can do is supply dessert."

Sara took a spoon and the chocolate syrup, scooting her chair closer to Janey's so she could be in easier reach of the calorie comfort. "What would I do without you?"

"I don't know." Janey took a big spoonful of ice cream, closing her eyes and moaning in sheer delight. "I can tell you one thing, though. Without you I'd still be a size eight. I've eaten so much ice cream in commiseration that none of my pants fit anymore. But you, you rat, haven't gained an ounce."

"Embarrassment burns a lot of calories," Sara said around a mouthful of ice cream. "I'm thinking of writing a diet book."

"I don't think it'll catch on."

"It's not the most pleasant way to lose weight."

Janey shook her head. "It's just that most women can't stick to a diet for six days. You've been embarrassing yourself over Max ever since you came to Erskine."

"Six years." Sara set her spoon in the carton and sat back in her chair. Hearing it like that made the egg roll and ice cream in her stomach simmer and stir unpleasantly. Not that it wasn't the truth, but having the past half decade of her life boiled down to that one basic truth made her feel like throwing up.

She'd met Max Devlin when she was nineteen, a bright-eyed, eager sophomore at Boston College. Max had been a senior, there on a track scholarship, and her student advisor; he'd always known somehow when she needed a sympathetic ear or a comforting shoulder, and he'd never failed to provide it—for the short time he could.

Before midterms, Max received news that his grandfather had died suddenly. Sara had ached for him, but even if she could have found a way to help him through his grief, there'd been no opportunity. He'd lost his father to a riding accident before he'd graduated from high school, and his mother had remarried and moved to Europe. With his grandfather gone, there'd been no one to run the ranch, and Max had been faced with a choice—sell or stay home. He never came back to Boston.

Time passed, Max married, and Sara convinced herself that what she'd felt for him was nothing but gratitude for the kindness he'd shown a shy, sheltered young woman out on her own in the world. They'd kept in touch, but the frequency had dropped significantly; Max didn't have a lot of free time on his hands.

Not that Sara did, either. After graduating from college with a degree in education, her father convinced her to take a job in his company, training men and women with master's and doctorate degrees how to use software systems they fobbed off on their admins anyway.

When Max's marriage ended, leaving him with a two-year-old to look after and a ranch to run, Sara hadn't hesitated. She'd arrived in Montana, a city girl so far out of her element she'd wondered how the ranchers punched cows without hurting their hands. She'd only planned to stay long enough to help Max get things under control, but every time she mentioned leaving, he got such a look of abandonment on his face she hadn't had the heart to go through with it. In the end, it was her heart that had kept her there.

Looking back now, she could barely remember the decisions she'd made in those first confusing weeks after she realized she was in love with Max. Not that she regretted taking a job teaching third grade; she'd always longed to teach children anyway. Her new job was so much more rewarding than what she'd been doing in Boston. And it had just made sense for her to move into the old, unused bunkhouse on Max's ranch so she could be closer to Joey. And Max. Someday, she'd hoped, he would fall in love with her and make them a family.

But it seemed that Julia had taken something with her, after all, when she'd walked out of Max's life. His heart.

"I'm sorry, Sara," Janey said, "I didn't mean to hurt your feelings."

Sara dismissed that nonsense with a wave of her hand. "My feelings aren't hurt, Janey. I'm just beginning to wonder what I've been doing here all these years."

"Sounds like you've been talking to your mother again."

Sara looked up, surprised. "I talk to my mother every week."

"And she always campaigns for you to move back to Boston, so what's different this time?"

"Maybe she's right. Maybe Max won't ever see me as more than a friend."

Janey's spoon clattered to the tabletop, her mouth and eyes going wide in overdone shock—which went ignored.

"Besides, Joey's always been my excuse for staying, and he's been self-sufficient for a while now," Sara said, admitting it aloud for the first time, although she'd been thinking it more and more often. "Max really doesn't need me around anymore, and my contract is up for renewal this year...."

"He'd be devastated if you went away."

"Would he?"

"You're a huge part of his life, Sara. He loves you."

"As a friend." Sara threw herself out of her chair, pacing

the generous confines of the kitchen. "I want more, Janey. I want it all. What if he never wants the same from me?"

"Maybe he won't, but you'll never know unless you push him to make a choice."

Sara snorted softly. "You know Max. If I force him to choose, I'll lose his friendship."

"Or gain his love. Look, Sara, in some ways your mom is right. You've spent six years—"

"'Wasted' is how Mom put it. I've wasted six years."

"So it's time to take the bull by the horns and tell Max how you feel."

"Like you're doing with Jessie's father?"

"That's different." Janey slumped in her chair, scooping up a huge, half-melted glob of ice cream and letting it drip back into the carton. "I called him when I found out I was pregnant. He never called me back."

"He should still know he has a daughter."

"We're talking about you."

"Not anymore," Sara said, then gave a little bittersweet laugh. "We're quite a pair, Janey. Two young, attractive women with nothing to do but sit around and feel sorry for ourselves. There has to be a bright side to this."

"There is—for Ben & Jerry's."

"Seriously, Janey. It's time we stopped moping around and did something about what's wrong with our lives. There have to be a couple of men out there who want a home and family—"

"Whoa!" Janey held her hands up, palms out. "I have a home, and Jessie is the only family I need. Despite my recent tendency to wallow, I see no reason to shackle myself to some burping, farting, dirty-laundry machine."

Sara dropped back into her chair, tracing the pattern on the antique lace tablecloth with one fingernail. "Aren't you ever lonely?"

"Sure, but that's no excuse to get married. It's a known fact that ninety-nine percent of men completely stop talking within five days of their own wedding anyway."

"I'm not buying it." Sara had learned early on that Janey's tough exterior was only a defense mechanism to protect her soft heart. "You want to meet someone and get married as much as any woman. You just aren't ready to admit it yet."

"If I ever do, slap me."

Janey put on a belligerent face, but the look in her eyes nearly brought Sara to tears.

"But, hey," Janey continued, sitting up suddenly. "You definitely need to change a few things. It's only a matter of time before someone's seriously injured or you're completely bankrupt or both."

"Yeah, a short time," Sara agreed. "I almost wish…" She let the thought hang, then shook her head.

"What?"

"Never mind."

"Uh-uh," Janey said. "I just ingested a couple thousand calories for you. Spit it out."

"Well…there was this moment when I was superglued to Max— Stop smirking, Janey."

"You have to admit it's funny."

Sara couldn't help grinning a little. "Okay, so it was funny. After. But there was this moment where I almost wished I could—" She swallowed, then said the rest on a rush. "I almost wished I could stop loving Max."

Janey burst out laughing, holding her stomach and sliding down in her chair.

Sara crossed her arms and glared until her best friend got herself under control. "It sounds stupid, but the way I feel about Max is the root of all my problems. If I could stop loving him so desperately and just accept that he'll only ever be my friend, I could still be a part of Joey's life, but I could be happy, too. The only problem is, how do I do it?"

Janey put her elbows on the table and rested her chin in her hands. "Considering my ex-boyfriends, falling out of love was never a problem for me. But Max is such a great guy. And he is drop-dead gorgeous. Just seeing him is enough to make any woman fall in love." She shot Sara a teasing look out of the corner of her eye. "I'd be tempted to go after him myself, but thankfully I don't see him all that often."

Sara leaped out of her chair. "That's it!"

"What?"

"It just might work." She began to pace, gnawing on a thumbnail.

"What?"

"All my accidents happen when Max is around, right?"

"Yeah."

"Well, if I stop seeing him, I won't have any more accidents."

"And how does that make you fall out of love with him?"

"I don't know," Sara said, her elation dimming a bit at the thought of how empty her life was going to be when Max didn't fill it anymore. "I only know that seeing him all the time keeps me hoping. Maybe if he's out of my life physically, my heart will forget about him." It didn't make any sense, even to her own ears, but she was desperate.

"That's the saddest thing I've ever heard." Janey got up and hugged her hard, then handed her a tissue.

"So how are you going to stop seeing him when you live about five feet from his back door? And when the man relies on you for everything but sex, and you'd be giving him that, too, if he'd ever asked."

"Jeez, Janey, just say what you think."

"You don't want to know what I really think. And you haven't answered my question."

"I guess I'll just have to avoid him," Sara said with a shrug. "And when he asks for something, I'll just say no."

"Would you like me to write it on the back of your hand so you don't forget how to spell it?"

"I think I can manage," Sara said. "I have to."

Chapter Three

After the Chinese food and ice cream, they'd moved on to Jack Daniel's, the only man, according to Janey, who really knew how to comfort a woman. Sara was usually a rum-and-Coke woman, heavy on the Coke, or maybe a Baileys Irish Cream if she was feeling especially adventurous, but she had to admit Janey was right this time. The first shot of whiskey burned her throat and turned her stomach. The second still had her gasping for air, but it hit her bloodstream like a warm massage. By the third she was singing "R-E-S-P-E-C-T," and doing her tap routine from when she was eleven years old. It wasn't the song she'd tap-danced to—the two didn't even go together very well—and she had to imagine the tapping sounds because her loafers didn't really do the job on Janey's linoleum. But that song just demanded some life-affirming action and the one she'd chosen wasn't going into effect until she saw Max.

Her pleasant buzz started to fade after that. By the time Janey, who'd appointed herself deignated driver and switched to coffee early on, pulled into Max's driveway, Sara was already rethinking her get-it-over-with-now strategy.

"Shhh," she said to Janey, putting her finger over her pursed lips when the tires crunched and popped on the gravel drive.

It didn't do anything to lessen the noise but it made her feel better.

"Having second thoughts?"

"Second? It's more like..." She looked at her hands, fingers spread, then lifted her feet, one at a time. "I can't count that high just now."

Janey chuckled.

"I know that laugh," Sara mumbled. "You don't think I'll do it, but I will. I'll just do it tomorrow."

"I don't think you'll remember any of this tomorrow." Janey turned off the lights and eased past Max's house.

She pulled up in front of the old bunkhouse Sara had converted into a little cottage, complete with a white picket fence and a generous garden, the frost-browned vines and bare trees decorated like a graveyard for Halloween. Every year when Sara put up the wooden gravestones with funny sayings, she'd secretly dedicated one to her perpetually broken heart. Well, that was going to change. "When New Year's Day rolls around, I won't need a resolution," she said to Janey. "I'll already be over Max."

"From the look of things, you won't have to wait till tomorrow to get started on that resolution."

Sara twisted around in her seat, this way and that, groaning when she realized what Janey was talking about. Either Bigfoot was coming toward her car or Max was. She would've preferred Bigfoot. A three-hundred-pound ape-man with an unpredictable temperament would've been much easier to face.

Janey glanced over at Sara, muttering, "I'll buy you a couple of minutes to get it together, then you're on your own," and she popped out of the car, crossing her arms on the top of the door.

Max pulled up short when he saw it was her rather than Sara. He turned toward the passenger side of the windshield, but the way Janey was staring at him was a challenge he couldn't ignore. "Don't you have someplace else to be?" he asked her.

"Jessie is spending the night at Mrs. Halliwell's."

Max frowned. "That doesn't explain why you're here."

Janey lifted up a shoulder, and gave him a crooked smile. "Moral support," she said. "And entertainment—at your expense, hopefully."

Max just shook his head. They had a…unique relationship. No matter what he said or did, Janey would roll her eyes or huff out a breath, as if he had absolutely no clue about anything. Max wrote if off as a kind of younger sister/older brother thing that came from knowing each other their entire lives. If it had been anything else, Janey would've told him, he figured. She was nothing if not outspoken.

He went around to the other side of the car. At least with Sara, he knew where he stood. "I figured you were at Janey's," he said once she'd rolled the window down. "I wish you'd called, though."

Sara tried to defend herself, but she had to put her head down first. Jack Daniel's, loyal and thoughtful guy that he was, suddenly wanted to come to her rescue, and not in a good way. Then again, throwing up at Max's feet would definitely send him running in the other direction. Or maybe not.

Considering the kind of man he was, Max would almost certainly see her tucked up safely in bed, maybe sit with her for a while to make sure she wasn't going to get sick and choke on her own vomit. The picture that went along with that thought—minus the vomit—had her sitting up in her seat. Smiling. Max in her bedroom, inches away from her bed. Within easy touching distance. All she'd have to do was take his hand, invite him into her bed and indulge every fantasy she'd ever had. It might mean losing him forever—or it might mean that he'd finally acknowledge her real feelings and consider the possibility that he could grow to love her, too. It was a risk she'd never been willing to take before, but with Jack Daniel's to help her...

Jack was supposed to help her do something else, Sara thought fuzzily, something entirely different. Wasn't he? Her head spun like a roulette wheel, risk opposite caution, fear across from courage, all of them separated by big sections of necessity. By the time Max knocked on her window, necessity had shoved all those other pesky options out of the picture.

Sara took a deep breath and looked up at him. Her heart lurched like it always did, but only a little. It was too heavy to give a really good lurch.

He opened the door and offered to help her out. Sara ignored his hand. She waited until he dropped it and stepped back before she levered herself out of the car, awkwardly but on her own.

"You okay?" he asked, all concern, from the deep timbre of his voice to the slight frown between his eyes.

She nodded.

"I was getting worried, Sara. After this afternoon..." He reached for her again.

She held up both hands to ward him off, bending into the car to gather her purse and her courage. And then her balance. She had something to say to Max. It wasn't going to be easy, but it had to be done or he'd never give her the space she needed to get over him. Just once, she told herself. If she did it right, she'd only have to do it once. She straightened slowly, grabbing on to the open door so she wouldn't have to wait for her head to stop spinning. "Max—"

"Why don't you come in the house? We're eating popcorn and watching *The Mummy* for the umpteenth time."

The Mummy was one of her favorite movies, but not for the

action or the really amazing special effects, or even the bumbling hero and endangered heroine. She always found herself hoping those two dead Egyptians in love for thousands of years would find a way to be together.

"Come inside," Max said softly, homing in on her indecision. "Joey is worried about you, too."

Sara closed her eyes, stifling the intentionally rude thing she'd been about to say. She'd forgotten about Joey. Max would eventually understand why she'd had to stop being his friend until she could be *only* his friend. But she was going to have to be very careful about how she alienated the father if she was going to avoid hurting the son. She turned to face him, taking a step forward so he couldn't possibly misunderstand her. "I don't wanna watch a movie. I'm going t'bed."

Max took a step back, waving a hand in front of his face. "Are you drunk?"

And she'd enunciated so carefully, too. "Maybe just a li'l."

He glared over at Janey. "This is your idea of making her feel better?"

"Now I have somewhere else to be," Janey said. She slid into the car and fired it up.

Max took Sara's purse and slid his hand under her elbow, steering her out of the way as Janey peeled off in a small shower of gravel. "Leave it to Janey to get you drunk."

Sara wrenched her arm out of his hand, then had to catch herself before she spun completely around. "It's not Janey's fault. I got myself drunk."

"She should've called me. I'd have come to get you." He tried to take her arm again.

Sara stepped back and, just for good measure, snatched her purse from his hand. It took her two tries, but it still felt good. "Janey's not responsible for me, Max. Neither are you."

He stopped in midstride. "I know that, Sara," he said, his voice very deep and solemn. Hurt. "But I think of you as a—"

"Don't say it!" She winced as her own screeching voice cut through her head like a railroad spike. Apparently she was getting started on the hangover already. Great. That meant she was sobering up. But drunk or sober or somewhere in between, she had to finish what she'd started before Jack deserted her entirely. "I'm not your sister, Max. I'm thirty, no twenty-nine, years old and more'n capa-capa—I've been making my own decisions and my own mistakes for a long time.

"Of course, nooooobody forgets the mistakes, but why can't you remember that at least eighty—seventy—" She stopped and thought really hard, but she seemed to be having an awful lot of trouble with numbers tonight. "Most of the time I manage to live my life without tripping over anything or gluing myself to anyone. But does anybody notice that? No, you all congregate at the Ersk Inn—and by the way that's the stupidest name I've ever heard for anything—and you sit around and drink beer and talk about when Sara Lewis is going to damage the town again."

Max rubbed at the spot on his chest where she'd been poking him to make her point, his handsome face creased in lines of confusion. "I've spent my share of time at the inn, Sara. You got the sitting around and drinking beer part right, but mostly we just watch whatever sporting event is on the big screen. Hardly anyone ever brings up your name, and I've never bought one of those squares."

"No, but you always seem to be around when someone wins."

"So it's my fault?"

Sara sank her teeth into her bottom lip, realizing what she'd said. If Max figured out that he played some role in her clumsiness, he'd wonder why. It was a question she didn't want him asking. Not now that she'd finally found the strength to let go of her dream instead of sitting around waiting for it to come true while life passed her by. The decision made her sick to her stomach, but empowerment was so liberating—it was as if she'd taken her first deep breath after a lifetime of struggling for oxygen. "No, Max, it's not your fault. I just want it to stop. I can't live like this anymore."

"Aw, Sara."

She almost stepped into Max's outstretched arms, one last brotherly hug that she could fantasize meant something else entirely. Instead she stepped around him and headed for her front door. "Just go away, Max."

"But—"

"Please, just leave me alone."

She slipped inside and closed the door behind her, then leaned back against it as tears started to stream down her face.

Jack Daniel's was a whiz at courage, but he wasn't very good at deadening the pain.

MAX SCOOPED UP one last bucket of grain and dumped it into the trough for the milk cows, then opened the fifty-gallon drum of cracked corn to fill the chickens' feed pan. Joey usually did both chores, but he and Jason Hartfield had been trading off sleepovers just about every Saturday night, and this weekend was Joey's turn to stay over there.

He missed Joey, but he knew his son would be back in the morning. Sara wouldn't.

Oh, she was still living at the ranch, but she hadn't said more than hello and goodbye since that last unfortunate incident Halloween week. It was almost Thanksgiving. Max was beginning to wonder who was going to cook the turkey. Okay, he allowed, that sounded a little self-serving, but that was what friends did, they took care of each other, compensated for one another's shortcomings. Sara helped him muddle through the domestic side of life and he did stuff like shovel her walk in the winter, change the oil in her car, chop wood…

The sound of an ax thwacking home drifted to him, and Max realized it had been going on for some time while he'd been moping, a kind of somber background music for his self-pity. It puzzled him for a second. None of his neighbors lived close enough for it to be coming from another ranch, and while they all got along pretty well, none of them liked him enough to just drop by and chop a stack of wood—which meant it had to be Sara. She'd finally emerged from her house.

With an ax in her hand.

He dropped the pan of chicken feed. Cracked corn poured into his boots and scattered over the floor. Max ignored the mess and the discomfort, racing out of the barn and across the yard, plowing through knee-deep drifts of snow. He skidded around the corner of her cottage on one foot, arms flung out for balance, his mouth opened on a shout that would have worked a lot better if he'd had any breath left in his body.

He gulped in a huge, painfully cold lungful of air and yelled "Sara!" just as she lifted the ax.

With a shriek she froze on the upstroke and kept going, the heavy ax dragging her over to sprawl flat on her back. The powdery snow puffed up around her, then drifted back down like her own miniblizzard, dusting her in white, face and all. Max pinned his lips between his teeth and slogged over to help her to her feet.

Sara ignored his hand. Her cutting glare might even have made him feel a little bit chastened if she hadn't spent the next couple of minutes floundering around in her puffy green coat like a turned-over turtle. She finally managed to roll onto her side, then crawl to her feet, leaving behind a snow angel that looked more like a Lizzie Borden silhouette, complete with murder weapon.

Max's amusement completely evaporated when she bent, picked up the ax and tried to walk around him. "What do you think you're doing?" he asked, stepping between her and the woodpile.

"Chopping wood," she said in her best third-grade teacher's voice, reasonable and patient. "I use it to heat my house, remember?"

"How could I forget when I always chop it for you?"

"Well, now you won't have to." She lifted the ax and took a step forward.

He crossed his arms and held his ground. "You're not chopping wood, Sara. That's my job."

"Not anymore." But she dropped the ax head to rest on the ground. Safely. "Weren't you listening three weeks ago?"

"Well, yeah, but…you were drunk."

Sara's breath puffed out in a cloud of white. "That doesn't mean I didn't know what I was saying. Or that I don't remember what you said."

"I really didn't mean to imply you couldn't take care of yourself, but…" *You're Sara,* he finished to himself, *Clumsy, artless, scattered-as-a-handful-of-packing-popcorn-in-a-windstorm Sara.* His best friend in the whole world. "I'm sorry if I offended you."

"You didn't offend me, Max. I'm used to people thinking of me as hopeless. What bothers me more is that you didn't really hear what I said."

That was exactly what his ex-wife had always accused him of, but Max shook off the thought almost as soon as it reared its ugly head. Sara and Julia were nothing alike.

"Of course I remember what you said." He shut one eye and tried to remember. "You said, 'I can't live like this anymore.' But like I said, Sara, I thought you were—" He got a good look at her face and swallowed the word "drunk," and, just to be safe, decided against mentioning her unfortunate tendency to leave chaos in her path every once in a while—which was the other reason he'd decided that statement had nothing to do with him. Now he had the sneaking suspicion she'd aimed that dart much closer to home—and he was wearing the bull's-eye. "What did I do wrong?"

The way she nibbled on her lower lip and looked away confirmed it.

"Just tell me and I'll take it back or apologize for it or fix it or…" He spread his hands. "I'll do whatever I can to get things back to normal, Sara. I miss you." More than he'd ever believed possible, enough to drag that confession from him, which was really saying something for a man who considered "hi" an emotional outburst.

Baring his heart, however, only seemed to have saddened her more. "It's not you, Max."

"Then it's the accidents?"

Sara lifted her shoulders and let them droop in a dejected shrug. "I'm not too pleased with making a fool of myself every few weeks, but the accidents are just the symptom of a bigger problem."

"So what's the bigger problem?"

"It's me."

"What the hell does that mean?"

"Don't yell at me."

"Don't—" Max shoved his cold-reddened hands back through his hair, pacing away then back. "You want me to listen to you, but you're not saying anything. You've been sulking for weeks and when I ask you why—"

"I haven't been sulking!"

"Really? I used to talk to you every day, but I've barely seen you since Halloween. You're hardly ever home before dark, and even when you are here you only come out of your house to get in your car and leave again. If that's not sulking, then what is it?"

"I've been busy," she muttered.

"Everyone's busy. If I did something to make you angry, that's fine, but at least tell me why I'm being punished."

"I'm not punishing you."

But she couldn't look at him, either, Max noticed. "It feels like it."

"I'm sorry for that, but you just have to understand that I can't—I don't—I'm unhappy."

"You're unhappy?" She seemed relieved to have that off her chest, but all that revelation did was heat his temper up a few more degrees. Julia had said that a lot. And then she'd left. He paced away, hands in pockets, kicking at the drifts of snow. "If you expect me to say anything remotely helpful, you're going to have to give me more to work with." He thought he'd said that in an incredibly even tone of voice, but when he turned back, Sara didn't seem all that impressed. She appeared…irritated. She sounded it, too.

"I made the decision to come here six years ago, Max. It was my choice and I'd do it again in a heartbeat."

"And we're grateful, Sara. More than grateful. I don't know what I'd have done without you. If I haven't said that enough—"

"It's not that," she said, shoving his gratitude aside with a wave of her mittened hands. "Much as I lo—" Her eyes lifted to his, then skipped away before he got any clue as to what was going on inside her. "Much as I'd love to spend the rest of my life taking care of you and Joey," she said so fast the words tumbled over one another, "I want a home and family of my own."

"Damn it," Max said on an outrush of breath that emptied his lungs and left him gasping. And damn her for catching him

off guard with something he hadn't thought about in years—
six to be exact. A home and family were what he'd wanted
when he married Julia, and he'd gotten them—not the way
he'd hoped, and he wouldn't trade Joey for anything in the
world—but damn Sara for reminding him that Joey would be
an only child. "Nobody's preventing you from having those
things, Sara."

She looked up at him, her eyes narrowing in a very un-
Sara-like way. "So it's okay if I just move out, get on with my
life? You should've told me a long time ago that you didn't
care if I was around or not."

"Who said that?"

"You did."

"No, I didn't."

She snorted. "You're hardly broken up at the prospect of
me leaving, Max. How am I supposed to take that?"

"I was trying to be supportive."

"You mean you were humoring me."

"No, I wasn't…." He rubbed at his temples. It felt as if his
head was going to explode. "You've been so confused lately.
I just…didn't think you were serious." He dug at a half-buried
log with the toe of his boot and jammed his hands in his coat
pockets, looking up at her without lifting his head. "Are you?"

"Would you be upset if I left?"

"Joey—"

"I'm not talking about Joey." Sara closed the distance between them, waiting until he met her eyes. "How would you
feel, Max?"

Max found himself standing behind the woodpile without
knowing how he'd gotten there, except that panic had something to do with it. One minute everything was fine, then suddenly Sara was unhappy. Talking about leaving. The next
thing he knew, she'd be out the door, exactly like Julia. Ex-

cept in Sara's case she'd go back to her family in Boston, probably marry some junior VP handpicked by her father. And when she left, he'd have to pick up the pieces as he'd done before. Unless he made sure he wasn't breakable this time.

"What do my feelings have to do with it?" he demanded.

"They just do, Max."

"It doesn't sound to me like you even know how you feel about it."

She tried to answer, but he walked away while he still could.

"Let me know if you ever figure it out," he said over his shoulder.

Chapter Four

Sara took down the rest of the papier-mâché turkeys her students had made, looping the strings that had attached them to the ceiling around her fingers as she went about the task. She really should have done it earlier in the week, so the children would have their handmade decorations to grace their tables for the big day tomorrow. Instead, she'd kept putting it off so she wouldn't have to think about the holiday looming like a big question mark at the end of the week.

But there were paper Santas, stuffed with cotton batting and stapled at the edges, to be hung. Life went on, time passed and memories weren't supposed to hurt as much. But they did.

Despite the ray of hope it had provided, the argument with Max haunted her. Here it was, the day before Thanksgiving, and for the first time in six years, she didn't know if she'd be cooking a turkey with all the trimmings for Max and Joey, or eating a solitary meal in a lonely house. She didn't like being on bad terms with anyone, and when it was Max…well, it felt as if somebody was ripping her heart out, and the pain of it was giving her second thoughts.

She'd tried to forget about the difficult path she'd chosen by focusing on the destination, but she really wasn't all that eager for things to change if that change might mean leaving

Max for good. Still, being alone couldn't be any worse than being in love alone.

"Look who I found."

Sara gasped in surprise, and slapped a turkey-festooned hand over her suddenly racing heart. "Jeez, Janey, I hate it when you sneak up on me like…" She spun around to confront her best friend, but her focus immediately shifted to the boy standing so uneasily under Janey's casually slung arm. "Hey, Joey, what's up?"

He shrugged, burying his mittened hands deep in the pockets of his coat.

Sara looked at Janey.

Janey made a face and gave a slight you-got-me shake of her head.

"Did you miss the bus?" Sara asked Joey as she unstrung her hand and laid the turkeys on her desk.

"No. Dad's picking me up."

Sara peered out her window, which faced the street and the parking lot. There wasn't a car or truck in sight. "I think he might have forgotten."

"He didn't forget. He's just late." Joey ducked out from under Janey's arm and went to the window. He crossed his arms on the sill and dropped his chin to rest on them, staring out at the empty road.

Sara's heart broke for him. She knew how he felt—oh, not that Max had ever forgotten about her. It was more a case of not thinking of her at all. She could be his boots or his coat: not to be given another thought as long as she fit his life. And perhaps to be just as easily replaced now that she didn't. But that was too dismal and self-serving a thought to be having while there was a child in pain.

She grabbed a chair and carried it across the room, sitting next to Joey. He sidled a couple of steps away.

So, there was more going on here than simply Joey being upset that his dad had forgotten him. "What's wrong, Joey?"

"Nothing." But he hunched his shoulders, concentrating very hard on the view out the window.

If he'd shouted at her to go away, she couldn't have gotten the message any clearer. She wasn't about to back off. "Why didn't you let me know your dad hadn't come? You know I'll drive you home."

"No—I mean, Dad's in town, helping put up the Christmas decorations."

"And it's been snowing on and off all day, so he probably didn't finish in time," Sara mused.

"I was gonna walk into town and find him, but *she*—" he jerked his head toward Janey "—brought me down here instead."

Janey rolled her eyes, spun on her heel and left.

"You know the rules, kiddo. You're not allowed to leave school property unless you're on the bus or an adult comes for you."

"Yeah," he sighed. "Rules."

"Well, I'm an adult, and it's only a few blocks into town. Since you don't want me to drive you home, how about we walk into town and find your dad?"

Joey stared at the hand she held out, so patently miserable that Sara couldn't bear it. She gathered him close, shutting her eyes and sighing out a breath when he threw his arms around her neck. Oh, how she'd missed hugging that compact little body, smoothing her hand over his unruly hair. "Want to tell me what I did wrong?" she asked, lifting his face when he refused to look at her. "Why don't you want me to take you into town?"

"Dad told me to leave you alone. He said you needed space."

Sara went hot and cold all at once. That Max would say

such a thing to an eight-year-old, give him the impression she didn't want him around.

She looked down at her aching hands, surprised to find them curled into fists. "Did he tell you why?" she asked, grating the words a little as she forced her hands to open.

"I asked him, but he said he doesn't know." Joey stared up at her, his blue eyes wide and confused. "There's practically nothing but space in Montana, Sara, so why do you want more?"

"I… You won't understand until you're grown-up."

Joey snorted. "That's what adults say when they don't want to explain something. Like when it has to do with sex."

Sara's first reaction was shock at hearing that word out of Joey's mouth. Her second reaction was that he'd hit the nail square on the head. It was about sex, since that was just about the only role she didn't play in Max's life, and if she got her wish, that would be the only thing added to their relationship. That and love.

"You're right, Joey, and so is your dad. I need some time to myself right now, and it's not something I can really explain to you."

"Does that mean you can't come over and watch a movie with me, or play Scrabble, or bake cookies, or…anything?"

"It means I won't be doing any of those things at your house."

His face fell, the cute little boy copy of Max's features crumpling on the verge of tears. Sara gathered him close once again, then cupped his chin and looked him square in the eyes. "It doesn't have anything to do with you, Joey, I promise you that. You and I are always going to be best friends. If you ever need anything, all you have to do is ask. Besides, just because I won't be spending a whole lot of time at your house doesn't mean you can't come over to mine."

"But I like it when you come to our house, Sara. It's like…" He turned away, his cheeks heating.

"I know what you mean." She had to swallow back her tears. "You'll always be my family, no matter what. Deal?"

He took the hand she stuck out, shook it solemnly. "Deal."

"Now, how about we go find that father of yours?"

He started toward the coat closet with her, but his feet were dragging. "Maybe I should go by myself."

"Maybe we can stop at the Five-and-Dime on the way, see if they have a sale on ice cream."

His face brightened immediately. Sara wished ice cream could cure all his hurts. He'd never let on that he was aware of the tension between the two adults in his life, but for the first time she got an inkling of how deeply Joey might be hurt if she didn't handle this situation exactly right.

Max wasn't helping. When she thought of him telling Joey that she didn't want to see him, the oddest feeling began to build inside her. The anger she recognized, but it was unlike anything she'd felt before. This anger was a heat that filled her from the soles of her feet to the roots of her hair, made her head throb and red crowd in at the edges of her vision. She followed Joey out of the school and into the kind of blue-sky cold that cut to the bone. She didn't even feel it, though her coat was unbuttoned; she just shaded her eyes against the glare of the sun on the snowdrifts and set off toward the main part of town.

She barely noticed how beautiful Erskine looked, the false-fronted buildings outlined in tiny lights that glowed against the gray clouds and purply white-capped mountains off in the distance. Or how festive the light poles were, half of them already twined with evergreen boughs, red and white ribbons and more lights. She strode down Main Street, shooting a glance over her shoulder every now and again to make sure Joey was keeping up with her. The fact that he had to trot didn't seem to bother him, so she didn't let it bother her. He obviously wasn't winded enough to keep him from chattering nonstop.

"Can we stop in the toy store?" he asked for at least the third time.

"Not today. We need to find your dad." Oh, did they ever, she added silently, before she lost this head of steam. "Maybe he'll take you to the toy store later." If he could still stand to show his face in town after she got through with him.

"Look, Sara, there's the feed store. I want to see if the kittens are ready to go home. And I need fish food."

"Not right now." By the time she got done cutting Max into little pieces, fish food wouldn't be a problem.

"Can I—"

"No, Joey." She caught his sleeve, checked the flow of pedestrian and automobile traffic, and shepherded him across the street, all without changing stride, causing a car accident or tripping anyone—including herself. The satisfaction was enormous, even with a layer of temper blurring it.

She hit the door of the Five-and-Dime with the heel of her palm, Joey still in tow, and weaved her way through the displays without so much as setting one of the card carousels spinning. "Hey, Lucy," she said in greeting to the girl behind the dinette counter. "Can you keep an eye on Joey for a little while? I need to find Max."

"Aw, jeez, I want to come and watch," the girl muttered.

Sara's temper spiked dangerously. She wrestled it down with a reminder that this teenager wasn't the one responsible for it. Neither was the general populace of Erskine; they merely got a heap of entertainment out of it. Well, those days were over. "No one's winning the pool today, Lucy, so you can stay right here and do your job. Give Joey whatever he wants and I'll be in to get him in a little while. Or Max will, just as soon as I track the—" She looked at Joey, poring happily over the menu, and censored herself. "One of us will pick him up later."

She turned on her heel, leaving a gleeful eight-year-old and a whining teenager at the old-fashioned soda fountain in the Five-and-Dime. She marched down Main Street, plunging through the preholiday crowds like a Boston steel plow through the rich Montana soil. It helped that people scurried out of her way, some even crossing the street, shopping bags rattling and swinging as they hurried their Christmas purchases out of the path of the town's klutz. Of course, about half of them fell in behind her on the chance they could liven up their Christmas shopping—and maybe pay off their credit cards.

Sara hoped they enjoyed their dancing cowboy Santas, electric socks and brand-spanking-new Levi's. Being inexperienced in this anger business, she just didn't have enough to spare for everyone who hoped to fund their holiday through her misfortune. It was already hard enough to keep track of who she was mad at.

A part of her realized that her anger stemmed from more than just Max telling Joey to steer clear of her outside of school. Some of that anger—okay, a hell of a lot of that anger—represented six years of accumulated frustration and pent-up hurt that Max was too blind to see what was right under his nose. And, Sara allowed grudgingly, she had to take responsibility for some of what churned inside her. She'd been too much of a coward to tell him outright how she felt. She had always seen it as a chance to lose everything rather than a chance to have everything. So she'd settled. That was on her shoulders. The rest belonged to Max.

She spotted him coming out of the hardware store just then, and it was no wonder her feet almost tangled up. Anyone carrying that heavy an emotional load was bound to be clumsy. But then the anger kicked back in, wrapping around her nerves and propping her up. "Devlin!"

He stopped dead and turned to face her. So did everyone else within hearing distance, and that happened to be a lot of people.

Sara didn't care, for once, that she'd drawn a crowd. Let them watch, she thought, as she crossed the street to confront Max. She could have sworn she heard a collective groan of disappointment when she made it to the other side without causing a three-car pileup.

"Hey, Max."

Sara looked up, noticing for the first time the ladder leaning against the nearby light pole, Ted Delancey teetering on the top step, hanging Christmas decorations.

"Before you, uh—" he made an apologetic face in Sara's direction, then appealed to Max. "Can you hand me that twine? This stuff is slipping."

"You're just going to have to wait, Ted," Sara called.

"But it's cold up here."

Max raised one hand. "Just hold on a couple of minutes, Ted."

"That's about all it should take," Sara muttered. She went toe-to-toe with Max, ramming her index finger into his chest, which didn't do her finger any good and barely made a dent in his heavy wool coat. "When were you planning on picking up your son from school?"

"School's not over yet, is it?" He sidled back and peered at his watch, shaking it, then putting it up to his ear. "Battery must have died. Or frozen."

Sara went at him again. "Joey's been sitting in the office for an hour, waiting for you." Her voice quavered before she could finish the rest of that tirade, her anger thinning a little at the sad picture of Joey alone and forgotten. "He wouldn't come and tell me because you told him not to bother me."

Max took a step to the side, a completely male, completely evasive action. "You're the one who needed time to figure things out, Sara."

"Don't you blame this on me! I never—"

"Hold it right there." Max moved back toward her, closing his gloved hands over her upper arms. "I don't know why you're angry with me—"

"Joey—"

"That's not what's really upsetting you, Sara. Why don't we go somewhere—" he nodded toward the crowd "—private and clear it up?"

Sara gazed up into blue, blue eyes full of worry and affection. Just that fast, the heat moving through her found its source in an entirely different place. Her anger sifted away like so much sand, the emptiness filled the way it had always been. By Max.

Distance, her panicked mind shrieked, and her body overreacted. She tore free of Max's grip, lost her balance and stumbled backward. Right into the ladder leaning up against the wrought-iron light pole behind her.

Ted Delancey threw his arms around the pole's decorative horizontal arm and hung there, swinging like an overgrown kid on overgrown monkey bars, yelling for help and kicking his feet in a vain attempt to wrap them around the pole. The ladder crashed into the middle of the street, landing in front of a passing truck, but no one gave it a second glance. All eyes were on Sara, festooned with the merrily twinkling Christmas lights, evergreen garlands, wide plastic ribbons and enormous ornaments Ted had dropped in an attempt to save his own life.

"I could really use some help," Ted called down into the stunned silence.

The ladder was now in pieces roughly the size of toothpicks, but before anyone could run into the hardware store to borrow another one, Ted had managed to swing his legs around the pole and slide down. It would've been perfect if he hadn't hit a patch of ice at the bottom and fallen on his butt.

Someone in the crowd laughed, the hilarity spreading when Ted sprang to his feet and made a flamboyant bow. As he straightened, he motioned to Sara, à la Vanna White. The audience went wild, laughing and calling out silly questions— like was she a Douglas fir or a blue spruce, and even sillier suggestions like maybe she needed to be watered, and wasn't there a spot on her right sleeve that could use some tinsel.

Even Sara had to admit she must look like a Christmas tree, her puffy green coat decorated with all the finery that was to have been twined around the twelve-foot-tall light pole. Instead of feeling humiliated or embarrassed, she found herself laughing along with everyone else. Oddly enough it felt good, like coming home.

Max moved forward just then, and her heart nearly burst with love for him. She was doomed to love him for the rest of her life, she decided in that instant, and as long as she loved him, she could stand anything. It was a peaceful notion, for the little while it lasted.

The crowd began to disperse, to her relief, and she settled in to enjoy the way Max was clucking his tongue and shaking his head, exasperated with her, but amused and relieved, too. Like old times.

"Hey, what happened?" Joey asked as he ran up to join them.

"I was clumsy again." Sara ducked her head so Max could untangle two strands of lights from around her shoulders.

"You look just like a Christmas tree, Sara." He tweaked one of the big, plastic bulbs hanging from her left sleeve. "All you need is an angel on top."

"What point would there be in putting an angel on top of

an angel?" Max said with a wide smile, his eyes twinkling with fondness if not love.

"Well, she should have some kind of ornament up there, like a tree topper."

"There's a big clump of mistletoe on her head."

Sara peered up. Sure enough, she could see the edge of something green nestled in the copper-colored curls sticking out of her hood. The little white berries in the greenery confirmed it. Mistletoe. She went very still, her eyes going to Max's face.

"Isn't that the stuff they hang in the town hall at Christmas?" Joey asked. "Then all the old ladies try to kiss me and stuff. Hey, Dad," he said as a thought occurred to him. "Don't that mean you have to kiss Sara?"

It never occurred to Sara to correct Joey's grammar. She was too busy watching Max. He straightened from where he was unwrapping lights from around her waist, his gaze rising, very slowly, to hers. She saw the humor fade from his eyes, could swear the blue darkened as they dropped to her mouth, lingered, lingered, then lifted to her cheek. By the time his eyes rose to meet hers again, there was nothing in the sparkling blue depths but amusement, and she was already wondering if she'd seen anything else. Or if she'd just spun it out of her fantasies.

"I think she'd rather have a kiss from her best guy instead," Max said.

Joey's face went about three shades of red, but he threw his arms around her waist and hugged her tight for a long moment.

"So," Max said nonchalantly, "is everything back to normal?"

Sara looked at the sprig of mistletoe in Max's hand, thought about her cold lips and aching heart and said, "Yes, everything is back to normal."

Chapter Five

Even when she drove down Main Street that evening and saw the single bare pole, like an unlit candle on a birthday cake, Sara couldn't count the day a total disaster. Yes, she'd been embarrassed and humiliated in front of the entire town yet again, and yes, Max had compounded that with his allergic reaction to being confronted with her and mistletoe at the same time, but at least she'd come out of it with a new purpose.

She was going to tell Max she loved him. It was time to stop being wishy-washy, to stop waiting and hoping he'd suddenly figure out that he couldn't live without her. He'd probably run in the other direction, but if he had feelings for her, he'd come back. And if he didn't, well, that would be an answer, too.

And she was flying solo this time—no Jack Daniel's to help her out, just Janey Walters, who admittedly didn't have a long tradition of bottled courage to lend her credibility, but she knew what was what in Sara's love life. And she knew Max.

Within moments of being divested of her Christmas finery that afternoon, Sara had burst through her best friend's front door and told her the whole sorry tale, ending with, "He didn't even want to kiss me on the cheek."

"Hell, Sara, the man's beauty might only be skin-deep, but

his emotions are buried so far down it's a wonder he even got within a mile of that mistletoe. You know that better than anyone."

A note of exasperation crept into Janey's voice—not that Sara blamed her. If she was sick of whining about Max, how tired of it must Janey be? Tired enough, it had turned out, to give Sara the bottom line without Ben & Jerry's to sugarcoat it.

"Stop complaining about the way things are and do something to change them."

"I tried," Sara had said. "It didn't work."

"Then try something else."

"The only thing I haven't tried is telling him I love him." And that, Sara recalled was where she'd slapped a hand over her mouth because she wasn't sure what other far-fetched and totally crazy ideas might jump out if she didn't. "I don't know where that notion came from, but there's no way I'm doing it."

"Why not?" Janey had asked. "It's a risk, sure, but you said yourself that you're tired of being his friend, so what have you got to lose? If he loves you, you get your wish. If not—oh, hell, Sara, take it from me, the guy loves you."

That last comment had been so startling it knocked the pessimism right out of her. "What makes you think Max loves me, Janey?"

"Have you ever seen him date anyone else?"

"Of course." Though Sara hadn't given it too much thought. The idea of Max with another woman didn't exactly make her top-ten list of fun things to ponder.

"Lately, Sara. Have you seen him date anyone in, oh, say the last three years?"

"No, but I figured he ran out of women to ask. Erskine is a small town."

"Erskine isn't the entire world, which you should have no

trouble remembering since you're not even from here. Trust me, the man's already found the right woman. He'll probably realize it himself—"

Sara snorted. "When pigs fly."

"They can clone 'em ," Janey pointed out. "It's just a matter of time before some egghead slaps wings on 'em, too."

Sara gave her a look, mouth tight and one brow arched.

"My suggestion is, tell the man how you feel and then get out your frilly underwear. Or better yet, don't bother. You won't be wearing them long, seeing as how Max hasn't dated in three years and you...well, it's a wonder you haven't melted down into a puddle of raging hormones at his feet by now."

Sara had decided to ignore the lewd remark and the disgusting metaphor that went with it, which was easy until she recalled that moment—okay, split second—when Max had been holding the mistletoe and his eyes had met hers. She could have sworn she'd seen something there besides friendship, something deeper.

That fleeting connection had turned into the holy grail for Sara, a light in Max's window that drew her to his ranch, even when her courage faltered and she wanted to turn around and hide out in Janey's basement rather than go through with her plan.

The closer she got to the ranch, the more tempting that basement began to look. By the time she pulled into the driveway her nerves were strung tight enough to play Beethoven's *Fifth*. It would have made pretty good background music, too, seeing as how Max must have been waiting for her because he was already there, big and solid and mind-numbingly handsome. He opened her car door and *da-da-da-daaaaaa,* ran through her mind. Despite Janey's certainty about Max's feelings, Sara really, *really,* didn't want to talk to him anymore.

"I just want to take a long, hot bath and get into bed," she said as she climbed from her car.

She expected Max to back out of her way like he usually did, what with his reluctance to touch her and all. But he didn't move. Worse yet, he braced one hand on the door, the other on the roof of the car, which put him so close her senses went haywire.

Sara didn't know how she kept her footing with her knees wobbling as much as they were, or how she managed to draw any breath with her throat closed and her chest aching. But she definitely couldn't tell Max she loved him when his scent alone was enough to make her tongue stick to the roof of her mouth.

"Have you been drinking with Janey again?" Max asked, although she noticed he made no attempt to steady her as he had the last time. That touching thing again.

"I haven't had anything to drink."

"Are you sure?"

Sara shot him a look, then ducked under his arm and headed for her house.

Max stepped in front of her. "Because I could certainly understand why you might want to forget... Uh, I mean, after what happened today...well, you don't always have to go to Janey. You could talk to me."

Sara opened her mouth, but all that emerged was a strangled sound because the words got lodged in the back of her throat, behind a big lump of indignation. *Talk to Max?* He couldn't even bring himself to make the simplest physical contact, let alone get in touch with her feelings. The extent of their conversation for the past six years had centered on Joey—the ranch and Joey—and suddenly he wanted her to unburden herself to him? If he had any idea what kind of unburdening she had in mind, he'd run screaming in the other direction. She probably wouldn't make it past "I" before he disappeared into the pitch-black, frigidly cold Montana night. Well, Sara decided, she might just as well save him the trip. She shoved by him and started up the brick walkway that led to her cottage.

"Please come inside," Max called after her. "Joey's worried about you."

She stopped dead in her tracks, all the encouragement Max needed to join her.

"After the way you ran off this afternoon…" He cupped her elbow, barely a brush of his fingers to her coat sleeve, but it was so surprising she let him turn her and guide her back toward his house. "I don't think he's ever seen you cry, Sara. Neither have I."

"I wasn't crying."

"Okay," he said, obviously relieved. And then he looked at her face.

Sara could only imagine what her expression must be for Max to go all pale and shocked like that.

"Because if you were crying," he went on, "and if it was something I did, I wish you'd tell me."

He sounded so upset, so sweetly earnest, that she risked a glance up into his face. The sincerity in his eyes, the need to comfort, made her heart pound and her mind spin for entirely different reasons than her usual upheaval. She'd missed it before because, frankly, it was simply too amazing to believe, but when Max suggested for the second time that she tell him her problems, well, jeez! He was finally reaching out past the emotional barrier he'd erected between himself and the world when his marriage fell apart. Sara had been waiting years for this moment and now that it had finally arrived her mind had gone almost totally blank.

"Umm, there was something I wanted to talk to you about."

"Okay." Max ushered her in the back door of the ranch

house. "I could use a hot drink first, how about you? Yeah, a hot drink would really hit the spot on a cold day like this. Sort of, I don't know, warm up your insides and kind of…loosen things up. Coffee always helps me, uh, talk."

Coffee? It seemed to Sara that fear made him talk—or babble, more accurately. Max sure as heck didn't want to talk if there was going to be a mention of her feelings anywhere in the conversation. But he was willing to do it anyway.

And then she remembered what she wanted to tell him. She began to shake so violently she couldn't have run if she'd wanted to. It was a struggle to put one foot in front of the other in the direction she was already headed. The sight that greeted her when she walked into the warm, well-lit kitchen, however, calmed her immediately.

Joey sat at the scrubbed pine table, stuffing his face. She couldn't drop a bomb on Max with Joey sitting right there, could she? She couldn't manufacture an excuse to get rid of him, either. Joey was too smart to fall for a line, and considering recent events, she refused to let him think she didn't want him around. No, baring her heart would have to wait.

"What are you eating, kiddo?" she asked, shoving her gloves in her pockets and hanging her coat by the back door, then sliding into a chair across the table from him.

"A meat pie," Joey mumbled around a mouthful. He swallowed, took a long pull from the straw sticking out of his chocolate milk, chewed a little more and swallowed again, eyeing Sara the whole time with a combination of accusation and pleading. "It's the last one."

"Then I guess I'll just have to make another batch, won't I?"

Max set a cup of coffee in front of her, an indication of how off balance he was feeling. Given her normal state of edginess, caffeine had always seemed like overkill so she rarely indulged. Max knew that better than anyone, but in light of what else she had to say, it didn't seem all that important to remind him. And at least the coffee was warm.

She wrapped her hands around the cup and let the heat seep in while the kitchen settled into a cozy, if slightly strained, silence. Sara was fond of her little bunkhouse-turned-cottage, but she had loved the main ranch house from the moment she'd first seen it. It had always felt like home to her, which was no surprise since she considered Max and Joey her family.

And of all the rooms in the rambling old stone-and-wood house, the kitchen was her favorite. It was a hodgepodge of styles, from the scrubbed pine table that had been created by the same Devlin who'd built the ranch house a century and a half before, to the side-by-side refrigerator-freezer Max had bought secondhand just a few months ago.

If it were up to Sara, she would have begged him to strip the peeling linoleum and refinish the hardwood floor beneath. But it wasn't her house, so unless Max asked her advice she wouldn't volunteer it. That would feel too much like crossing a line she'd fought very hard to respect. Of course, any moment now she'd be stepping over that line big-time, but then it would be up to Max whether he kept his floors to himself or gave her the chance to state her opinion about refinishing versus recovering with the authority of someone who might have to look at them on a permanent basis.

"Hey, pal, did you feed the menagerie?" Max asked Joey.

His deep voice strummed every tightly strung nerve in Sara's body simultaneously, almost launching her out of her seat. There was no way he could have missed her reaction, since her chair clattered back at least a foot and she had to mop up some of her coffee, but he made a big show of keeping his eyes on his son.

Joey slid her a puzzled glance, then shrugged off her behavior as weird adult stuff. "Yeah, I fed 'em, Dad." He stuffed the last bite of meat pie in his mouth and chugged down his milk, wincing and slapping a hand to his head. "Brain freeze," he gasped. The older of his two dogs, a shepherd mix named Lucas in honor of another Hollywood icon, George Lucas, whined and nosed Joey's hand in sympathy while Max watched him with a slight grin.

The very ordinariness of the scene settled her again, so that when the doorbell rang a few seconds later, she barely twitched. Joey dumped his plate and glass into the old porcelain sink and ran out of the kitchen to look through the big front window, the dogs yipping at his heels. "It's some people I've never seen before," he called.

Max looked at Sara. She looked back, neither of them moving until the bell rang again, the person on the front porch pushing on the button long enough to give the normally cheerful buzz a bit of attitude.

Max straightened away from where he'd been leaning against the counter and took off for the front door. He wasn't eager to hear whatever had been upsetting Sara so much over the past few weeks, but he'd strip down and dance naked in the snow if it meant getting her back to her old, happy-go-lucky self. From the expression on her face he figured what she wanted to say wasn't going to be a pleasant experience.

Neither was opening his front door. A middle-aged couple stood on the front porch. The man, tall and distinguished, could have graced the cover of *GQ*. Despite the wings of silver at his temples, he was fit and trim, his dark suit and wool overcoat fitting him as if they were made for him, which they probably were. The woman looked…like an older version of Sara. She had the same soft eyes and pretty features, the same kind and open manner, and although her hair was laced with subtle blond highlights and cut into a short, chic style, Max could tell it had once been coppery and curly.

A month of living without Sara as a part of his daily life had taught him that he didn't like it. He'd finally come to the conclusion that she was never going back to the easy friendship they'd shared for so long, that if he wanted her in his life, things would have to change. And that change would have to come, at least in part, from him.

Now, just when he'd reconciled himself to finding out what it would take to keep her around, here were two people who wanted just the opposite. And they wouldn't have any problem using emotion to get it.

"Who is it?" Joey asked, coming to stand beside his father.

Max dropped a hand to his son's shoulder. Not because he thought Joey needed the connection—but because he needed it himself. "Mr. and Mrs. Lewis," he said. They'd met once, the first year Sara came to Erskine. They hadn't been successful in convincing her to go back to Boston then. Max wondered if things would end differently this time. "Come in," he said, opening the door wider and stepping back.

Mr. Lewis ushered his wife in before him, then thrust out his hand. Max shook it, turning to greet Sara's mother next, but Mrs. Lewis was looking past him, into the depths of the house.

"Is Sara here?" she asked Max. "We went to her little house, but she didn't answer the door."

Sara poked her head around the door leading from the kitchen into the front room, gave a shriek and ran over to hug her mother and father. "I thought I heard your voices," she said, and hugged them both again.

"You remember Max, of course," she said, turning to indicate him, "and this is Joey."

John Lewis hunkered down. "You've grown," he said to Joey. "The last time I saw you, you were about this tall." He held his hand three feet off the floor.

Joey didn't seem impressed. Normally, Sara would've

been concerned about how he was taking this unexpected arrival, but she was busy watching her mother. Maureen Lewis was studying Max's front room. The furniture, rugs and knickknacks that had been in his family for generations must look shabby compared to what she was used to, but Sara suspected that wasn't the reason for the tears in her mother's eyes.

"Why don't we go to my house and catch up," she said, taking her parents each by an arm and urging them through the front door. She paused on the threshold, looking back at Max.

"We'll talk another time," Max said, his arm still around Joey's shoulders. "Do what you need to do, Sara."

She tried to produce a reassuring smile, and failed miserably. What she needed to do was stay and explain to Max why her parents were there, but she didn't know herself. What she did know was that her mother wouldn't want to cry in front of Max. And Sara didn't want Max to think her mother was crying because of him.

She stepped out and Max swung the door shut behind her; it caught with a soft and final click. She almost turned back again, but her dad settled his coat around her shoulders just then, and she remembered that Max would still be there tomorrow.

"I'm sorry we barged in like this," John said as they made the short walk to Sara's house. "We had to come—"

"Everything's okay?" she asked, suddenly frightened. "Brad and Ben?"

"Your brothers are fine." Maureen took her daughter's face between her cold hands. "I just needed to see you," she said through a fresh wave of tears. "It's been so long."

Sara wanted to laugh and cry at the same time. "I was home for two weeks in the summer."

"I know." Her mother dug into her coat pocket, coming up with a linen handkerchief.

"And we talk on the phone at least once a week." Sara went into her house, her parents following.

"It's not the same thing, Sara." Maureen dabbed carefully at her eyes.

"You're right, Mom. It's good to see you both, but…what are you doing here?"

"It was a spur-of-the-moment decision," John said. "Your brothers are both out of town for the holiday, and your mother couldn't bear the thought of being stuck alone with me for the whole weekend, so she nagged me into bringing her to Montana for Thanksgiving dinner with you. I hear the Erskine Hotel has worked its way up to two stars."

"John." Maureen rolled her eyes. "We missed you," she said to Sara, "but your father thinks Lewis Exports will go bankrupt if he shuts down for two whole days, so we're only going to be in town until tomorrow evening."

"Thanksgiving's not a holiday in Europe," John said, his wife parroting him silently.

Sara had always enjoyed her parents' good-natured contention, but she had no trouble keeping a straight face this time, especially since they wouldn't like what she was about to tell them. "Max and Joey are expecting me to have dinner with them. I can't leave them hanging at the last minute." She chose not to mention that, until a few hours ago, they would have been on their own anyway. But now everything was…not back to normal, but a lot closer than it had been.

John made an impatient face. "Why can't that friend of yours—"

"Janice," Maureen supplied.

"Janey," Sara said.

"The point is," John continued, "she's single, right? She could invite Max and his son for dinner and you could come with us."

As always, her father had it all worked out. There was just one problem—or maybe two—that he hadn't considered. "I'd love to go to have dinner with you at the hotel, Dad, really I would. But Joey's been so upset lately…"

"Sweetheart, he's not your son," her mother said gently.

No, but it felt like he was. And because of that, Sara could understand how her parents felt. If Joey chose to go and live halfway across the country, with someone she believed didn't even love him, she'd want an explanation, which was no less than her parents deserved. It was what they'd come all this way for. "Max and I had a fight," she began. "We weren't speaking for a while, and I'm afraid Joey got caught in the middle."

Maureen shared a look with her husband. "That's why you've sounded so unhappy on the phone lately."

"I…have some things to work out." Like her entire future. And if she chose dinner with her parents over Max and Joey, it would send the wrong message. She took a deep breath and said what she had to say before she could think of any reasons not to. "Before you arrived I was going to tell Max I love him—"

Her mother gave a little sob, covering her mouth with the handkerchief. Sara went instantly to comfort her, but she mumbled something about being exhausted and disappeared into the bedroom.

Her father caught Sara's arm before she could follow. "Your mother was hoping you'd come home with us," he said, pulling out one of the chairs at the small kitchen table for her and taking the other himself.

She simply stood there a moment, torn and miserable, while her mother cried and her father watched her with expectant, hopeful eyes. A part of her wanted to go with them, desperately, to put all the heartache and uncertainty behind her and return to a place of unquestioning support and love, a place where no one teased her for being who she was and where she'd have all the time in the world to decide what to do next. The rest of her was just too stubborn to walk away from her feelings for Max until all hope was gone.

No matter what path she chose, she'd be hurting people she loved—her parents and brothers, Joey and the friends she'd made in Erskine.

"Maybe we shouldn't have come," John said.

Sara went over and hugged him around the shoulders. "I'm glad you did. It's good to see you."

"But we could have picked a better time."

"I'm sorry, Dad." She sat in the chair he'd pulled out, taking in a slow, deliberate breath and letting it out. "I feel as if I'm picking my way through a minefield. I don't even know what my next step will be, so how can I tell you?" And how did she tell him that their coming here only made it harder for her? Max had just begun to open up, and now he'd probably close right down again.

"We just want you to be happy, Sara."

"You want me to be happy according to your rules," she corrected him ruefully.

"What's wrong with that? What's wrong with wanting you close by, with a man who can give you all the things you deserve?"

"Did Mom marry you because you could give her nice things?"

"Of course not. Lewis Exports was doing pretty well when we met—" John smiled, acknowledging that he'd been outmaneuvered "—but I had to convince her she couldn't live without me."

Sara offered him a crooked smile. "I can understand how you must have felt."

Her father's smile faded. "And what if you can't convince

him? He'd be a fool to let you walk away, but it's been six years, Sara. Maybe—"

"He's been hurt, Dad. He just needs to be pushed out of his shell."

"And you're going to do that by telling him you're in love with him?"

Sara stared down at her hands, wondering how they could be so calmly folded when she was all churned up inside. "One way or another, I'll get my answer."

"And if it's not the answer you want to hear?"

"I...don't know."

"I hope you'll think about coming home. To Boston, I mean."

She looked up and saw on her father's face the hurt she'd heard in his voice. "I'm sorry, Dad. I haven't thought that far ahead."

"And even if you had, you wouldn't want to leave Joey."

It wasn't a question, and Sara felt no need to respond to it.

John reached across the table and took his daughter's hands. "Have you considered the possibility that you might be hurting the boy by staying here? If Max isn't interested in you—" Sara's hands clenched in his and he paused. "If he gets involved with another woman, it'll only be harder for Joey to warm up to her if you're still in the picture."

"Max doesn't even date," she protested.

"Of course not. As long as you're taking care of the two of them, Max has no reason to move on. You feel guilty even talking about the possibility of leaving Montana, Sara, but you're not the kind of woman who'll stay on the sidelines indefinitely. The fact that you're ready to prod Max into taking a stand proves that. If he can't or won't say he loves you, the time will come when you'll meet someone else and you'll follow your heart, just as you're doing now. How do you think Joey will feel then, after he's had that many more months or years of you in his life?"

He said it gently, but it hurt so much she couldn't breathe. The idea of Max falling in love with someone other than her was bad enough, but the idea that she might hold them both back, that she might trap them all into the limbo of an almost-family instead of freeing them to find the real thing, was infinitely sadder.

Hurting Joey was the last thing she wanted to do, but she realized she couldn't avoid that, no matter what decision she made. The best thing for them all, it seemed, was for her to go through with her plan to tell Max how she felt. And if he couldn't love her back, she had to leave—and not just the ranch. She had to leave town.

"You're right, Dad. If Max doesn't…if he can't…" She couldn't say it, but she knew her father understood. "Of course I'll come home, at least for a little while."

"A little while." John smiled thinly. "Your mother and I have often wondered if we aren't responsible—at least partly—for you being out here."

"What?"

"We pushed you too hard after you graduated from college, Sara. I knew you told me you wanted to teach children and instead of listening, I strong-armed you into working for me. And your mother—"

"Stop right there," Sara said. "No offense, Dad, but what's happening here has nothing to do with you and Mom—unless you mean the fact that you raised me to be who I am. I didn't fall in love with Max as an escape from my life in Boston. I fell in love with Max because of the kind of person he is, and because—" she spread her hands "—I guess it was just meant to be, like you and Mom. I don't know what's going to happen next, or whether we'll end up together, but no matter what, I'll be okay." And for the first time in weeks, she believed it.

Max might choose to get over his past and open up his heart, or not. And even if he did, he might not open his heart to her. Sara couldn't control that. What she could control, what she was determined to control, was how she handled herself through it all, and she'd be damned if she folded up into a ball of self-pity and ran back to her parents so they could fix everything.

She would hurt, deeply, if Max couldn't love her. But she'd live, and she wouldn't do it the way he had, behind a wall.

Chapter Six

It didn't take much for Sara to talk her parents into coming over for Thanksgiving dinner, although it probably would've made them more comfortable to have it at her place. It definitely would've made Max more comfortable, Sara thought. But her parents had come a long way to see her, and even if she could have found a way to make everyone happy, for once in her life she wasn't about to try.

Her house was too small to cook the meal, let alone serve it, and if it was up to her, they were all going to be family one day anyway. Might as well get a head start on the bonding, she figured, and what better time to do that than on a national holiday that had come to represent an endless supply of football on TV and enough food to put everyone into a stupor for a week?

For this day, this one day, Sara decided, she'd simply be grateful for what she had, and not wish for more. After the upheaval of the past few weeks, seeing her parents was just the pick-me-up she needed, and she refused to think about whether the days to come would bring happiness or disappointment.

Once the heavy-duty meal preparation got underway, she didn't have time to think about that kind of thing anyway. The house filled with mouthwatering aromas, the windows fogged with steam from the pots bubbling on the stove, and Joey haunted the kitchen, trying to scam a taste every time she basted the turkey. Max popped in and out, dividing his time between a sick horse in the barn and whatever football game was on the television in the front room. And when her parents arrived, her dad staked out a prime space in front of the TV and settled in to watch with Joey. Sara smiled when she heard his young voice giving a rundown of the season to a man who probably hadn't missed a second of it, but who never let on.

Even her mom seemed determined to make the day a good one, tying a dish towel over her raw silk slacks and pitching in to wash the dishes that already crowded the sink.

"What?" Maureen asked when she saw the look her daughter sent her. "You don't think I know how to wash a few dishes?"

"Of course I do," Sara said. "It's just… I was worried about you. Last night—"

Maureen waved off her concern, launching a gob of soap bubbles onto the window over the sink. "I'm sorry about that, sweetheart. Hearing you say you loved Max… I hoped we'd be able to persuade you to come home, but you're not ready."

"It's more than that, Mom. What else is worrying you?"

Maureen leaned forward to swipe the suds from the window, concentrating a little too long on the simple task for it to be anything but an excuse to pull her thoughts together. "I know your father presented you with any number of reasons why you should think long and hard about staying here." She gave her daughter a slightly amused, slightly sheepish smile. "He practiced on the plane. But that's because he's worried you'll mistake his concern for interference," she rushed to add. "He needs to be very sure you know exactly what your decision will mean, Sara, not because he doesn't trust you or doesn't think you're capable of making your own decisions. It's for his peace of mind.

"But there are things about this way of life even he doesn't understand." Maureen's expression turned wistful, and Sara knew she was remembering her childhood on her parents' farm in Pennsylvania. "There's something so simple, so good, about this kind of life," she said at last. "But it's not an easy one, Sara. The bad years outnumber the good years, and there's never enough money coming in to keep up with day-to-day expenses, let alone the kind of maintenance an old place like this needs."

"I know. Max is forever fixing something around here," Sara said, but she said it fondly. The place was ancient, no doubt about that. The porches sagged, the floors creaked and if there wasn't a leak in one place, then dry rot had set in somewhere else. And if it wasn't the house, it was the barn or one of the other outbuildings. Sara no longer noticed any of that.

She loved the creaky old staircases with their risers hollowed out by generations of Devlin feet, and the squeaky wood floors with the rag rugs handmade by Devlin women long gone. She loved the leaky parts and the dried-out parts, and she found the cluster of buildings comforting, a protective hug against the overwhelming and often inhospitable emptiness of the land. "I know you want me to marry someone more…East Coast."

"Well, you'd be closer, at least."

"That life was never right for me," Sara said gently.

"No." Maureen sighed, but the corners of her mouth turned up. "When you were little and your father was still building his business in Europe, I used to travel with him whenever I could, especially in the summer. We sent you and your brothers to stay on the farm with my parents."

"And I used to cry when you came to pick me up," Sara said, smiling. "I remember." She knew how hard her father worked to give his family the best of everything, but she had never felt as if she fit into the world of upwardly mobile professionals and entrepreneurs that her parents and brothers seemed to enjoy so much. She loved her family and her home, but she'd cherished the time she'd spent on her grandparents' farm in Pennsylvania, the quiet beauty of the land and the simplicity of people who accepted a shy young girl no matter if she wore the latest fashions or knew all the right people. "I was an ungrateful little monster, wasn't I?"

"Of course not." Maureen dried her hands on her towel apron, then turned to face her daughter. "I always knew you preferred the farm over the city, but I hoped you'd meet the right man and make a place for yourself in Boston, near us."

"I've met the right man, and I want to make a place for myself here. I know it's not what you and Dad would have chosen for me, but I love this place."

"And you love Max." Maureen glanced in her husband's direction. "You'll fight for love, Sara. I wouldn't expect any less of my daughter."

Sara hugged her, whispering, "Thank you for understanding."

Maureen sniffed and managed a wavery smile. "We want you to know we'll be there for you, no matter what."

"I know that, Mom." Sara hugged her again, blinking away her own tears.

"What's this all about?" John Lewis asked, coming into the kitchen.

Maureen sent her daughter a wink. "The turkey's done," she said, slipping her hands into mitts and opening the oven door.

"Let's have a look." John slung an arm around Sara's shoulders and pulled her close. "You don't think we came here just to talk you into coming back home, do you?"

Sara felt a rush of cool air, and the bottom dropped out of her brightening mood. She didn't need to turn around to know

Max had just come in from the barn, and she could tell from the quality of the silence that he'd heard what her father had said.

Joey appeared in the opposite doorway, alerted, no doubt, by the squeaking of the oven door. "Is dinner ready?" he asked, oblivious to the tension. "I'm starving."

Maureen Lewis bent to take the big enameled roaster out of the oven, but her husband grabbed a dish towel and lifted the heavy pan himself. Sara jerked into motion, poking a fork into the simmering potatoes and pronouncing them done in a voice that was a little too chipper.

"Let's get out of the way while the ladies work," John said, shooing Joey back into the other room.

None of them looked at Max, which was just fine with him. It wasn't as if he hadn't expected there to be some awkward moments today, and it wasn't as if he hadn't already realized why Sara's parents had come to Montana.

Hadn't he been telling himself for years that this moment would come? Sara was from a world where incomes were tied to the stock market, not the stockyards. The eligible bachelors in her social circle were headed for careers in boardrooms or courtrooms, and her parents probably had one of them all picked out for her. Every time she went home for a visit, Max wondered if she'd come back, and every time she came back, he wondered how long she'd be content to stay in a tiny house in a tiny little town in Middle-of-Nowhere, Montana. As much as Max would've liked things to go on the way they were forever, it wouldn't be fair of him to hold her back from the life she deserved, any more than it would have been fair of him to hold Julia back from the fame and fortune she'd craved six years ago.

But then there was Joey. When Julia left, Joey hadn't been old enough to really feel the loss. Oh, he'd known his mother was gone, but then Sara had come, and she was so good with children, Joey had settled right in. In his memory, Sara had always been there. If she left...

When she left. Max had to face it. She wanted—no, she needed a change. Those were her words. She was unhappy. She couldn't live like this anymore—more of her words. And it wasn't just her words, it was her actions. She'd been avoiding him, and even he wasn't clueless enough to miss the fact that there was something she wanted to tell him, something she was afraid to tell him. He was beginning to see a pattern he was all too familiar with.

Max slipped off his coat and hung it on the hooks in the back breezeway, wondering how both of them, he and Joey, were going to survive it. For the time being, though, there was dinner to get through. Yesterday he'd been happy about another Thanksgiving with Sara; today he'd be grateful to have it over with.

Sara, as usual, came to the rescue. "I'm thankful," she said after Joey had finished leading them all in his version of grace, "to be sharing this meal with people who mean so much to me." Her gaze went around the table, resting on each and every one of them for a moment. When she got to Max, he swore he saw hope in her eyes.

Leave it to Sara, Max thought, to make such an awkward situation feel comfortable with a few simple words. Even his mood lightened considerably after that, though it wasn't easy to listen to Sara and her parents talk about people and things she missed in Boston.

"How are Ben and Brad?" she asked her parents, turning to Joey to explain, "they're my twin brothers. Ben was the big troublemaker and Brad was constantly daydreaming—he couldn't walk across a room without falling over his own feet because his mind was always somewhere else."

Her eyes were bright and shining with laughter. It made

Max ache to see her so happy when she'd been so somber lately.

"Now Ben's an assistant district attorney in Boston, and Brad is helping design spacecraft for the Mars mission."

"And Alison is pregnant," Maureen put in. "Brad's wife," she explained for Max and Joey's benefit. "We found out just before we left Boston."

"They must be so excited. I'll call tomorrow and congratulate them," Sara said, but her smile dimmed a bit. Her gaze met Max's and he could see it was wistfulness she felt.

He felt a little of that himself. The happiest day of his life had been the day Joey was born. To never know that kind of joy again was sad enough for him, but for Sara, a woman with so much to give, never to know it at all would be a real crime.

It made him really think about their relationship for the first time since she'd come to Erskine six years ago. The rest of the meal passed that way, Max content to be on the outskirts of a conversation that didn't require his input except for the occasional nod or grunt of assent, which gave him plenty of time to ruminate over the path of his future. His and Joey's and Sara's.

Before he knew it, the table was cleared, the dishes were done, and her parents were turning down dessert in favor of catching their plane back to Boston. Max held Maureen's coat while she slipped into it, but just when he smelled freedom, Maureen pulled him aside.

The last thing he wanted was to have a private conversation with Sara's mother, but he didn't see any graceful way to avoid it.

"Thank you for letting us invite ourselves to dinner," she said, flicking a glance to where her husband and daughter stood by the door, putting on their coats.

"It made Sara happy to have you here," he said.

"But not you, I think. No, don't apologize for that. I didn't mean it as a criticism. We didn't give you any notice, and that's inexcusable, but…" She looked over at Sara and sighed. "She's so far away, and she doesn't come home nearly often enough. She's my only daughter, and I miss her terribly." She smiled at Max, truly smiled at him for the first time since she'd arrived. "I'm sure you understand."

It was Max's turn to look over at Sara. "I do understand."

WHEN SARA GOT BACK from walking her parents to their car and seeing them off, Max had gone to the barn to check on the sick horse. Joey was sitting at the kitchen table, working on his second piece of pie—lemon meringue this time. "Something wrong with the pie?" she asked when she realized he was only playing with it. "Too sour?"

"No." Joey laid his fork down on the plate. "I guess I'm full."

A number of responses ran through Sara's mind, mostly disbelief that he could ever get enough to eat, but she kept them to herself. She knew Joey better, probably, than his own father when it came to how he felt and how he dealt with his feelings. Asking wouldn't work; neither would manipulation. He'd talk when and if he was ready.

"Your mom seemed kind of sad," he said after a quiet moment. "So do you."

So, she thought, he wasn't as unaware as everyone presumed. "We miss each other, Joey. Like your dad misses you the nights you sleep over at Jason's."

"Is that why Dad looked like he ate something rotten? Because he figured you were going back to Boston with your mom and dad?"

"Who said I was going to Boston?"

He shrugged. "Didn't they want you to go?"

"Well, yes, but I have responsibilities here."

"Oh." He picked up his fork and plowed furrows in the meringue on his pie. "Am I a responsibility?"

Sara took a moment so he'd know she'd considered her answer, not just handed him an easy and insincere denial. Kids were smarter than people gave them credit for about picking up on that sort of thing. "A responsibility is something you have to do," she said. "I love spending time with you, Joey."

He ducked his head, cheeks flushing with pleasure. Sara's heart warmed, but Joey turned serious again.

"Are you going away, Sara? Ever?"

She wanted to tell Joey she'd stay in her little house forever, but it would be a lie. If she stayed, it would be under different circumstances than in the past, and if the circumstances didn't change, she couldn't stay. And since she had a lot more faith in the second possibility, better that he be prepared than caught off guard. "I'd like to stay, Joey, but it might not be possible. I want to get married someday—"

"Why don't you marry Dad?"

"Well…we're just friends, Joey. It usually takes more than that for two people to get married."

"So you might leave?"

"I have a lot of things to think about, and there are some decisions I need to make," she said. "I'm not really sure what I'll do."

She could all but see him digesting that, fitting it into the cracks that must have suddenly appeared in his safe little world. Thankfully, he decided not to delve too deep. Sort of like his father. "Do you want to watch *Star Wars* with me?" he asked as if they hadn't just had a potentially life altering conversation.

When they settled on the couch, he snuggled against her side, and even after he fell asleep halfway through the movie, she sat there savoring the feel of his head nestled in the crook of her arm. And waited for Max.

When she woke up on his couch in the morning, he still hadn't come in from the barn.

HE'D WANTED TO KISS HER, there on Main Street. With half the town watching, including his son, Max had wanted to kiss Sara. And not just a friendly, there's-mistletoe-on-your-head peck on the lips. An all-out, spit-swapping, hearts-pounding-against-each-other kiss. A kiss that might lead to something. Something Max wasn't allowed to want with Sara.

As if that wasn't bad enough, he'd wanted to know what had made her cry and, if he'd caused the tear-fest, what he could do to make it stop. He'd been careful not to touch her, though, because if he touched her he'd be right back to Detour One on the strange new path his life had suddenly taken, where he wasn't sure anymore if kissing Sara would be such a terrible mistake.

But then her parents had shown up and reality had knocked him over the head. Having Sara in his life had been like wearing a set of dark glasses—the sun was out, but he knew it was dangerous to look directly at it without protection. She was an inch from walking out of his life, and while there was a part of him that wanted to take off those glasses and see, just for once, what his world could be like without her, he had to think about what was best for Joey. And for Sara.

There weren't going to be any easy solutions, either. Max didn't know much, but he was absolutely certain of that. Skulking between the house and the barn for the past two days hadn't solved his problem any more than avoiding him had solved Sara's. Anyway, the horse was healing, and hiding in the barn was beginning to create some serious self-respect issues. He knew what he had to do and putting it off wouldn't make it any easier. He'd done a lot of thinking and he'd come to one inescapable conclusion. He had to let Sara go.

He couldn't give her what she wanted, that much was painfully obvious, and it wasn't fair to let her sacrifice another year of her life to his family. Eight was still a little young for Joey to be completely self-sufficient, but he was a responsible kid. He knew how to microwave meals—meals that Sara made and froze for when she had to stay late at school or when she went to Boston to visit her family. Well, Max thought, he'd have to spend more time in the frozen-food section at the market, or make extra on the nights he forced himself to cook and freeze it the way Sara did. But he wasn't looking forward to it.

And he hadn't expected her to be there when he came in from the barn.

"Mrs. Hartfield called and asked if she could pick Joey up early," she said, pretending not to notice how he'd stopped dead inside the back door as soon as he saw her in the kitchen. "He figured you were too busy to see him off, and he didn't want to leave without somebody knowing he was gone."

"I guess we raised him right," Max said. It was the first thing that had popped into his head. He wished he could have stuffed it back in there.

Sara seemed to be suddenly fascinated by the view out the window. Max wasn't quite sure what to do with his feet—or his mouth—so he just stood there.

"How's the horse?" she finally asked.

"Fine," he said, and he had to clear his throat.

"Good."

This was awkward. All the times he'd rehearsed this conversation over the past two days, it had never been awkward. He'd explained his position calmly and rationally—that should've been his first clue that he'd been hallucinating. He'd never handled any conversation about his feelings calmly and rationally. In fact, they'd all started out awkward and gone downhill from there. "Why don't we sit down?"

She sat at the table and Max took the chair opposite her. Quiet fell, a silence so profound the ticktock of the old tambour mantel clock in the front room seemed like doom tolling.

"It's selfish of me to keep you here," Max began.

"Before you leave again—" Sara said at the same time. Her eyes lifted to his, dropped to contemplate the table again.

There was another minute of ticking doom-filled silence.

"You were saying?"

"No, Max." She didn't look at him. "You go ahead."

"You first, Sara."

"It's not that important," she said miserably.

Max took a deep breath. One of them had to go first. "You should move back to Boston—" he said at the same time Sara blurted out, "I love you."

She came out of her chair, eyes wide. "What did you say?"

Max lurched to his feet, too, then had to brace both hands on the table when his legs threatened to give out on him. He felt as if someone had sucked all the oxygen out of the room. He knew Sara was talking, he could see her lips moving, but he couldn't have repeated a single word she'd said—except those first three. *I love you.*

"Wait a minute, wait a minute." He stumbled out the back door. His breath steamed in the frigid air, but he didn't feel the cold. He stared at the ranch yard and wanted to laugh hysterically. How could everything appear so normal when the whole world had just shifted beneath his feet?

And then he glanced over his shoulder and saw Sara watching him through the window. The look on her face was the same sad, lost, hurting look he'd seen on her face after the mistletoe incident. When he hadn't kissed her.

He dragged his eyes away from her as the pieces of the puzzle fell into place at last. He could finally see the whole picture—even if he had no idea what to do about it. "I don't want to hold you back from having a home and family of your own" hardly seemed appropriate after finding out it was *his* home and family she wanted.

"I'm sorry, Max."

He whipped around to discover her standing behind him. She had her arms wrapped around her waist, but he doubted she was feeling the cold, either.

"I shouldn't have dropped it on you like that."

"Sara—"

"No, let me say what I have to say."

"We should at least go inside."

She nodded, but when he came toward her, reaching out to rest his hand at the small of her back, Sara shied away, scooting inside before he could touch her. She was half a heartbeat from tears; if he touched her she'd throw herself into his arms and let them come, and to hell with what needed to be said.

"When I came here to help you six years ago, I didn't love you—at least I didn't know I did. I mean, I had a crush on you in college." She ran herself a glass of water she didn't want, cradling it between her hands to keep them from shaking. She knew she was babbling, but Max still had that shell-shocked look on his face. "Do you understand what I'm saying?"

He nodded, though his eyes were filled with such bafflement she couldn't continue to meet them.

"I don't want you to think I came here because I was hoping… All I felt for you was friendship, Max. At least, that's what I thought." She took a sip of water, after all, her throat achingly dry. "I wasn't here very long before I realized I was in love with you. I should've told you sooner, but I was afraid…" Sara closed her eyes and took a deep breath. She knew she was making a mess of this. Max wasn't even looking at her anymore, but she blundered on. "Even if I'd known it would end this way, I wouldn't wish the last six years away. Except maybe for the accidents."

His head came up at that, his gaze stabbing into hers.

She took another drink of the lukewarm water, needing some sort of strength for what she was about to confess. "I kept telling myself that I could settle for your friendship, but my body has always admitted the truth. Every time I look at you, I forget...everything but how you make me feel. Before I know it, I've humiliated myself and embarrassed some other poor, innocent soul, damaged personal property and generally wreaked havoc wherever I happen to be at the moment. The townspeople have always forgiven me because I pay for the damage, and because—"

"They all know you're in love with me?"

Sara nodded miserably. "I'm sorry, Max, but whenever something happens, you're there."

"And they made the connection I've been too blind to see." He shoved his hands into his pockets and turned to look out the window. There was nothing to see but the Montana winter night, as bleak and unfathomable as his own heart seemed to be. "Why didn't anyone tell me?"

"I guess they thought you knew, and I...I didn't have the courage until now."

"I don't know what to say."

"You don't have to say anything."

"But I should have seen it. You're my best friend. I'm an idiot, Sara. It's a wonder you can stand to look at me after...so long."

She swallowed a couple of times to relieve the tightness in her throat. "Don't beat yourself up, Max. I went to a lot of trouble to hide it from you."

He heard her voice coming closer, could feel her standing behind him. He turned and, without thinking, tried to take her into his arms, needing to comfort her as much as he craved this one bit of stability in a world that had suddenly turned inside out.

She braced her hands on his chest, denying them both that moment of peace.

He looked her in the eyes, seeing the pain and heartbreak there, and a fierce light of determination that puzzled him. "Sara—"

"I don't want your pity, and I can't live with just your friendship any longer."

"What does that mean?"

"I think you're right. I should go back to Boston as soon as the school year is over."

He groaned, finally remembering what he'd said. "Forget that, Sara. I didn't know—"

"Shhh," she said, laying her fingers softly over his mouth. "I'm glad you did, Max. It would be a mistake for you to keep the truth to yourself so you wouldn't hurt my feelings."

She spoke in a rush—as if he could have said anything with his mind bouncing between the certainty that he was right to set her free, and the stark and frightening idea of not having her in his life anymore. He thought he'd been prepared for it, but now that the moment had arrived... He caught her wrist, pulled her hand away from his tingling mouth. "What about Joey?"

Sara's determination wavered for the first time since she'd walked in the door, tears threatening to destroy the cloak of calmness she'd pulled around herself. After everything she'd told Max, he still wouldn't ask her to stay for himself. "I'll call Joey and e-mail him, and I'll come back once in a while," she said.

But they both knew she wouldn't, at least not right away. She had to cut the ties that had held her in their lives for so long. Her heart was going to bleed, but she'd mend. And in time, maybe she'd find a man she could love, one who loved her.

"You can't leave, Sara."

"We both know I have to, Max, but…there's something…" Her courage faltered, but she knew she'd always regret it if she let this moment pass. She rose onto her toes, slipped a hand behind his neck and pulled his face the rest of the way down to hers. Her mouth met his in a kiss that was achingly soft and sweet, everything she'd always dreamed kissing Max would be.

And then the world caught fire.

Chapter Seven

The instant Sara's mouth touched his, the air around them seemed to burst into flames. Max gulped in great, ragged breaths, the fire inside him surging and growing with each rush of oxygen. He kissed her wildly and she met him the same way. He thought he knew everything there was to know about Sara, but he never would've guessed that her tongue would tangle and spar with his, or that she'd taste so sweet and intoxicating she'd make his head reel. He wouldn't have believed she'd know how and where to touch him, that her hands could bring such exquisite pain and pleasure. He never would have expected her skin to feel like hot silk beneath his hands, that her scent could make his heart pound, that she would be so softly yielding, so supple and graceful and so beautiful in her abandon that she would literally take his breath away.

He would have known, if he'd ever let himself think about it, that she'd give him everything she had to give. But not that she would demand so much of him in return.

It was Sara who took the kiss to the next level, clenching her hands in his shirt and tearing it open as she backed him up against the kitchen counter. Her mouth dropped to his neck, his chest, her hands moving down to his backside, pulling him hard against her.

He peeled her snowman sweater over her head and tossed it away, pulled her bra straps down and took a moment to savor the sight of her, milky skin flushed, her desire for him clear and compelling. Irresistible. He dropped his mouth to her neck, savoring the taste of her skin and the way she shuddered beneath the subtle rasp of his tongue. Then he lifted his mouth to hers, drinking in the sounds of her pleasure as his hands roamed, skimming the curves of her breasts and slipping over the slender rib cage as he learned by touch what he'd never so much as allowed himself to imagine before.

Sara was anything but submissive. Her hands ran boldly over his body, and she met him kiss for kiss. When their mouths parted, her husky pleas and throaty moans guided him ever closer to a place from which there'd be no retreat. The feel of her unbuckling his belt was all it took to push him over the edge.

One moment they were both still half-dressed, the next he was in her, her back braced against the kitchen wall, her legs around his waist. He moved and she shuddered violently, clamping her legs around him so he couldn't move again unless she allowed it. Her strength surprised him; the way she looked at him from under her tousled, coppery curls all but made his knees buckle. Her lips, swollen and moist, curved into a wanton smile, her eyes glowing with heat and knowledge—the elemental power that every woman knew instinctively how to wield.

And no man could resist.

Max began to move, her body wrapping around him, moving with him, driving him to a place that was nowhere and everywhere, pain and pleasure, heaven and hell. She braced one hand on his hip, draped the other around his neck, her eyes locking on his until they both went blind with the pleasure, tumbled over the edge of ecstasy and clung tightly to each other as the storm blew itself out.

Max smiled smugly at the sight of her, head thrown back, her skin flushed and rosy. His eyes roamed over her lovely bare breasts—her black lace bra still hooked but around her waist now—down to where their bodies were still joined.

It seemed to Sara there was some sort of secret physical communication going on, independent of thought and reason and control.

But then, if just the *possibility* of having his mouth and hands on her could steal her wits, why had she assumed she could actually kiss him and keep her sanity? Shame and embarrassment gave way to a deep sense of satisfaction. She would never forget making love with Max, even if all the love had been on her side. She only hoped he could understand why she'd thrown herself at him like this, why—now that their friendship had been destroyed forever—she had needed to be with him, just once.

"Max, I—"

"No," he said, his deep voice sending shivers down her spine. He cupped her face, rubbing his thumb across her bottom lip. "If you're about to apologize, don't. If you're analyzing this, Sara, just let it go." He helped her up, and when she tried to straighten her clothes, he helped her out of them instead. The genuine approval on his face as he looked at her naked body, his absolute lack of self-consciousness, stripped her embarrassment away. "Let's not talk or even think about anything but here and now."

He held out his hand and she took it without hesitation, let him lead her into the bedroom and lay her down on the bed, let him worship her body from head to toe and then worshiped him in turn until they were both limp as rags, tangled together and wrung out by pleasure.

And afterward, Sara cried.

MAX WOKE UP feeling as if he hadn't slept in years, muscles heavy with fatigue, eyes gritty, his head buzzing—no, that was the alarm. He rolled over to shut it off and found his way blocked by a warm body. Joey, he assumed at first, brought there by a nightmare. But this body was a lot bigger than Joey's. And naked. And female.

Sara.

He reached for her, then thought better of it. She had to be as exhausted as he was. It brought a smile to his face, a warm glow to the rest of him. He propped himself up on one elbow, reaching over her to shut off the alarm, all the while gazing into the pale oval of her face. It was the same face he'd seen practically every day of the past six years, the same freckle-dusted skin, same nose and eyes and lips, and yet she seemed so different now. Or maybe *he* was different.

Just looking didn't seem to be enough, so he ran a finger over the soft skin of her cheek with the excuse of brushing back her tousled hair.

She groaned softly and swatted at his hand.

Charmed, Max tugged at one of her curls, tickling her nose with the ends of it.

She stuck out her lower lip and blew.

He feathered a fingertip along the curve of her bottom lip, and forgot it was a game. He bent down to put his mouth where his hands had been, hazily noting the glaring red glow of the alarm clock: 6:04 a.m.

Six-oh-four! He flopped onto his back, desire wrestling with reality for a moment—which was all it took to make his hormones cry uncle, considering the workout they'd had. And considering he was already an hour late for chores. "Being self-employed means never getting a day off," he muttered, dropping a kiss on her lips and slipping out of bed before he could change his mind. He didn't touch Sara again, didn't even look at her for fear he wouldn't be able to leave her.

He hit the bathroom, throwing on pants and a shirt from the hamper rather than risking a return to the bedroom for clean ones. Too bad he couldn't use the same logic for the chores, he caught himself thinking, but you couldn't just leave cows somewhere until you had time to milk them. No, it had to be done every day, morning and evening, or all hell would break loose, and he was on the hook no matter which way things played out. For the first time since he'd chosen this way of life, Max found himself resenting the responsibility of it.

He'd always been a morning person, even when his morning had to start at five o'clock. By the time breakfast rolled around, he'd already accomplished more than most people could show for an entire day. Every task he performed contributed directly to the welfare of his little family, and every task had to be completed to the best of his ability, because it reflected directly on him. No half measures for Max Devlin; nothing was ever just good enough, and there was no such thing as a shortcut.

That didn't mean chores had to take him three hours *every* morning.

Suddenly he could think of all sorts of ways to cut corners without sacrificing quality. For instance, if he spilt a little milk because he was carrying two buckets in each hand instead of one, that just meant he didn't have to feed the barn cats. And if he accidentally shoved an extra bale of hay out of the loft because he'd been thinking of Sara when he should've been paying attention to what he was doing, he would need one less bale tomorrow.

The sky had pearled to gray when he left the barn, a weak, diffuse yellow patch where the sun had dragged itself over the southeastern horizon and was trying to peek through a lightly falling snow. Despite his rush to get back to Sara, Max stopped in the middle of the yard and looked around at what was his, just as he did every morning. The chimneys on his house and Sara's plumed smoke, chickens clucked and pecked the ground around the coop, and cattle were nudging each other for a turn at the feed or water troughs. Nothing had changed but everything was different.

Grinning like a fool, Max hurried to the house, shucked off his coat and boots and threw a pound of bacon in a frying pan. The smell of it sizzling made him so ravenous his stomach knotted. He stirred it around with a fork, pulled a chair out, then decided there was no reason to eat alone. Sara had to be hungry, too, he figured, and she could do things with eggs, mysterious things involving all those little pots of herbs she kept on the windowsill. He took the stairs two at a time and shouldered his way through the bedroom door—

It was empty.

It took a moment to register, and then he simply stood there, staring at the bed. She'd made it; the sheets were tucked in, blankets pulled up, the quilt in place. Just the way he liked it.

Except he didn't like it. There ought to be some proof to show that Sara had been there, Max thought—dents in the pillows, some little bit of female fluff on the nightstand or dresser. He'd settle for finding her.

Not that her absence was all that surprising. Knowing Sara, she was probably feeling shy after last night, and considering some of the things they'd done...

The rest of that thought didn't just wander off, it burst into flames.

Max found himself downstairs, boots on and halfway out the door before he noticed the smell of burning bacon. He spun on his heel, raced around the table—and sprawled over the chair he'd left pulled out. Luckily, he grabbed on to the protruding chair leg just in time to cushion the blow to his face. Not that his fist was that much softer than the wood, but at least he didn't put an eye out. Head ringing, his left cheekbone throbbing, he jumped to his feet, turned off the stove and dashed out the door, wading through knee-deep snow because he was in too much of a hurry to use the shoveled walkways.

No one answered his knock, but Sara never locked her door, so he opened it and went inside. And knew without a doubt that she was gone—not merely away from home. Gone.

The little house felt empty, desolate, abandoned. All the furniture Sara had rescued from the storage loft in the barn and lovingly refinished was still there. The refrigerator in the kitchen still hummed softly and warmth radiated from the wood stove in the main room, but the place seemed cold.

For the first time in his life, Max went into Sara's tiny bedroom. He opened the old-fashioned armoire and found most of her clothes missing. Her sweaters and wool skirts had disappeared from the closet. That should've been enough to convince him of the truth, but he opened her dresser drawers anyway, one after another. Empty, empty, empty, except for a bit of harlot-red lace peeking over the far back edge of one of them. Max tugged free a pair of silk panties that had gotten wedged behind the drawer and crushed them in his hand.

Sara *couldn't* be gone; he was just jumping to the wrong conclusion. He had to be. When Julia had walked out of his life, he'd vowed never to put himself in that position again, never to open himself up to that kind of hurt.

And yet he had. Without even realizing it, he'd let Sara into every corner of his life. And then he'd said one stupid thing.

Oh my God, he thought, shambling out of her bedroom, *I told Sara she should move back to Boston.* That wasn't just stupid, it was…he couldn't think of anything bad enough to describe it. And then he'd told her to forget it. Like that was going to happen.

Max slumped into one of the chairs at her little dining table and saw a square white envelope propped against the Santa and Mrs. Claus salt and pepper shakers. He reached for it, catching sight of the panties still clutched in his other hand. Reality versus fantasy. It made him hesitate for a moment, but only a moment, before he consigned the fantasy to his back pocket and opened the envelope, bracing himself for reality.

I've gone to stay with Janey Walters. You were right last night, Max. Not about being selfish—I stayed here because it was what I wanted to do. You and Joey have been able to take care of each other for quite a while now, so it's time I let you. I'm going back to Boston as soon as the school year is over. I know how hard it is for you to talk about your feelings. Thank you for being honest with me. Sara.

He read it again, and a third time, but he couldn't make the words mean anything but what they said. She'd left him. After the most incredible, earth-shattering night any man could fantasize about, let alone hope to experience, Sara had walked out with no warning, without even giving him a chance to explain. She didn't like the way things were, so out the door she went. It was Julia all over again.

Only this time he wasn't going to sit back and take it. Not from Sara, damn it. Unlike Julia, she'd been happy here, and suddenly she said she was going back to Boston as soon as school ended? If she thought she was leaving town after what she'd told him in words yesterday and shown him by her actions last night, then she had another think coming.

He dropped the note and stalked out the door, the ringing of his boot heels on the polished wood floor like the sound of applause at his determination to find Sara and get some answers.

The cold air made his sore eye sting and throb, but that wasn't what made him turn around. It was the sight of Joey's baby shoes, hanging from the rearview mirror of his truck. He wasn't like Sara; he couldn't just up and leave. He had responsibilities—to himself, to the ranch and most of all to his son.

He went to his own house and took some aspirin for his eye, then called the Hartfields and asked them if Joey could stay a little longer. No problem, Tom Hartfield said. No problem. Sure, what did Tom have to complain about? He'd been with the same woman since high school. He didn't have to worry about turning his back and finding her gone.

And he didn't have to worry about going through Janey Walters to discover why she'd disappeared.

"SARA'S NOT HERE," Janey said when she found him standing on her front porch. "What happened to your eye?"

"Nothing. Where is she?"

"It doesn't look like nothing, Max. It looks like someone punched you."

"Nobody punched me, Janey, I tripped over a chair. I need to find Sara."

"Why, did she push you?"

"Could you just forget about the black eye and tell me where she is?"

Janey made a face. "You're taking all the fun out of this for me."

Max glared at her.

"C'mon, Max, you know I can't tell you where Sara is. She's my friend."

"And I'm not? We've known each other all our lives. We went to school together—"

"I wouldn't be bringing that up, considering the way you treated me in school."

Max winced, not because of the good, clean fun he'd had teasing Janey, but because he was about to throw himself on the altar of past humiliations. It would be worth it, though, if it got him what he wanted. "You didn't get teased any more than anyone else, Janey. Don't you remember what they used to call me?"

"Yeah." Janey grinned. "I trust you've taken care of that little problem."

"It only happened that one time—look, I really need to talk to Sara."

"I'm sure you will, just as soon as she's ready to talk to you." She crossed her arms, but not, Max thought, because it was cold and she was coatless. "Listen, Max, you've been stringing Sara along all this time—"

"I didn't even know she was in love with me. How could I be stringing her along?"

"By hanging on to the past while she was hoping you'd fall in love with her, that's how. It doesn't make any sense," she said before he could. "I know that, but logic is hardly the most important thing to consider when your heart is breaking."

Max lifted a hand and rubbed at his chest, but before he could put a name to the sudden pang he felt, or even wonder about it, Janey interrupted his train of thought.

"I'd like to help you, Max," she said. "Believe it or not, I want to see the two of you together, if only to make Sara happy. But you guys are going to have to settle this on your own. I'm staying out of it." She stepped back but didn't close the door. "I will tell you one thing, though, and only because you look so damned pathetic. Whatever you do, it better be good."

"Is she that mad?"

"Determined," Janey corrected. "She's made her mind up that she's leaving town."

"Then I'll just convince her to stay."

"I don't know, Devlin. The last time she set her heart on something, it was you. It's taken her six years to give up on that. What does that say for your odds?"

Chapter Eight

Sara had heard that Max was looking for her all over town. He'd even gone so far as to peek in the door of the ladies' room at the Crimp 'N Cut, right at the strategic moment when Mrs. Erskine-Lippert, Joey's principal and the scourge of the town, was bent over adjusting her panty hose. She'd straightened suddenly, cracking her head on the bathroom counter, and as the town's clinic was closed on Saturday, the veterinarian had been called in to stitch her up. By all accounts, she was sporting seven stitches, dead center in a bald spot no ratting and combing could hope to cover. And she was eager to have a conversation with Max.

Thank heaven it wasn't her fault, was all Sara thought when she heard about it—at least not directly. Max had been searching for *her*, after all.

She hadn't been avoiding him exactly, but the Ersk Inn was the last place she expected to find him, huddled over a beer and looking for all the world like he'd lost his best friend. But then maybe he had—they both had, after last night.

She had a hard time mustering up any regret. Last night had been... Sara didn't have the words to describe it. She certainly hadn't meant to sleep with Max, but gosh, just looking at him was enough to turn her into bumbling, brainless mush. When he'd kissed her like that and touched her like that… She shivered involuntarily. Max might not love her, but he'd wanted her last night with a desperation that still took her breath away. She should have said no, but the shocking and arousing things he'd whispered in her ear as his hands had rushed over her body….

There was no way she could have resisted the temptation to fulfill so many fantasies. And no way she could have risked facing him at the ranch that morning, seeing the regret and apology in his eyes as he tried to let her down easy. She still wasn't up to facing it. In fact, once her vision adjusted to the afternoon gloom inside the bar, she made a point of not looking at him at all.

She perused the room instead, surprised to find that hardly anybody was interested in her unprecedented visitation, and the few who did glance over avoided her eyes the way she'd avoided Max's. Their gazes automatically shifted to the big-screen football game when she looked their way. For the life of her, she'd never understand what was so thrilling about a bunch of men turning themselves into human battering rams just to move an ugly leather ball a few yards in one direction or another.

But that was irrelevant. She'd come to the Ersk Inn with a mission and, Max or no Max, she was going to carry it out.

She turned around and almost ran straight into Maisie Cunningham, the one and only daytime waitress. Sara stopped dead, but Maisie began to back away, as if clumsiness were contagious. Maybe it was, Sara thought as she plucked the full tray from Maisie's hands before the woman bumped into a table crowded with tourists, who must have come to see the scandalous window, since they were all having the Mountain Man special that came with the tour package. Sara set down the tray and grabbed Maisie by the wrist just as she was about to tumble into the lap of one of the tourists. That earned her a disgruntled look from the man with the empty lap, a grateful smile from the man's wife and a collective sigh of relief from the rest of the room. Or maybe it was disappointment that, for once, she'd prevented an accident rather than causing one. If that was the case, they'd better get used to it, because her days as the laughingstock of Erskine, Montana, were over. It wasn't just a plan this time; conviction filled her like a white-hot core of solid steel. It was all she felt—all she would allow herself to feel.

Despite her determination, she glanced experimentally at Max, bracing herself for the rush of yearning that always put her off balance. It didn't come. Neither did the warm flood of love. She felt numb inside, as if a blanket of insulation surrounded her heart and no feelings could leak in or out. All the time she was agonizing over telling him how she felt and he was already done with her. And she couldn't even get angry about it.

"Uh, Miss Lewis?"

Sara took a deep, calming breath. There was nothing she could do about the emotional black hole she'd been sucked into, nothing she wanted to do, truth be told. After so many years of heartache, the numbness felt good.

She turned around to find the proprietor of the Ersk Inn and creator of her namesake pool watching her with the mixture of deference and apprehension usually reserved for much bigger celebrities. Or mass murderers. "Hello, Mr. Shasta."

"Can I get you anything?"

"No, thank you, but I would like to say something to everyone, if you don't mind."

"Anything for you, Miss Lewis." He wiped his hands on the towel slung beneath his truly remarkable beer belly, then gingerly took her elbow and led her to stand in front of the big screen.

Sara had to shield her face from the glare of the projectors until they cut off suddenly. When her eyes adjusted and she saw everyone staring at her, her voice froze in her throat.

"Hey, Mike," someone yelled out. "Did you shut off the TV or did Sara break the projector?"

There was a smattering of laughter and one loud, disgusted groan. "Aw, man, if you'd just waited another thirteen minutes, I'd have won the pool. I could have bought Emmy Lou that brand new gen-u-ine fake leather sofa she wants so bad."

"Naw, Mort O'Hara has this square so he gets the money."

"Mort O'Hara is in a nursing home down Casper way. What's he gonna do with that kind of dough?"

"Beats me, but his granddaughter bought it for him for his ninetieth birthday. The last time she caught her husband fooling around she tried to scalp him. I don't know about you, but I wouldn't want to mess with her."

Sara shut out the laughter and commentary that followed, but she couldn't help noticing that the tourists were whispering among themselves and sending her curious looks, until a thoughtful Erskinite filled them in, and then they all laughed, too.

Yep, Sara wanted to yell at them, *I'm the one who broke the window. I'm the one who superglued myself to another human being. I'm the one stubborn enough to keep loving a man who will never—*

A loud thump ended her detour into self-pity. Like everyone else in the bar, Sara turned toward the source of the sound, her stomach tensing when she saw Max scowling around the room, his fist still resting on the tabletop. She had the quiet she needed to speak her piece, but her conviction was fading fast. The people of Erskine would never let her forget her past, and she didn't have the heart to be bitter about it when she understood the reasons so well. Even if she never caused another moment of embarrassment or another dime's worth of damage, nothing in this small town would ever be as entertaining as her exploits, so what point was there in making a stand?

She turned toward the door, glancing at Max in an automatic reflex she hadn't yet trained herself out of. His gaze bounced off hers, landing on the beer mug cradled in his hands. He took a healthy swig before he lifted his eyes back to hers.

Oddly enough, she found her strength in the man who'd broken her heart. Even in the dim lighting, she noted the grim set to his jaw, read the regret in his eyes, mingled with a sort of sick realization that he had to say something to her that he didn't want to say and she didn't want to hear. Something like, "Last night was a mistake."

She spun on her heel and headed for the bar, then deliberately slowed her steps when she realized she was trying to outrun that dismal inevitability. In a town the size of Erskine, she couldn't avoid Max forever. What she could do—what she was determined to do—was abdicate her throne as queen of the klutzes. Having an accident now would be just a bit counterproductive to that goal.

She made it through the maze of tables and chairs without getting her feet tangled or bumping into anyone, and stopped at the service station in the center of the bar. "I'd like to buy everyone a drink," she said, her eyes panning over the surprised faces of the patrons and skimming Max's bent head before resting on the far wall beside the door. "You can use the money you've already collected on the pool, Mr. Shasta, because it's the last time that poster board over there is going to pay off."

The place went so quiet it felt as if the silence had a life of its own, buzzing in her ears with the shock and confusion of everyone there. Sara's first instinct was to walk through the doorway and let them figure it out on their own. She stayed where she was. Her life had changed in so many bad ways, she was determined that at least one good thing would come from her broken heart. "I've lived in this town for six years, taught most of your children at one time or another, and I've been the butt of your jokes—not that I haven't given you reason. I didn't mind, really, but, well, I'm asking… I know the teasing is meant in good fun, but I just can't live like this anymore."

She could have been speaking to a painting for all the reaction she got. She spread her hands, at a loss as to what else she could say to make them understand how she felt. Thankfully, she didn't have to.

"Looks like the Sara Lewis Pool is officially closed," Mike Shasta announced.

That got a reaction, mostly in the form of groans and doleful expressions. But Sara did see one or two apologetic smiles aimed in her direction. No one objected, at least, which meant that she'd accomplished her task, since the rest of the town would probably get the message before she could make it the four blocks to Janey's house. She murmured a heartfelt thank-you and turned to go.

"Sara."

The sound of her name called out in Max's deep voice stopped her. She steeled herself before she turned to face him, but there was no jolt when she met his eyes, just a slight ache that went away when she lifted her chin and refused to acknowledge it. She held his attention for a moment, held her breath, too, waiting for him to say something, do something, besides stare at her. He simply sat there, and then Maisie and her freshly loaded tray stepped between them and the spell was broken.

Sara shouldered the door open and stepped outside.

"Wait!" Max lurched to his feet and started after her, but his eyes were dazzled by the light streaming in the door, reflected by the snowbanks that lined the street. When it slammed shut, all he could see were little squares of white dancing in his vision. He wasn't about to let a little temporary blindness stop him, though. Max made a beeline for the door, but his foot caught on a chair leg and he tripped. Both hands shot out to break his fall. His right met only empty air, but his left hand slammed down on the edge of the fully loaded tray Maisie had just set down on the table in front of him.

The tray flipped, launching its contents into the air and sending Max hurtling to the floor. He managed to twist so he landed on his backside rather than his face, but he hit the ground hard enough to jar his spine all the way up to the crown of his head. That was nothing compared to the shock of being pelted by the peanuts and pretzels that had been on the tray, then showered with beer and cold soda. A burger with all the trimmings bounced off his shoulder, and the accompanying fries, complete with chili and cheese, splatted into his lap seconds before a heavy glass beer mug hit his thigh. It missed his groin, but it still hurt enough to have him hissing in a breath, then letting it out on a curse.

He sat there for a moment, but the fact that he was wearing lunch for four didn't seem so important measured against the compulsion to get to Sara before she locked herself inside Janey's house. He reached into his back pocket and pulled out his bandanna so he could mop some of the beer from his face. It went suddenly quiet in the room, except for the sound of chairs scraping back. Max was too busy wiping chili out of his lap to notice.

"Uh, Max?"

"Yeah, Mike," he replied distractedly to the gravel-voiced question.

"Did you just wipe your face with a pair of women's panties?"

Max tossed a handful of soggy French fries aside and peered at what he'd thought was his bandanna. Instead of faded red-and-white printed cotton he discovered that his hand was full of black silk trimmed with harlot-red lace. The panties he'd shoved in his back pocket that morning, he remembered. Sara's panties.

A ball of fire exploded in his belly and shot heat out to every extremity at once. He felt all feverish and itchy, as if he'd contracted some rare disease that only Sara could cure. And she'd just walked out of his life. Again. He stuffed the panties back into his pocket and climbed to his feet, ignoring the fact that he'd become the center of attention for the whole bar.

"Hey, Max?"

"What, Mike?"

"Where'd you get the black eye?"

He'd forgotten about that, too, but at the reminder it began to throb and ache. "I fell at home, if it's any of your business."

"Was Miss Lewis around?"

"Nope," he said. But he'd been thinking about her at the time—not that it meant anything, since he'd been thinking about nothing but her since he'd opened his eyes that morning.

"Um…Max?"

He set his teeth. "Yeah, Maisie."

"Rita Jenkins from the Crimp 'N Cut was in here a while ago. Did you really go into the ladies' room there this morning?"

"I only peeked inside the door," he muttered, his eyes on the exit as he fought to get his wallet out of the soaking-wet back pocket of his jeans.

"Rita said that Mabel Erskine-Lippert was in there." Maisie, seeing that she had everyone's attention, went on to recount the whole incident, filtered through enough mouths that instead of a few stitches, Mabel was in a coma, her loved ones faced with the difficult decision to pull the plug or pray for a miracle.

Max tossed a couple of dollars onto the table where he'd been sitting and started to leave, only someone must have asked why he'd been looking in the ladies' room at the Crimp 'N Cut or who he'd been looking for because Maisie said "Sara."

That was all Max heard, just "Sara," but her name—or rather her memory—hit him midstride and had him lurching unsteadily. He stepped on the remains of the hamburger and skidded a couple of feet, arms flailing for balance. Somehow he managed to stay upright.

Everyone in the bar laughed, but Max just scraped the sludge off his boot on the nearest chair rung and headed for the door. All that mattered was Sara. As soon as he talked her out of her anger, his life could get back to normal.

Better than normal, he amended, his mind already spinning fantasies of the cozy evenings and even cozier nights to come.

As soon as the door shut behind Max, Mike Shasta reached for the heavy black marker he kept by the register and clamped the cap between his teeth to pull it off, the last of the laughter dying away as he crossed the room and stopped in front of the betting wall.

It was a pure shame the Sara Lewis Pool had to end, but even if he was callous enough to ignore the poor girl's request, his wife would have his head when she found out about it—and she would find out. Dory Shasta wasn't just a stop on the information highway that kept Erskine's gossip traveling, she was a major intersection. That didn't mean she'd want to see someone hurt for her enjoyment, and if he'd had a hand in it, well, Mike had no desire to find out just how comfortable the old couch in his office was.

But keeping his wife happy didn't mean he had to give up the single most lucrative attraction the inn had ever had, or that the people of Erskine had to lose the best entertainment to hit town since cable television had brought back *I Love Lucy* reruns. Besides, if Mike was any judge of recent events, he'd have bet the show wasn't over yet. And if he could help it along a little, well, wasn't that his civic duty?

He blacked out Sara Lewis's name and scrawled a replacement, grinning like a fool as pandemonium broke out. Shouts of amazement and hoots of laughter mingled with the crash of chairs colliding as just about everyone shoved back from their tables at once. A few people raced out the door to spread the news, but most of them crowded up to the bar, everyone clamoring to be the first to lay down five dollars and put their name on the brand new pool, headlined with the only name that could possibly top Sara's.

Max Devlin.

Chapter Nine

Sara thought the last person she wanted to see was Max. She was wrong. The last person she wanted to see was Joey. Max she knew how to deal with. Joey was another story entirely; if she didn't have the emotional stamina to deal with Max at the moment, that was at least partly his fault. If she let Joey down, she'd never be able to forgive herself.

Her first impulse was to give him some excuse and take him into town to find his dad. But she'd hate herself for it. She swung open Janey's front door and stepped out onto the porch, knowing she'd made the right decision when his face lit up and he ran the rest of the way up the walk, not stopping until he threw himself into her arms.

She laughed, despite the tightness in her throat when she hugged his little body. "What are you doing here, kiddo?"

"Mr. Hartfield had to come into town, and since Dad said he was going to Janey's to see you, Mr. Hartfield said he'd save everyone the trip and drop me off here."

Sara looked up, waving to Jason's dad, which he saw as an invitation to take off. Sara closed her eyes for a second. It looked as if she was going to have to deal with Max after all. But not right now.

"Where's Dad?" Joey asked as she scooted him through the front door.

"He's not here."

"Oh. Then I can drive back to the ranch with you."

Sara let her shoulders slump. Joey didn't know she'd moved in with Janey, and she had two choices—tell him the truth or stall him until Max got there. "Um…how about we have a snack first?" she asked, waiting while he pulled off his coat and jumped to hang it on the very top of the coat tree in the entryway. "Janey just made a batch of her extra-special double-chocolate-chip cookies."

"Won't they spoil my supper?"

"Smart aleck," she said, reaching out to ruffle his hair.

He ducked away, shooting her a grin over his shoulder as he went down the hall and into the kitchen. "Where's Jessie?"

"She has a sore throat, so Janey took her over to Doc's."

"Oh," Joey said, obviously disappointed. He was a bit younger than Jessie, but the two were good friends. "How come you're staying here if Janey's not here?"

So much for stalling, Sara thought, hating what she had to tell Joey. Hating that it had to be this way at all. "I can't take you to the ranch, Joey," she said before the lump in her throat got too big to talk past.

He shrugged, sitting at the kitchen table. "Then I'll go with Dad and you can come later."

She put a plate of cookies in front of him and went to get the milk out of the refrigerator. "I'm not going later."

"When are you going home?"

"I am home, Joey." She turned slowly to face him. "At least for now."

She'd been afraid he'd cry. His reaction was even worse. She watched the reality dawn on his face, saw his gaze lift slowly to hers and fill with hurt and disappointment. And hope. He leaned forward slightly, and she could almost feel him willing her to say she didn't mean it, that she was only kidding. When she didn't, the tears came.

"I'm sorry, Joey." She sat next to him at the table. "I wish it could be different."

He looked up at her, blue eyes pleading. "You and Dad used to be friends. Don't you like him anymore?"

For a moment, just a moment, she wondered why she was putting everyone through this. They could all go back to the way things used to be, right? And everyone would be happy again.

Except her. And Max. Even if she could've settled for friendship after last night, she wouldn't get it. Max would pull back, there'd be tension, and eventually Joey would suffer for it anyway.

Caving in now wouldn't do a thing except prolong the agony for everyone. She smiled sadly. "I like him too much."

"How can you like someone too much?"

"Sometimes one person likes the other person more…" No, she couldn't give Joey the impression that it was all Max's fault. She poured milk into a glass, took it to the table and sat down next to him. "Your dad and I have been friends for a long time, but…I don't think he wants the same things I do."

"What things?"

"I'm not going to answer that," Sara said. "It's better that I don't."

"I'll understand when I'm an adult, right?" Joey gave a half sigh, then sucked in his breath, his eyes on hers. "My dad's an adult, so maybe if you tell him what you want, he can do it."

It sounded so simple the way Joey put it, with the clear, uncomplicated logic of a child. Ask for what you want and you'd get it—or at least get an explanation of why you couldn't have it. That was Joey's experience. And it worked when you were talking about a sleepover or another piece of pie or a colt of your own.

Feelings weren't quite so neat and tidy. They didn't appear or disappear on request, and sometimes they were all but impossible to explain. In Joey's case she wouldn't even try. She didn't know how to tell him she was in love with his father without making Max the bad guy, and she wouldn't do that. Better that Joey think badly of her than ruin the relationship between father and son.

"You're going to have to trust me and your dad to work this out," she said.

"But I don't understand why things can't go back to the way they were."

"Too much has changed, Joey. Things have been said that can't be unsaid." And actions taken that couldn't be undone. She'd promised herself she would never regret telling Max she loved him, that she would never consider the night she'd spent in his arms a mistake, but she almost did. For Joey's sake, she almost did.

"So what's going to happen now?"

"I'm going to stay with Janey while I finish out the school year. And after that…" She shrugged, looking away from the sadness on his face. "I'm not sure."

"So, you might stay?"

"Yes—no—I don't know." Sara dropped her chin into her hands, giving Joey a sad smile. "I'd like to tell you I'll never leave Erskine, but I don't know if that's the truth."

"Can't you at least come back to the ranch to live?"

"No," Sara said. She wanted, desperately, to put Joey's mind at rest, but peace now would come at a higher expense down the line. She wasn't only afraid moving back to the ranch would be a mistake—she knew it would be.

She'd like to believe that what had passed between her and

Max last night meant something to him besides sex, but only moments before that kiss, he'd been prepared to let her go. If she came back to the ranch, it would be too easy for him—and for her—to fall into the old pattern, or worse. She'd already shown how weak she was; he'd only have to touch her and she'd end up giving him everything she had. And nothing would be resolved.

It had taken all her strength to leave in the first place; she didn't think she'd be able to do it again. "It's going to take a while before I know what I have to do."

Joey looked over at her and said, with the long-suffering tone of a kid who had no choice but to indulge the strange behavior of the adults in his life, "You need more space."

"Yes," Sara said, but it was really Max who needed the space—space and distance—and maybe then he'd realize he wanted her in his life.

And maybe he wouldn't.

BEFORE MAX EVEN GOT out of his truck, Sara opened Janey's door and stood at the top of the step, arms crossed, Joey nowhere in sight. That couldn't be good, Max thought as he crossed the street and walked through the gate. It *wasn't* good, he amended when he got close enough to see her expression. There was no sparkle in her eyes, no curve to her lips, not the slightest concern over his black eye. He wasn't sure she even noticed. "Where's Joey?"

Sara stared off over his head. "Inside. I told him he could watch TV until we were done talking."

Max didn't like the sound of that.

"I told him I moved out."

He liked the sound of that even less. "How did he take it?"

"He was upset at first, but we talked for a while and he seemed better." Her eyes connected with his for no more than a second or two, but he saw the cloud that passed over her face. "He's still troubled, though. It's going to take him a while to get used to this."

"If he ever does." Max looked toward the front window of the house. "He feels like he's losing you, Sara."

"And what about you, Max. How do you feel?"

Like someone had pulled the world out from under his feet, but he couldn't bring himself to say that out loud. "Why did you leave?"

"If you don't know, there's no point in trying to explain it to you."

Her cryptic responses sent his temper inching up. Max curbed it. Letting her drag him into an argument wasn't going to get him the answers he needed. It would just give her an excuse to end the conversation. "If I understood any of this, I wouldn't be asking."

"I said everything I needed to say yesterday. So did you."

"But that was before last night—"

"Last night was a mistake, Max. I won't say I regret it, and I'm not blaming you, or myself, for that matter. We both got caught up in the moment. But the moment's over."

Max knew he was gaping, but he really couldn't help it. She could have been talking about a fender bender for all the depth of emotion she exhibited—as if, instead of giving him the most incredible night of his life, she'd hit him with her car and dented his bumper, and just as soon as they traded insurance information they could go their separate ways.

Not only was it infuriating and hurtful, it was weird. Unbelievably weird. "So you're saying last night didn't mean anything to you? I don't buy it, Sara. You said you loved me—"

"And you told me to go back to Boston."

"I was wrong."

That got her attention. Her expression was still stony, but

something flickered in the depths of her brown eyes. "What makes you say that?"

"Because I hurt you."

She flinched. Max had the impression he'd hurt her again, though he had no idea how.

"You're not responsible for my feelings," she said. "You didn't ask me to fall in love with you, and I don't expect you to tell me what I want to hear just to spare me some pain."

"But last night, you and I—"

"Sex and love aren't the same thing, Max." She reached for the door handle.

"No, listen to me, Sara. Please."

She stopped and turned around, her breath rushing out on a white cloud.

Max was stunned by how beautiful she was, and not just the lovely face and sexy figure. He wondered how he could have missed the beauty shining like a beacon from her heart and soul, marveled at the passion she'd hidden beneath her bubbly, slightly quirky exterior.

"I'm listening, Max."

And he knew if he didn't handle this just right, all that beauty and passion would slip through his hands. "I...you've been so...different lately. Unhappy." Great, Max thought while he tried to untwist his tongue. Whatever was wrong with his feet was spreading. He glanced down at the offending appendages and found that his mind cleared almost immediately. He didn't really figure his feet had anything to do with it, but he kept his eyes on them just to be safe. "After all you've sacrificed for Joey and me—"

"I don't consider it a sacrifice."

He held up a hand, refusing to be sidetracked by semantics. "You told me you wanted a home and family of your own, Sara, and when your parents came, I thought..."

"You thought I was going to leave."

Just like Julia. They remained unspoken, those three words, but they hung there between them. So did *I love you,* three more words Max couldn't bring himself to say—as if keeping them to himself would make this hurt any less.

"Well, you were right," Sara said into the heavy silence. "I left."

Max kept his head down. Hearing the pain in her voice was enough; he didn't need to see it on her face. "I'm sorry about all of this, Sara. I'm sorry you were hurt, but I only said what I thought was the best thing for you."

"The best thing for me would be to stay here with you and Joey, but you're too stuck in the past to ever believe that, Max. There'll always be a part of you that's waiting for me to walk away, a part of you that's closed off. There are women who can live with that, but I'm not one of them. I've already begun to resent you for thinking you have to protect yourself from me. If I went to the ranch with you, we'd only end up in the same mess again, eventually."

"I wish I could take back what I said yesterday, Sara, but it's too late for that and all I can do is ask you to try and understand."

"I do understand, Max."

"Then tell me you're not leaving."

She gave him a small, sad smile. "Do you think this was an easy decision for me to make? I'll miss you and Joey more than I can even imagine, but it's time we both lived our own lives. Joey is pretty self-sufficient now, and together you can figure the rest of it out. You'll be fine without me, I promise."

Max scrubbed a hand over his face. "There's nothing I can say to change your mind, then?"

"Nothing you're willing to say."

"I…" He lowered his eyes to his feet again, but it didn't help this time, because this time he wasn't trying to organize his thoughts, he was trying to organize his heart, and a man who hadn't been in touch with his feelings for so long couldn't, between one breath and the next, suddenly find the words to express them.

It didn't help that Sara's sweet, light scent rode the cold winter breeze like a tropical current, that the bright winter sun paled in comparison to the fire of her hair and the glow of her skin. He remembered how soft and warm that skin had felt beneath his hands, the planes and curves of her body, the way her breath caught when he touched her, then sighed out into a throaty moan that aroused him to such a state of blind, burning hunger that all he could think of was making love to her again. The idea that she might listen to reason afterward would be a definite bonus, but the driving motivation was just to get his hands on her again—and get hers on him.

It would be a mistake, though. He knew it before he so much as made a move in her direction. He tore his eyes off her—it was the only way he could gather his wits—but he could feel her watching him, waiting for the answer to a question he couldn't even remember. He kicked at the chunks of ice lining Janey's walkway, watching them skitter out of reach, just like his thoughts and feelings. And Sara.

"Why did you come here, Max? Besides Joey?"

"Finding you gone this morning…" He stopped, unable to put the depth of his betrayal and hurt into words without comparing her to Julia, which would hardly help the situation. "Finding you gone made everything feel different," he finished. "Wrong. I just want my friend back."

"You want everything to be the way it was?" she asked. "Before?"

"We can hardly go back to just friendship, can we?"

"Then you want sex, too?"

"I didn't mean it that way." But Max found himself remembering, and the heat of embarrassment turned…warmer. He'd liked the way she'd looked in his bed this morning, liked dropping a kiss on her lips before he'd gone out, looking forward to seeing her when he came back in the house—and not just for sex.

"That's the way it feels," she said as if she'd read his mind.

"I can't pretend last night never happened."

"Neither can I," she said softly. "But I want more than your nights."

He frowned. "We always see each other during the day, and we have dinner together almost every night—"

"At the ranch. But if our relationship changes the way you want it to, how are we going to treat each other when we're in town together?"

"We're in town together all the time, Sara."

"I'm not talking about you, me and Joey at the diner, Max. I'm talking about a date."

"Uh…"

"Okay, that's obviously too much right off the bat." She thought for a moment, chewing on her bottom lip.

Max had to look away before he forgot how much was riding on this discussion.

"What if we begin with something simple, like holding hands?" she asked.

"We can hold hands."

"Really?" She thrust hers out.

Max looked at it, up at her face, then down at her hand again.

"I guess not," Sara said, letting it fall back at her side. "You want to sleep with me, but you won't even hold my hand on a side street in town. Are we friends who are only satisfying a mutual need, or are we lovers who started out as friends?"

"Yes—no—" Max threw his hands up in the air. "I don't know. This is all moving so fast, Sara."

"Is it? Where do you think *this* is going?"

Max spun around, pacing the length of the sidewalk and back, though it did little to ease his frustration. "Do we have to decide that now?"

"I've been waiting six years—"

"But it's only been one day for me, Sara."

"You're right." All the fire he'd worked so hard to bring out in her seemed to drain away suddenly, leaving her fragile looking, as exhausted as he felt. "We're a long way apart, Max. Maybe too far."

"We don't have to be," he said, knowing she heard the edge of desperation in his voice and not caring. Maybe it would reach the part of her she'd closed off. "If you'd move back to the ranch—"

"No."

Max opened his mouth, but nothing came out for a second, and then he sounded like a damned parrot. "No?" he squawked. "That's all, just *no?* Why not?"

"Because it won't solve anything," she said. "If I move back there, everything will revert to the way it was—oh, not at first. I'll make resolutions and you'll make promises. We'll both keep them for a little while, but sooner or later you'll catch me at a weak moment." Her gaze moved to his mouth and color came up in her cheeks, color that had nothing to do with the brisk winter air. "Before I know it, we'll have a repeat performance of last night."

"Would that be so bad?" he asked, climbing the first step, then the second, so that he stood eye-to-eye with her. Mouth to mouth. "Come back to the ranch, Sara. We'll take it slow."

"That's just the problem," she said. "We've been moving by your timetable all along and look where it's gotten us."

"But—"

She held up a hand. "When Julia left, you forgot how to trust."

"This has nothing to do with Julia," Max grumbled.

"It has everything to do with how you've been protecting yourself since your divorce, but you're right, Max. This is about you and me. We have to figure out where to go from here."

"Home," he said.

Sara shook her head. "I won't go backward, Max. I can't. When you're ready to have a normal relationship, you'll know where to find me."

He shoved his hands back through his hair, wondering why she couldn't understand how he felt when she was the only one who could possibly know. First she walked out on him, and now she wanted him to run his personal affairs with a standing-room-only audience. "I won't conduct my private life in front of Janey Walters and the whole town."

"And I won't be someone you sneak across the yard to see after your son has gone to bed."

"I wouldn't do that to you, Sara."

She crossed her arms, one slim eyebrow inching up.

He had the good grace to look away. "So where does this leave us?"

"Nowhere," Sara said, her voice heavy. "It leaves us nowhere, Max."

Chapter Ten

"Go, go, *go!*" Max shouted at the portable television in the kitchen. He banged the side of the TV and managed to clear the picture long enough to see Michigan's running back tackled on USC's twenty-eight yard line before static clouded the screen again. Fourth down, Michigan was losing by three with seventeen seconds remaining on the clock. Any coach who valued his job would have dropped back, taken the field goal and sent the game into overtime. Instead the players were lining up for a running or passing play.

Max placed one hand on top of the television, raised the other in the air and lifted his left foot, wiggling around until the picture came into focus. The players lined up, the screen panning to shots of the fans, the sidelined players and finally the coaches, everyone silent, their eyes glued to the field. Then the cameras went back to the line of scrimmage, the ball was snapped and a couple thousand pounds of human flesh collided with an audible crunch. The quarterback danced in place, arm poised, searching for an open receiver while the crowd screamed, the coach chewed his thumbnail and the clock ran down, six seconds, five, four…he drew his arm back and launched the ball—

There was a loud hissing sound, and a cloud of steam that

quickly turned into black smoke filled the kitchen. "Damn!" Without thinking, Max raced to the stove, stopped short and looked back at the television. The screen was a blizzard of static again. He almost ignored the overboiling pot, but he'd never get himself pretzeled into the perfect human antenna position fast enough to see the end of the play. Or the instant replay, for that matter. Christmas Day football had been a lot more fun when he wasn't doing the cooking, too.

He stomped across the kitchen and grabbed the pot, then dropped it immediately, sucking a breath in through his teeth. Its contents sloshed over the side and another cloud of steam and smoke billowed up. Grumbling out a choice phrase or two, Max bunched up the skirt of the frilly apron tied around his waist and used it to buffer his hand from the red-hot handle. Heat leached through to aggravate his burned palm, so he set the pot aside and went to run cold water over it.

It wasn't blistering, he noted as he studied the burn under the running water. That was something, at least. He shut off the TV and retrieved the first-aid kit he'd taken to leaving in the kitchen, wondering if he should bandage it or leave it uncovered. Sara would know. He was halfway to the back door before he remembered she wouldn't be in her cottage.

Max wrapped a clean towel around his hand. He still couldn't get used to her being gone, or believe that one person's absence could make such a huge difference in his life. When Julia left, he'd hardly noticed.

Because Sara had been there to pick up the pieces.

Sara had been there to look after Joey, to worry that the curtains were clean and put little felt pads on the bottoms of the new lamps so they wouldn't scratch the tables. Sara had been there to mend things and clean things and remind him that he had neighbors, and that he needed to sympathize with them in times of grief and celebrate in times of joy, and to be grateful there were more of the latter than the former. Sara had made his house feel like a home, a place where he and Joey could feel completely welcome, completely at ease, and, though he hadn't considered his life in those terms before, completely happy.

He could go on without her, learn to cook and clean and handle all the little things she'd done to make his and Joey's physical existence more pleasant, but the sunshine would still be gone from their lives.

No, it was worse than that. His life had become a total disaster. Every time he thought of Sara, he lost track of place and time and before he knew it, all hell had broken loose. The other day he'd caught sight of her house, which had reminded him of the last time he'd been there, which reminded him of her panties. By the time he'd remembered he was driving the tractor, he'd taken out about twenty feet of the south corral fence.

Then there was the hose he'd left running in the barn. The water had trickled out the door and into the chicken coop for a good portion of the night. It resulted in a nice little skating rink for the chickens—if chickens could skate.

There wasn't a square inch of the ranch that didn't hold a memory of Sara, or proof of what those memories did to him, from the new fender on his pickup truck to the old vacuum cleaner he'd had to resurrect after he'd sucked up a few feet of drapery and blown up the current one.

As bad as those accidents were, however, they didn't hold a candle to humiliating himself in front of half the town at the Ersk Inn. He didn't even want to think about the Max Devlin Pool.

He'd gotten his fill of Erskine's brand of fame when Julia walked out on him—the endless questions, the whispers and finger-pointing every time he showed his face in town, the pity for poor, motherless Joey. He'd sworn never to conduct his private life in public again, but damned if he didn't go and get involved with the one woman guaranteed to put him right back in the center of attention. If he could just get her alone, and then manage to *think,* despite the heat his body always generated when he was around her—

Crash!

But that was tomorrow's problem. At the moment it was all he could do to get through Christmas Day.

"Joey?"

"Everything's fine, Dad," he called back from the great room.

Sure, everything's fine, Max thought. As long as *fine* was another word for chaos....

Joey had spent Christmas Eve with Sara. She'd brought him back last night, coming inside for only a few minutes to get the sleeping eight-year-old to bed and drop off some presents and then she was gone, without even addressing his concerns about her driving back to town in a heavy snowfall. Max had been up half the night decorating the tree and getting the gifts under it, and the other half worrying whether Sara had gotten home all right, only to have Joey wake him up about three minutes after he'd finally managed to fall asleep.

Chores came first, even on Christmas, but once they were done, Joey opened his gifts under the tree in record time, then ignored them all except Sara's, one of those robotic dogs that drove the real dogs and kittens—and fathers—crazy. The morning and early afternoon had passed in an earsplitting cacophony of mechanical barking, real barking and feline hissing, spitting and yowling. Various assorted pets alternated between cowering against Max's shins and making courage-fueled dashes into the living room to confront the odd-smelling beast that had invaded their home. He would have prayed for the batteries to run out, but Sara had supplied extras. She was thoughtful like that.

"Joey, shut that thing off—and leave it off this time. Find something else to do for a while."

The noise cut off before he could draw another breath, the silence so sudden Max's ears continued to ring. He rested his hands on the counter, letting his head hang down while he enjoyed the quiet. But only for a moment. There was still Christmas dinner to put on the table, which he was making compliments of Sara's present to him: a cookbook. He'd decided there might be some significance to the gift—it was as if she thought he only wanted her around to make his life easier. After seeing firsthand all the work involved in pulling off a holiday like Christmas, that would be a damn good reason, but he'd want her back even if she never cooked another meal again, or helped Joey make a flour-paste map, or refilled those little bowls of dried stuff that made the house smell so good.

Anyway, he wasn't doing too bad. The house was clean if he didn't count the closets. He hadn't ruined any of the laundry in at least a week. And Christmas dinner was in the bag, thanks to Betty Crocker and a bottle of whiskey. A pot roast, complete with potatoes and carrots, was baking away in the oven, and there'd be gravy and rolls. He'd planned to make pumpkin pie, taken one look at the piecrust recipe and opted instead for bread pudding with hard sauce—which was where the whiskey came in—if he ever figured out the difference between simmer and boil. He'd already discovered scorched through trial and error.

He emptied out the burned sauce, filled the pan with soapy water and set it to soak in the sink. Then he dug out the double boiler, filled the bottom with water and put it on the gas burner to heat up. It might take him all afternoon to make the sauce this way, Max thought, but he'd be damned if he burned anything else today. He picked up the whiskey bottle and upended the last of it into a big glass measuring cup, consulted the red measurements on the side, drank some of it, consulted and drank again—

"What's that funny smell?"

Max snorted the last mouthful. Even with the coughing fit, he managed to shove the bottle behind some other stuff before he turned around to face Joey, who was craning his head to see around his father.

"What're you doing, Dad?"

Max glanced behind him to make sure the bottle was hidden, coughed a couple more times and swiped at his watering eyes. "I'm making dinner."

Joey scrunched up his face. "Is it a turkey? It doesn't smell like turkey."

"It's pot roast. You like pot roast."

"Not on Christmas. Why aren't we having turkey? Sara always made a turkey for Christmas."

Because Sara always remembered to buy one, Max thought, but all he said was, "Anyone can make a turkey. This is—" he consulted the cookbook "—'a real American tradition, perfect for any occasion.' And that's a direct quote from Betty Crocker herself."

"I never heard of her."

"Well, she's famous. Like Chef Boyardee and, uh…"

"Emeril?"

"Who's he?"

"Bam!"

Max blinked a couple of times and shook his head.

"Jeez, Dad, you gotta watch more TV. Emeril has a cooking show—hey!" Joey ran out of the room and up the stairs, coming back a minute later with Sara's video camera. "We can make a cooking show, like on cable."

"No."

"Aw, c'mon, Dad. I have to practice or I'll never be a famous director."

"I thought you were taking movies of Spielberg."

"I am, but mostly he just stands there and chews stuff. And I don't get to yell 'action' or 'cut' or anything. He doesn't even understand 'whoa' yet."

Max made an effort not to laugh, but Joey was so serious he couldn't bring himself to seem as if he was poking fun.

"C'mon, Dad, please? It'll be quiet."

"Now there's a program I can get behind," Max said, ruffling his son's hair, "but no."

"Da-aa-aa-ad—" he protested, making it about four syllables long.

"I don't even like having my picture taken, Joey, let alone being taped." And then he'd want to take it for show-and-tell, and all the kids would run home and tell their parents that Mr. Devlin had been making like Martha Stewart and he'd be hearing about it for the next month, at least.

Of course, there was an upside. Sara would get to see just how great he was doing at this domesticity thing. That might raise her opinion of him a little. He pictured a scale, mentally weighing the two sides of the issue, but the potential for embarrassment was a heavy thing. "Why don't you watch TV in the living room," he told Joey. "Maybe Emeril is on."

Joey sighed heavily. "Okay," he said, and turned to go.

Max felt bad for sending him off, but someone had to get dinner on the table. "And leave that camera where I can see it. Put it over by the door where it'll be out of harm's way. We don't want it getting broken." Which was likely to happen if he got anywhere near it. "Sara's trusting you to take care of it."

Joey crossed the room and put down the camera, then looked back over his shoulder. "Dad?"

Max gazed into his son's eyes and knew what he was thinking. "It's all right to say it, Joey."

"I miss her."

"So do I."

"Is she ever coming back?"

Max flirted with the idea of telling Joey about Sara's intention to leave town, but it was Christmas, and besides, he was determined to keep her from moving away. "I'm trying to fix it, Joey."

Joey relaxed perceptibly, half running across the room to throw his arms around his father. The hug was unusual enough, but when Joey looked up and said, "I love you, Dad." Max's eyes began to burn.

He hugged his son back, then put him at arm's length and took a good, long look. He was amazed at what he saw—not the face that resembled his, but the clarity and honesty in Joey's eyes. Maybe it was the fact that he was eight and hadn't really been exposed to that much bad stuff, but whatever the reason, Max found himself wishing he could recapture a little of that innocence himself. "I love you, too, Joey."

"And Sara, too, right, Dad? You love Sara, too."

Hearing Sara's name in that context hit Max like a physical blow. Memories assaulted him, and not just the obvious ones of her in bed, making incredible love with him. He saw her walking down the street as he'd seen her hundreds of times, copper curls bouncing and the smile on her face that made him feel like the sun was shining, even on a rainy day. He remembered the immense patience she'd always shown his son—and him, for that matter—the love that shone from all the little things she'd done for them.

And he remembered the day he'd held that mistletoe over her head and stared down at her, aching to touch his mouth to hers, but so comfortably buried in the status quo that he'd completely ignored the way her lips had trembled, the yearning in her eyes, the hurt when he'd rejected her. The same hurt he'd seen on her face at Janey's house the other day.

Six years of guilt slammed into him with all the suddenness and force of a tornado, shredding the illusion of the happy world he'd built for himself and Joey after Julia left. He yanked the towel from his back pocket and fired it fastball style at the counter, but even anger couldn't keep the memories from playing through his mind like an unflattering episode of *This Is Your Life.*

He saw it all now, in hindsight, all the times he'd shied away from touching Sara because touching her, he now knew, meant he couldn't hide from the desire he felt for her, and if he had to face the desire—

"Dad!" Joey shouted, pointing over Max's shoulder.

Max whipped around just as the dish towel burst into flame. He jumped to one side, grabbed the first thing that came to hand and threw its contents on the fire. The entire stove top and a good portion of the counter on either side ignited with a loud whoosh into a sheet of blue flames.

He looked down at his hand to find that he was clutching the glass measuring cup, and it was empty. He'd thrown a cup of whiskey on an open flame. He stared for a second, the shock of his own stupidity making him forget whether he should use water or salt or baking soda, or if he even had any baking soda. Meanwhile, the flames spread through the litter of cooking ingredients, canned goods and assorted paraphernalia crowding the counter. The edge of the cookbook began to brown nicely, the top pages curling up one by one and puffing into flame. Little white drifts of ash floated into the hot updraft of air as the fire crept over the backsplash and began to consume the wallpaper.

"I'm calling 911," Joey shouted, galvanizing Max into action.

"Just get out of the house," he yelled back. "I'll have this put out in a minute."

He grabbed the cookbook, tossed it into the sink and turned on the water, using his hands to splash the bottom of the curtains where they'd begun to smolder. He should have used the extinguisher, but the fire wasn't really that bad, and there was no way Joey was eating canned soup for Christmas; he'd worked too hard to make him a real holiday meal for that.

He started at the stove and worked his way methodically along the countertop, slapping the wet towel at the flames like a madman, chucking singed boxes and cans with their labels burned off into the garbage across the room. He picked up the whiskey bottle, searing his fingertips, but he refused to let it crash to the floor. All he needed was broken glass and stocking feet to make this catastrophe complete. So he juggled the bottle from hand to hand, hot-potato fashion, dancing across the kitchen and saying "ouch, ouch, ouch," before he dropped it into the garbage can—which promptly burst into flames. One of the cans, already swollen from the heat, exploded. Pumpkin pie filling geysered out, narrowly missing Max. The floor and ceiling weren't as lucky, but at least the watery pumpkin doused the fire in the garbage can, and he didn't have time to worry about anything else, not while somebody was breaking down his front door.

Glass broke and wood splintered. Max felt a blast of frigid air followed by the sound of someone shouting "Fire department!"

He whipped off Sara's apron, leaned back against the counter and crossed his arms. Sure enough, a minute later, Tom Hartfield, fully outfitted in Erskine Volunteer Fire Department gear, appeared in the kitchen doorway, clutching the big metal end of a dripping fire hose in his asbestos-gloved hands. George Donaldson stood behind him, a loop of hose supported loosely in the crook of his arm, which meant that Sam Tucker would be manning the truck outside. Max would have been the fourth member of the team if not for the fact that he was hosting this little get-together.

"Cool! Hi, Mr. Hartfield," Joey said from the hallway leading to the back door.

"Hi, Joey. We came as soon as you called."

Max sent Joey a look that doused some of his excitement. "You got here fast, Tom."

"I think we set a record," Tom said. "Lucky for you, George and Sam were in town already and the roads were clear."

"Yeah, lucky," Max muttered. "Did you really need to break down the front door? It's not like there's smoke pouring out of the windows or anything."

Tom shrugged. "Nobody answered when we knocked. So where's the fire?"

"It's out already."

"That how you burned your hand?"

"Uh…yeah." Max curled his fingers over his palm before Tom could notice that the burn was exactly the same shape as the handle of his grandmother's saucepan.

"You oughta take care of that."

"It's fine. So's the kitchen, but I appreciate you guys coming out here on Christmas."

Tom did his one-shoulder shrug again. "We're here. We might as well take a look."

Max thought about trying to stop them, but then they'd wonder if he had something to hide. So he waved them in, stepping to one side so they could examine the scene for themselves and get out of there. "See? There's hardly any damage."

"It's still smoking in one or two places," Tom said. "We'd better check it out just to be safe."

"I think I can handle it."

"You know the drill, Max. The walls are scorched. We have to make sure there are no pockets of flame that could flare up later."

Max let out a breath. "Could you at least get rid of the fire hose? You're dripping water all over—uh…"

"Your clean floor?"

Max's gaze jumped from the peeling linoleum he'd laboriously cleaned the previous day, now dotted with pumpkiny puddles, to Tom's face, his expression a mixture of amusement and understanding.

Tom handed the hose back to George Donaldson, who was taking it all in—the fire, the floor, the orange circle of dripping goo on the ceiling—with a big smile on his face.

Max gritted his teeth. Tom wouldn't say a word about what had gone on here, even to his wife, but there wasn't a damn thing anybody could do, short of homicide, to stop George from blabbing, because he would see it as payback. Not that Max had ever actually *done* anything to George, except get the place on the high-school varsity football team he'd wanted. Twenty other guys had made the team, too, but since Max had been the only underclassman, George had always blamed him. Max had never considered him more than an annoyance; he had a feeling George was about to be upgraded to major pain in the ass.

"Take the hose back out to the pumper truck, Donaldson."

George took one last look around, committing it all to memory, probably embellishing it before he dragged the hose out the way they'd come. By the time he got on the phone, Joey would be suffering from second-degree burns instead of sitting at the table fiddling with Sara's video camera as if they had a fire every day, no big deal.

"Don't worry about him," Tom said as he started to check

the singed areas of the counter and walls. "Everybody knows he's a horse's butt. Half of what he says is a lie and the other half is rumor. Nobody'll pay him any mind."

"Yeah, sure," Max said, feeling marginally better. George did have a reputation for creative storytelling. He gathered the wet towels, mopped up the puddles and started for the sink.

"What's for supper?" Tom asked. "It doesn't smell like turkey. Sara would've made a turkey."

Max stumbled and had to catch himself on the counter. The towels splatted on the floor and Tom looked over at him, one eyebrow raised. "Need to replace the linoleum," Max said.

Tom nodded, pretending not to notice that the closest worn spot was at least a yard from where Max had actually tripped. "You know, you could've come to our house for supper. Nothing Mary loves more than a houseful of people to fuss over, and it would give Jason something to do besides play with that da—" he shot Joey a glance "—darned robotic dog he got for Christmas."

Max nodded in commiseration. "Joey got one, too. I appreciate the offer, Tom, but I've got it under control. Pot roast is Joey's favorite, so I don't think he'll miss the turkey, and I'm making bread pudding for dessert."

"With whiskey sauce?"

"Yeah, my grandmother used to make it every Christmas. I haven't had it since she died, and I thought this year, since everything's so different anyway, it was time to get back to doing things the way my family would have done them."

"Yeah, sure," George sneered from the doorway. "It has nothing to do with the fact that you have a problem hanging on to your women."

"Things change, people come and go," Max said, rounding on him. "There's nothing I can do about that. What I *can* do is see that Joey has a good Christmas and if I have to make like Betty Crocker to get the job done, that's exactly what I'm going to do."

As if to punctuate his statement, the stove timer dinged.

"What's that?" Tom asked.

"My roast is done," Max muttered. He ignored the laughter, shoved his hands into oven mitts and opened the oven door. He pulled out his grandmother's old enamelware roasting pan and cracked the cover. After the steam cleared, he peeked inside and couldn't stop the smile. It might not be a turkey, but it was just about the most perfect roast he'd ever seen.

"Smells good," Tom observed.

"Yeah," George agreed in a make-believe teary voice. He pretended to wipe his eyes on his sleeves. "Our little boy's all grown-up, Tom. Don't it make you want to cry?"

"I guess you're not one of those people who improve with age," Tom said to George. "Why don't you go out and secure that hose so we can leave?"

George looked as if he might object, then abruptly changed his mind. "Yeah, sure. Hey, kid, want to come out and see the truck?"

Max narrowed his eyes in George's direction, but he couldn't really see any reason to object. "Don't forget your coat, Joey."

"Okay, Dad." Joey bundled up then headed for the kitchen doorway.

"Why don't you bring the camera?" George suggested. "You can take some footage of a real fireman."

The other two men rolled their eyes.

George ignored them, taking the video camera from Joey and studied it as they left the room. "This is one of them new ones, ain't it? Them Palmcorders?" Max heard him ask Joey. "What's this red light for?" And then they were gone, out the front door.

"Looks like everything's okay here," Tom said.

"Thanks, I feel so much better now."

Tom grinned. "Enjoy the pot roast," he said, clapping Sam on the shoulder. "We're outta here."

Max heard the truck rumble away and a few seconds later Joey raced back into the kitchen. He set the video camera on the table along with a crisp ten-dollar bill, peeled out of his coat and went to hang it on the coatrack.

"Where did the ten-spot come from?" Max asked.

"Mr. Donaldson bought my video."

"Uh…run that by me again?"

"Mr. Donaldson said he heard I wanted to be a director. He said he could get me on television screens all over town."

Max was confused for a moment, then he went cold. "What's on the tape?"

"It's my tape of Spielberg."

"And?"

Joey's chin fell to his chest.

"You didn't videotape me cooking, did you?"

"Uh-uh."

"Joey!" He jumped and Max toned his voice down. He was angry but he wasn't having his own son afraid of him. "I asked you not to tape me cooking."

"I know, Dad, but you didn't say I couldn't tape the fire. I turned the camera on before I went to call 911 and Mr. Donaldson—"

"Never mind." Max slumped against the counter, tucking his hands in his armpits. He studied his stocking feet, but his toes weren't exactly known for their problem-solving abilities.

"Did I do something wrong, Dad?"

Max sighed. "No, kiddo. Why don't you get washed up for dinner?"

"Okay." Joey headed toward the bathroom, casting an apologetic look over his shoulder.

Max glanced at the phone but he didn't pick it up. George Donaldson was no fan of his, and the way his luck was running, that tape was probably already mass-produced and being handed out with every fill-up at the Gas 'N Snack on Route 21.

All in all it was shaping up to be a hell of a day. Thank God Christmas only came once a year.

Chapter Eleven

So this is it, Sara thought. Erskine's annual New Year's Eve party. She'd only been in the town hall once or twice since coming to town six years ago, and never to a gathering of this size. Humiliation was best taken in small doses. But she was there tonight, and so was everyone else within a fifty-mile radius—men, women, children, even a dog or two, all of them waiting, but not for midnight. No, they were waiting for Max Devlin to arrive, and though she would have preferred it not to matter, the prospect of seeing him had butterflies swarming in her stomach.

It wasn't anticipation fluttering around inside her. She hadn't come back far enough from her broken heart for that yet. She could manage fear, though; it was the only recognizable emotion in the jumble of her feelings. But was she afraid of reacting to Max, she wondered, or not reacting to him? And which would be worse, being hopelessly in love or just hopeless?

Max had hurt her, deeply, or maybe she'd hurt herself by clinging to her love for him long after she should have moved on. Whatever the reason, she never wanted to feel that tangle of despair and sorrow again, that sense of this-can't-be-happening, followed by the realization that she wasn't dreaming—that her dreams were, in fact, at an end.

Okay, now she was making herself ill. She pressed a hand to her midsection and tried not to think about it. The Erskine New Year's Eve party didn't offer much in the way of diversion, though. There was the obligatory potluck buffet laid out over three long tables, ninety-six square feet of Jell-O molds and casseroles, breads and pies, candied things, pickled things and frosted things. Sara didn't dare put any of it in her rolling stomach.

Then there was Big Ed's Rhythm Method, a local band that played everything from wakes to weddings. Sara had always wondered if Big Ed and his crew had something besides music in mind when they named their band, but the truth was, about all they had going for them was rhythm—there wasn't much in the way of melody. It didn't stop the dance floor from being cheek-to-cheek close, faces *and* bottoms.

She waved off an invitation to dance in the form of a raised eyebrow and a head jerk toward the shuffling crowd. Of course, Mr. Hodges was well over eighty, and he had a palsy, so maybe he didn't really want to dance, but Sara wasn't taking any chances. Dancing meant small talk and she wasn't up to any one-on-one with the townspeople, so she decided to play it safe. And since the only safe Erskinite was… Well, they were the ones hanging on the wall.

Sienna-hued photographs of grim-faced pioneers standing in front of mud-and-stick huts dotted the pine paneling, along with the antique farming implements that had probably given them those sour expressions. They were kind of depressing, but at least they weren't patting her hand in sympathy, sending her long, meaningful looks, or giving her heartfelt, and sometimes tearful, apologies.

Since she'd taken her stand in the Ersk Inn, the townspeople had stopped teasing and smirking and were throwing themselves wholeheartedly in the opposite direction. It seemed there was no happy middle ground in Erskine. Once, just once, she'd like to walk down the street in complete anonymity like any normal person. But then, normal was a concept that had completely bypassed this small town.

"Hey, Sara, did you see the tape?"

Point proved, she thought, forcing a smile as Percival Jenkins stepped in front of her, so close she had to back up a couple of steps. Percy hadn't quite gotten past the smirking stage, and that little quote-marks thing he did with his fingers when he said "the tape" was really irritating. The jet-black, Elvis-style wig didn't help either, what with his salt-and-pepper sideburns and the gray cast to his face that older men got with their five-o'clock shadows. She had to wonder why Rita let him out of the house looking like a bad advertisement for the Crimp 'N Cut. But then, maybe Rita was the one who wanted him to resemble Elvis, since she did favor that Priscilla Presley beehive-hairdo-from-the-sixties....

Sara shuddered at the mental picture that sneaked in before she cut off that thought. And when Percy sidled up and slung an arm over her shoulders, his hand hanging casually just about breast level, she figured it was her own fault for getting caught up in that kind of speculation when every woman in town knew to be on guard around him.

She managed to wriggle around until she thought she was out of cop-a-feel danger, but while she was doing it, he planted a long, disgustingly juicy kiss on her cheek.

"How you doing, baby," he said, Elvis-style. "You're lookin' mighty fine tonight."

He called every woman "baby," but it gave Sara the willies. "I'm all right, Percy. How are you?"

"Dead if Rita sees him." Janey's voice coincided with the weight of Percy's arm disappearing from Sara's shoulders. Sara spun around and sure enough Janey was holding Percy's wrist between her finger and thumb. "Go back to your wife, Percy," she said as she let go. "I didn't drag Sara here to be manhandled by you, even if you are the King."

Unfazed, Percy scoped out the crowd, then set out to intercept his next victim.

Sara tugged the napkin from around Janey's whiskey and water so she could scrub the feel of Percy off her cheek. "You didn't drag me here at all," she said. "I came here to make a statement."

"You're making one, all right."

"Not the one Percy got."

"Yeah, well, Percy isn't the only man here who's getting that message."

"Great."

"What did you expect to happen when you went from spinster schoolteacher to va-va-voom?"

"That's not the point of this," Sara said, making a two-handed pass up and down her body that was meant to indicate her attire: a black skirt that fell in a straight column to her ankles, topped with a clingy openwork lace blouse over a silk camisole in the same shade of gold. Class had been her aim, not to mention confidence and control. The old, klutzy, love-struck Sara was gone and a new woman had taken her place, a woman who didn't need her clothes to make a statement so everyone noticed them and not her. She'd meant to convey that she was in charge of her feelings, not the other way around.

All she'd managed to do was attract a creep like Percy Jenkins who'd never given her a second look before. And she was cold, to boot. Her tights might have been a bit juvenile, but they'd been a whole lot warmer than sheer hose. She felt as if there was a constant cold draft blowing up her skirt and the lace blouse was next to useless in terms of winterproofing.

Plus it made her itch, which put it at about a negative one on the comfort scale. Being braless had felt liberating at first, but now it seemed everyone was staring at her breasts. The fact that her nipples were perpetually peaked from the chill in the room didn't exactly detract from that notion.

"Earth to Sara."

She crossed her arms over her breasts and hugged herself against the cold. "You don't happen to have a sweater you could lend me, do you?"

"What? And miss seeing every guy here eat his heart out—including Max? Not on your life, Sara. The people in this town have enjoyed themselves at your expense long enough. You've told them it's over…"

A dull roar started at the doorway and rumbled its way through the room.

"…now's your chance to prove it to everyone," Janey finished, just as the crowd parted in a jagged line, as if an earthquake had hit Erskine, leaving Sara at one end of the fissure and Max at the other.

Her heart jumped, once, then settled into a nice, easy rhythm. She knew she ought to be happy about that, since it meant she wouldn't be making a fool of herself over Max tonight. But she missed the way her stomach used to drop when he walked into a room, the hot flush that was part goofy happiness, part desire so strong it made her blush just to remember it. Sure, there'd been pain along with all the wonderful stuff, but the pain had been worth it because she'd had hope.

"Stop it," Janey whispered.

"Stop what?"

"You look so—I don't know, alone, unhappy. Whatever it is, knock it off before you make me cry. I never cry and I'm not going to do it in front of the town busybodies."

"You're not the only one who hates being a public spectacle," Sara said, pointing her chin toward Max just as he began edging back away from the sea of staring faces.

But then his gaze met hers.

Max took her stance as a challenge, mouth set, arms crossed, her face devoid of emotion except for one eyebrow rising slowly upward. Why Sara seemed to think he should face down this humiliation, he didn't know. She should understand why he wanted to leave; she'd always felt the same way, hiding from everyone until the notoriety from her latest incident died down. And he'd always coaxed her out in public again, he recalled, thinking it was for her own good. Showed how much he knew. It felt entirely different when he was the notorious one—different, as in a lot harder to ignore.

He held Sara's eyes while the wheels in his head began to spin. He owed half the town favors for returning copies of that videotape George Donaldson had made, and he'd paid off some of those favors just by showing up tonight. It didn't take a fortune-teller to figure out why they wanted him in the same room with Sara, but he was going to prove everyone wrong. By dancing with her. Slow-dancing. Yep, he'd show 'em all that he was in charge of himself even with Sara plastered up against him. Then they'd stop watching him and go back to minding their own business, and he and Sara could handle their affairs privately.

He sent Joey off to play with the other kids and scanned the crowd, letting his smile go a bit smug because he had it all figured out. But that was before he looked at Sara again, because when he looked at Sara, sweat popped out on his upper lip and his feet were suddenly glued to the floor.

He hadn't noticed what she was wearing when he'd been looking her in the eyes, ordering his thoughts and formulating a plan of action. He couldn't have found a thought now if it jumped up and rapped him on the forehead, and his plan of action was simple: try not to drool.

His gaze slid down to the floor, then inched its way back up, over her shoes, some intricate tangle of straps that made his mouth water even more, up the slit in the skirt, which revealed just enough skin. And considering the way her nipples were straining against the fabric, he'd have bet her breasts were bare under that slinky gold top. Plain as day for anyone to see...

Max tore his gaze off Sara and scanned the crowd. Yeah, they were seeing, all right. The women were watching her for a reaction. The men couldn't have cared less what was going through her mind—or if she even had one.

Max suddenly found himself in front of her without remembering how he'd gotten there. He had only one thought—to put something over the front of her, even if it was himself. "Let's dance," he said, his voice gruff from a combination of desire and jealousy. He caught her hand and pulled her, unresisting, onto the dance floor. One dark glance sent Big Ed and his boys into action—a waltz judging from the beat. The melody was anyone's guess.

After a brief hesitation, Sara fell into step with him. They moved in perfect unison, but there was something wrong. Max brought her closer, until her body brushed his with every slow step they took, closer still, until her curves fit against him and soft, fragrant curls brushed his chin and cheek. Yeah, that was better. He curled her arm up between them until their intertwined hands rested over his heart, nestled his other hand in the small of her back and snuggled his cheek against her temple.

"Max."

"Hmm?" he murmured, not really caring what she'd said. He just wanted to feel her breath hot in his ear, feel the flames lick through his bloodstream with every brush of her body over his. He buried his face in her hair and took a long, deep breath of her warm, sunny scent—

"Max! Everyone's watching."

His eyes flew open. They were alone on the dance floor, completely ringed by silent, staring people. Without thinking, he shifted Sara away, missed her immediately and tried to bring her back against him. But she'd braced her hands on his shoulders already, her slim yet surprisingly strong arms holding them apart.

He looked into her face.

She stared placidly back.

"You had a nice Christmas?" he asked, aware that everyone in town was watching, and he couldn't simply stand there staring at her all night.

"It was…different. Very quiet." The slight smile teasing the corners of her mouth disappeared. She dropped her hands from his shoulders and moved back. "Not like yours."

"You saw the tape." He set his jaw. "Of course you saw the tape. Sara, the fire was an accident. Joey was never in any danger, I swear—"

"I know that, Max. You're taking wonderful care of Joey."

"So…"

Her brow inched up again. "So?"

"So you know I don't need you around to take care of us, right?"

"Yes, I got that from the tape." For the first time she looked away. "'Things change, people come and go, and there's nothing you can do about that.'"

Max closed his eyes. If he hadn't said exactly those words, they'd been pretty close. Thank God it didn't take a genius to figure out how Sara had interpreted it; his IQ seemed to be falling fast. "That was just something I said to make Donaldson go away."

"Well, you got what you wanted. I hope…" She shook her head slightly, and turned to leave.

"Sara."

She stopped, glanced over her shoulder at him, looking for all the world so completely unaffected by his nearness that it made him wonder, for one numbingly cold moment, if he'd destroyed her love.

But Max knew she wasn't as unmoved as she wanted everyone to think. He'd heard that little sigh when she'd settled against him while they were dancing, felt her pulse quicken where his thumb brushed her wrist. It was enough that he knew how she really felt; she didn't have to show it to everyone else.

Neither did he. She had him ready to get down on his knees and beg her to come back to the ranch, but he refused to ask her at all with the town hanging on every word. So he let her turn around and walk away, and then wanted that moment back so desperately he couldn't stand his own company, let alone anyone else's.

He headed for the door, calling himself every kind of fool for not dragging her out of there and straightening out this mess before it got any worse—as in Sara dancing with another man. Old Mr. Hodges certainly didn't waste any time, but there was no reason to be jealous of him. Then the song ended and Mr. Hodges tucked her hand into the crook of his elbow and escorted her off like the kindly old grandfather he was. Only before they could take two steps, Ted Delancey whirled her back out onto the dance floor without even asking, and she laughed! She was supposed to be as miserable as he was, not having the time of her life in the arms of some other guy—and a friend, no less!

Max forgot all about leaving and went to the bar instead, although why he thought alcohol would cool his temper or his blood he'd never know, because after she danced with Tom, she danced with Mike Shasta, then Mr. Landry, who owned the feed store, and then Sam Tucker. Twice. Whenever she took to the dance floor with a man who was single and even remotely close to her own age, the room seemed to heat up another degree. Max would have blamed it on the booze, but he'd switched to coffee a couple of hours back, right about the time his vision started to blur. He needed to see what Sara was doing and who she was doing it with, although for the life of him he didn't know what good it would do either of them.

What he did know was that seeing her in the arms of all those other men was killing him. Each time her slender body brushed against some other guy, each time she lifted her face to look up at a man who wasn't him—

"Hey there, Lone Ranger, why don't you holster those fists. There're no outlaws around these parts."

Sure there are, Max thought. There were several of them right out there on that dance floor, trying to steal his woman. "Go away, Janey."

"She's gotten pretty popular now that she's stopped mooning over you. 'Course she hasn't accepted any invitations. Until tonight."

If it had been any other woman, Max might have believed Sara was doing it on purpose to make him jealous, but she didn't have a deceitful or manipulative bone in her body. Janey, on the other hand… "You put her up to this."

"What makes you think she's 'up to' anything besides enjoying herself? Do you think she's going to be a nun after she leaves here?"

"She's not leaving."

"Oh, really? What are you doing to stop her?"

Max didn't answer, too busy watching all the men jockey over who got to dance with Sara next.

"It's almost midnight," Janey said. "This might be a good time to make your move. Before somebody else does."

He straightened out of his slouch, wanting nothing more than to walk over there and pull Sara into his arms so that he was the one dancing with her when the clock struck midnight. *Happy New Year, Sara, how about a kiss?*

But what if she said no? Worse yet, what if she said yes? If he put his hands on her he'd never be able to confine the contact to one Happy Holidays peck on the lips. Heat burst through him, most of it creeping up his neck to settle in his face at the thought of losing control in public.

By the time his panic receded, Sam Tucker was dancing with Sara again. "Sam's okay," he said.

"Yeah, Sam's all right. And he has that nice spread on the other side of town, almost as nice as yours, Max, and now that his domineering mother is out of the picture—God rest her soul—the field is clear for Sam to settle down...." Janey let the rest of that thought hang because Max was gone, pushing his way to the edge of the crowd surrounding the dance floor.

"That was low, Janey Walters."

She leaned her elbows on the bar and looked over her shoulder at Mike Shasta, letting her smile say it all.

"Especially when you've got this square in the Max Devlin Pool. And the next one," Mike said.

"Why, you're right, Mike."

"But that's not why you did this, is it?" he asked over the chorus of voices counting down to midnight.

"Ten, nine..."

Janey shrugged. "They're both being stubborn. Sara won't give in until Max says he loves her. At the rate he's going, she'll be long gone before he figures that out, so I gave him a little nudge."

"Why not just tell him what she wants to hear?"

Janey gave Mike a look that placed him in the clueless category right alongside Max. "He has to come to that conclusion on his own. Otherwise it's meaningless."

"And punching Sam will accomplish that?"

"You'd be amazed at what a little rampant jealousy can say to a woman." Janey slipped her arm into the crook of his elbow when he offered it, the two of them walking over to join the crowd, just as the old year came to an end.

"Happy New Year!" everyone shouted, exchanging kisses and hugs with their significant others before breaking apart to share good wishes with their friends and neighbors.

Max barely caught sight of Sara going into Sam's embrace and then he was engulfed by the jostling, milling crowd and had to work his way over to her, greeting by greeting. It wasn't easy smiling and pretending to care whether anybody's New Year was any different from the last one, when his showed every sign of being completely rotten. But he was pulling it off—until George Donaldson grabbed his hand and began to pump it enthusiastically.

"Happy New Year," George slurred. "No hard feelings over the tape and all, eh, Devlin?"

Max mumbled an acceptance, all the while craning his neck around George to keep Sara in sight, which was difficult with George weaving drunkenly from side to side. Max tried to liberate himself, but George only clung tighter, wrapping his other hand around Max's wrist for good measure while he blubbered something Max didn't want to hear, even if he'd been able to make it out through the combination of alcohol and self-pity thickening George's voice.

Max pried the fingers around his wrist loose, throwing all his weight back at the same time. His hand slipped free so suddenly he lost his balance and stumbled backward, bumping into Sam.

"What'd you do that for?" Sam asked.

"It was an accident, Sam."

"I'm not asking her to marry me. It was only a friendly dance—"

"I didn't do it on purpose," Max insisted.

"—and maybe a New Year's kiss, but no tonsil juggling, Max, I swear, although if you're dumb enough to let Sara get away I wouldn't mind taking her out—"

Max's temper went from zero to spoiling-for-a-fight in about a tenth of a second. "I'd rather see her leave town for good than wind up with a yahoo like you, Sam."

"Stop it!" Sara said, stepping out from behind Sam. "I thought you two were friends."

"We are, but that don't mean I'm going to stand here and let him insult me," Sam said.

Max snorted. "Like I'd waste my time."

He turned to walk away, but the mayor, sure there was going to be a fight, grabbed the town's antique crystal punch bowl and found himself bobbling fifteen pounds of crystal with liquid sloshing over the sides. He managed to save it by wrapping his arms under the bottom and hugging it to his chest. Sideways. He gave a high-pitched shriek as the ice-cold mixture of cranberry juice, orange juice and lemon-lime soda poured down his pants. And then he dropped the punch bowl. It landed on his foot and rolled away, unbroken, which was more than the mayor could say for his big toe.

Sam burst out laughing, as did the rest of the town. Max was just happy it wasn't him marinating in three different fruit juices and hopping around on one foot. He helped the mayor into a chair and left him with Doc Tyler.

"No hard feelings," Sam said, sticking his hand out.

Max shook it, but he was searching the crowd.

"She ran after Joey," Sam said. "Kid seemed upset about something."

Max picked his way through the slippery mess on the floor. By the time it was safe to look up, Joey was standing by the door to the coatroom. Alone.

"Sara left," Joey said.

Max frowned. Was he so transparent that everyone immediately knew he wanted to find Sara? Did it even matter, with Joey's face looking like that? "You heard what I said to Sam about her leaving town, didn't you?"

Joey shrugged, staring at the floor.

"I'm going to change her mind."

"You didn't change Mom's mind."

"That was different."

"How?" Joey demanded.

"It just is," Max said, partly because it was the only answer he had—but mostly because he wanted so badly for it to be true.

Chapter Twelve

Max eased into one of the chairs flanking the front of Mabel Erskine-Lippert's desk. His back grew damp immediately—industrial-grade vinyl, he told himself, but the ten-year-old still alive somewhere inside him knew better. Mabel Erskine-Lippert could make a statue sweat, no vinyl necessary.

Max returned her stare, refusing to be intimidated, even if, like everyone else in town, he was more than a little afraid of her. It seemed ridiculous considering that she looked like a summer breeze would knock her over. She was barely five feet tall, skinny as a scarecrow with all the stuffing gone. Her arms were thin and knobby as sticks under her clothes, her hands and face covered with skin as tough and faded as old burlap. A stranger might think her old and frail, until he got a look at her eyes.

Mabel Erskine-Lippert's eyes were dark and glittering, perpetually narrowed under brows that winged up from the bridge of her nose to her temples, black slashes that gave her a menacing look, which could only be intentional since she obviously drew them on herself with some mystical female product made especially for that purpose. Or maybe she used a grease pencil... Max didn't really know, but he felt himself starting to crack under the ominous gaze that had never failed to make even the toughest bully break down and confess on the spot. He might be grown up, but he wasn't immune, and being summoned to the principal's office just naturally made him believe he was in trouble. Except he hadn't done anything wrong—if he didn't count opening the ladies' room door at the Crimp 'N Cut at a strategic moment in Mabel's panty-hose maintenance.

Involuntarily his eyes lifted to her head. "I can barely see the bald spot anymore." His voice sounded like a bullhorn in the deathly still room. His voice? "Da— dar— sh— I said that out loud, didn't I?"

Mabel raised an eyebrow, so high the black slash disappeared beneath her hairline, pointing right to the scene of the crime.

Max hunched down in his chair, his damp shirt and the vinyl chair collaborating to produce a long, drawn-out groan. He couldn't have summed up his sentiments any better if he'd planned it.

Mabel's other brow shot up to join the first, forming a perfect V.

Max tore his gaze off her forehead, but he couldn't quite meet her eyes. "I'm sorry."

"For saying that out loud or for causing me five stitches?"

"Only five? I heard it was at least ten. Or more, depending on who you talk to—" He broke off. It was probably best not to remind her that she'd been the talk of the town for several days. Not that she should be any different from anyone else in this gossip-ridden place, but why bring it up when he was responsible for it? Sort of. "I'm sorry you hit your head," he said. Then he felt compelled to add, "It was an accident."

"That's what Miss Lewis always says."

Max flushed, his face topping out about ten degrees hotter than the rest of him. It could've been his normal reaction to her name, or the urge to defend Sara and himself, or a bit of both. Whatever the reason, Mabel seemed to get a kick out of it, if he was interpreting her grimace correctly.

"I thought you wanted to talk about Joey," he said. "If not—"

"Sit down, Mr. Devlin." Her voice was sharp enough to cut him off at the knees.

Max sank back into his seat.

"I did telephone you about your son, although if you ask me, a bit of advice on your love life might be in order." She held up a hand before he could so much as open his mouth. "I don't meddle in the private lives of my staff unless someone's job performance warrants it. Miss Lewis is much too professional to let personal matters interfere with her teaching, and as you are not a member of my staff, your happiness is none of my concern. Your son's is."

"Joey isn't unhappy."

"You're right, for the most part. Joseph has always been a good-natured, outgoing, nonconfrontational child, but lately…" She placed her hands flat on her desktop, seeming to choose her words carefully before she went on. "Joey had an altercation with Jason Hartfield on the playground today at recess. Loud voices, from what I've been told, and a bit of shoving."

Max glanced toward the closed door. Joey was sitting out in the hall, waiting while he talked to the principal—which Max had thought was the reason for the miserable look on the kid's face. Now he knew better. "Jason's his best friend."

"So I understand."

"You called me because he had an argument with his best friend?" Max couldn't really see the need for all this drama. Sure, Joey was upset now, but he and Jason would be friends again in no time. And it wasn't as if anyone had been hurt— "Jason's okay?"

Mrs. Erskine-Lippert nodded curtly.

"Did Joey say something he shouldn't have?"

"I don't know what was said. The playground monitor noticed the uproar from a distance, but neither boy would give her, or me, the particulars of the argument. In fact, both Joseph and Jason have claimed to be at fault, Jason for saying something mean, as he put it, and Joey for getting angry."

She looked sour over that admission, but Max had to stifle a smile. "It was just a disagreement between friends," he said. "They're not making a big deal of it, so maybe we should let it go, too."

"Usually I would agree with you, Mr. Devlin. However, I believe Joseph's behavior today is only a symptom of a bigger problem, and if the cause of that problem is not addressed, the behavior will escalate beyond name-calling and half-hearted shoving."

Max shook his head. "I don't believe that. If there's something bothering Joey that much, he'll come to me or—"

"Miss Lewis? I don't think so, and I'm not sure he'd go to you, either."

"Of course he would. We've always been able to talk."

"Under normal circumstances, perhaps, but I don't believe Joseph is comfortable bringing his concerns to either one of you without feeling he's betraying the other. I'm sure you don't want to hear this, Mr. Devlin, but your son is as confused and upset about the rift between you and Miss Lewis as any child would be when the parental figures in his life are going through a difficult time. He doesn't understand his own feelings, let alone yours."

Max hunched down in his chair, feeling belligerent if for no other reason than that the only discussions he'd ever had about his feelings had ended in really, really bad changes in his life. Like Sara walking out on him. He wasn't about to delve into the subject with Mabel Erskine-Lippert. He let the silence drag out until he couldn't stand it anymore. "What happens now?"

"I don't believe any punishment is warranted at this point, but I suggest that you and Miss Lewis sit down like adults and discuss the situation," she said.

Something in his face must have telegraphed his reluctance to approach Sara. And Mrs. Erskine-Lippert must have been aware of Sara's complete and utter aversion to talking to him—the whole town had to know about it by now. Ever since the New Year's party she'd taken to crossing the street whenever she saw him in town. And because Max had absolutely no idea what to say, he let her.

"Miss Lewis is Joseph's teacher," the principal reminded him. "If the two of you can't at least meet and get along for Joseph's benefit, how do you ever expect him to come to terms with the changes in his life?"

Max crossed his arms and scowled at her.

"You'll find Miss Lewis in her classroom." Mrs. Erskine-Lippert pulled a stack of papers in front of her and bent over them.

Max got to his feet. She'd effectively dismissed him, and as little as he was looking forward to what came next, he figured it would be best to get while the getting was good. He walked out into the hallway, wondering how in the world he was going to talk to Sara—and how he could face Joey if he didn't.

"What'd she say?" Joey asked, flashing a look at the principal's door in case she could hear his whispered question through solid wood and glass.

"You're going to have to apologize to Jason, and you're going to have to try to keep a lid on that temper of yours. And…she wants me to talk to…to your teacher. To Sara."

Joey jumped off the bench, such hope in his eyes it all but

destroyed Max to have to disappoint him. "I think you should wait for me here, Joey."

"But, Dad—"

"I'll come back for you when I'm done."

Joey just stood there, rebellion in every line of his body. Max hunkered down in front of him and waited until his son looked at him. "We're only going to talk about what happened at recess today. I know that's not what you want to hear, but we have to take care of this first. Okay?"

Joey nodded and sank back onto the bench to stare at the wall.

Max hated to leave his son there, alone and unhappy, but he had no choice. Talking to Sara would be hard enough without having to worry about how Joey was reading the conversation.

"Dad?"

He turned back.

"Tell Sara I'm sorry."

"You can tell her yourself, the next time you see her."

"Then…tell her…" His narrow shoulders slumped.

"I know exactly how you feel, son."

"Dad?"

Max turned around again.

"Don't mess up, okay?"

Out of the mouths of babes, Max thought. "I'll try not to," he said, hoping for some kind of divine intervention on the way to Sara's classroom.

But heaven wasn't helping, it seemed, because what little inspiration had managed to survive his apprehension was incinerated the moment he saw Sara. She wore one of her school outfits, a snowflake sweater and a jean skirt that hit her mid-thigh over dark blue tights. She looked just like the old Sara— it should've been easy to think of her as his best friend again—but he was too busy noticing things he'd never noticed about a friend before. Things like how her sweater draped over the swell of her breasts, how that skirt hugged the sleek lines of her hips and bottom. Memories ripped his resolve to shreds, memories of how it felt to shape those curves with his own hands, how perfectly their bodies fit together.

She bent to gather a stack of papers off her desk and little black dots began to dance in front of his eyes. It was all he could do not to back her up against that wall where she'd had him pressed all those weeks ago. Once he got her in his arms, she wouldn't be walking away, superglue or no superglue.

All of a sudden that ridiculous scene flooded back to Max, him spread-eagled against the wall with Sara all over him like foam on fresh milk. He caught himself smiling. It was one of the things he missed about having her in his life—the way she made him laugh.

He wished he could have done the same for her, but apparently he'd been more effective at hurting her, though in all fairness he hadn't really understood that until recently. There was a lot he hadn't understood until recently. In fact, if anyone had told him that one day his driving obsession would be to get Sara in just the sort of position she'd put them in by accident, he'd have said that person was crazy. Now he was kicking himself for blowing the opportunity—for blowing six years of opportunities.

But he wasn't wasting any more time. The past was gone, and tomorrow could take care of itself. Today was all that mattered. He focused on that as he walked into the room, kept his eyes on her as he searched for the words to convince her they belonged together. He never found them—never had to, because halfway across the room he ran smack-dab into the paint easel. It collapsed and fell over with all the noise and shock value of a firecracker. Paint shot up into the air like Old Faithful in Technicolor.

She spun around, her attention landing on the paint dripping down the front of his jeans and onto his workboots. Her eyes lifted, wide and wary, to his, and the papers she'd gathered began to slide out of her arms. She juggled a little and managed to catch them, but Max could tell she was flustered.

Sara took in his wide grin, the way he arched his brows as his gaze shifted down to the papers in her hand and back up to her face. She turned away and dropped her load of papers on the desk, her mind racing as furiously as her pulse.

She was no longer immune to Max; he'd just figured that out, but it was hardly news to her. She'd known ever since she'd danced with him on New Year's Eve. Touching him was like throwing a lit match on a pile of sawdust. Even the parts of her she was sure were dead forever had exploded back into instant and painful life, and she'd found herself wondering why she was being so stubborn. What would it hurt to give in, just a little, to the need to see Joey and be with Max again? Every now and then, when the loneliness got too much to bear.

But in her saner moments she knew that if she relented one iota, Max would suck her in completely and before she knew it she'd be right back where she started, sharing everything with him but her heart. She couldn't return to that perpetual limbo—not and keep her self-respect.

He had to be the one to give in this time, and Sara wasn't going to settle for some wishy-washy mumbled sentiment. She wanted a big, splashy declaration of love, wanted to know that she mattered to him more than his ranch, his reputation, even his phobia about being a public spectacle—everything but Joey. She wouldn't settle for less.

"You spoke to Mrs. Erskine-Lippert?" he asked, bending to pick up the pint-size paint shirt that had been hanging from the easel.

"I listened mostly," Sara said, trying not to notice his backside, or the way those paint-dampened jeans clung to the muscles of his thighs, bunching and flexing as he swabbed off his boots. She turned away, afraid he'd see the desire in her eyes and use it against her.

"Me, too."

"What did she decide to do about Joey?"

"This is it," Max said, spreading his hands. "You and I are supposed to talk."

"I don't see how that will help," she said. "Unless you're prepared to talk about something besides who won what ball game, or how many eggs the chickens laid, or how well you think your bull's going to show at the state fair this summer."

Max only stared at her, but the dam had broken, and Sara couldn't plug the leaks fast enough to keep six years of pent-up frustration from spilling out. "I know it hurt you when your marriage broke up, Max, but don't you think it's about time you started dealing with your feelings instead of walking around as if you don't have any?"

"I deal with my feelings," he snapped. "I just don't need to examine them every five seconds—"

"Or ever."

"—or walk around with them hanging out for the whole town to see."

Sara stalked over to him, hands on her hips. "Well, at least I don't have to live like a hermit because I'm afraid of what a bunch of meddlesome, bored people might say."

He leaned in, practically nose-to-nose with her. Definitely eye-to-eye. He wasn't about to give her the satisfaction of backing down. "At least I'm not the constant subject of gossip in this town."

"Have you checked lately?"

"If I am, it's your fault."

"*My* fault! You were carrying my panties around in your pocket! How is that my fault?"

"You left. Everything was fine the way it was, but you had to move to Janey's and turn my life upside down. Not to mention Joey's."

"Don't you bring Joey into this."

"Joey's right in the middle of this, in case you haven't noticed." He paced across the room and back again. "You can't ignore me without ignoring him."

"Well, let me tell you a thing or two, Mr. Devlin." She grabbed his arm so she could talk to him without feeling like she was at a tennis match. She knew instantly that she'd made a mistake. But it was too late, because he was touching her back and the world narrowed down to the feel of his fingertips on her cheek, his mouth covering hers, the hot, hard planes of his body burning against her.

She clenched both hands in his shirt and dove into the kiss. He pulled her hands down, locking them behind her with one of his, turning her around and backing her up against the desk. His mouth slid down to her neck, the stubble on his cheeks rasping over her skin in a way that had her twisting and shuddering in pleasure. She fought her hands free so she could touch him, then had to brace them on the desk behind her because he was arching her back over his arm, laying her down as he stepped between her thighs and locked their clothed lower bodies together. He leaned over her, sending papers and books crashing to the floor.

Sara shot upright, shoving him away and scrambling off her desk before he'd even begun to grasp that she was gone, let alone why. She opened a window and stuck her flaming face in the frigid draft of air that streamed in.

After a moment Max joined her and let the fresh air wash over him until it began to feel cold against his skin. Sara was shivering by that time, but when he placed a hand on her shoulder, she dashed across the room and stood there, arms wrapped around her waist.

"We can't go on like this." It wasn't what he'd intended to say, but frustration got the better of him. He didn't know how Sara had managed while being so off balance around him all these years, how she'd managed to keep so much need contained without bursting into flame, but he hated it. "These accidents—"

"I'm not having accidents anymore."

"So it's my problem? Maybe if you stopped being so stubborn—"

"I'm being stubborn? You know how I feel, Max. The whole town knows how I feel, as you pointed out."

"And you want some sort of declaration from me, is that it? Tell me what you want me to say and I'll say it."

She looked at him, the anger in her eyes dulling into misery. "If I have to put the words in your mouth they don't mean anything, do they?"

She waited, but he didn't say anything more. All this time apart, she thought, all this time hurting, and they'd gone nowhere at all.

"I'm sorry, Sara," he finally said. "I just wish I knew how to fix this."

You do, she wanted to shout at him, *by saying three simple words.* But they weren't simple words, not really. They represented trust and love and commitment, and she wouldn't want to hear them from Max until he could put all of that into them.

"I'm sorry, too," she said, crossing to right the easel. When she bent to gather the corners of the plastic dropcloth together, she noticed the paint on her skirt, like a modern-day version of Hester Prynne's *A,* only in her case it ought to be *F* for fool. She kept having this same conversation with Max, but nothing ever got settled. "There's one thing we can agree on. We both love Joey, and whatever else happens, Max, he'll be a part of both our lives. But we can't keep letting him get caught in the fallout from our disagreements."

"I don't want him in the middle of this any more than you do, but I don't really see a way to prevent it. Like you said, we both love him and he loves us. He can't help but be affected."

"You're right." Sara walked over to the far counter and set the edge of the dropcloth on the sink, letting the bottom corners fall open. Paint cups and brushes clattered into the stainless-steel basin, but her goal wasn't really cleaning up a mess. It just helped, somehow, to be doing something. "Joey heard what you said on New Year's about me leaving town," she said over the sound of running water. "I took him into the coatroom and tried to explain it to him. He seemed to understand, but—" she spread her hands, at a loss "—he hasn't been himself lately."

"As far as he's concerned you've already left."

"There's not a lot I can do about that at the moment."

Max clamped his mouth shut, a muscle in his jaw tensing. "At least come and spend some time with him, then."

"Joey can come over to Janey's and stay the night."

"That won't work. He needs to see things haven't changed that much."

"He needs to know they've changed for good."

"I think he got that message already, Sara."

She bit back what she'd been about to say. Her brain stopped churning out arguments for points he hadn't made yet. She'd accused Max of using Joey to get to her, but now she realized she was using Joey to keep her distance.

"Come out and have supper with us tonight, watch a movie like you used to every Friday night. It isn't that much to ask, and maybe it'll make Joey feel better."

Sara found herself actually considering it and took a mental step back. She'd get out there, make supper in Max's kitchen and fall under the spell of all those old dreams again, dreams of being a family with Max and Joey. The next thing she knew, she'd be in Max's arms, then his bed and it would be impossible to think after that.

"I'm busy tonight."

"Change your plans."

"No, I—I can't. It wouldn't be right."

"Why, what are you doing?"

"None of your business."

Max's eyes narrowed on her face. "Do you have a date with Sam Tucker?"

"If I did, you'd probably have heard it down at the hardware."

"Yeah," Max said with a heavy sigh. "That's the problem with this town. Everyone minds everyone's business but their own." And then he perked up because he'd just figured out that Sara hadn't replaced him, which meant— "I think you're afraid to come out to the ranch."

"Afraid? You want to talk about fear, Max? Why don't you bring Joey into town and we'll have supper at the diner, then drive over to the theater in Plains City and see whatever's playing there."

"Plains City's a two-hour drive, and what if there's an R-rated movie showing? And I really think Joey would prefer it if you came out and cooked something for him. I mean, I could make supper but despite Betty Crocker's best efforts, Joey's not all that wild about my cooking and…" He trailed off when he saw the way she was looking at him, kind of disappointed and sad, and he could have sworn her eyes misted over before she turned away. "Okay, so maybe we both have issues."

"Why doesn't that make me feel any better?"

"YOU WERE ARGUING," Joey said sullenly, accusingly, when Max came to collect him from the bench outside the principal's office. "I heard you."

"Yeah." Max handed Joey his coat, waiting while he slipped it on. "I don't seem to be able to say the right thing anymore."

"Yelling probably didn't help.

The understatement of the century, Max thought, but Joey was eight—and unhappy to boot—so he was allowed to state the obvious. "We were both yelling."

"Did you yell at Mom? Is that why she left?"

Max stopped midstride, turning to look back at his son. "Is that what you think?"

Joey shrugged, his face set in an expression Max had never seen before, but one he knew all too well. Joey was angry, upset, hurt, but he was turning all those emotions inward, assuming, somehow, that it was his fault.

"Your mom and I, we wanted different things, Joey. I can't imagine living anywhere else but here. Your mom...she didn't want to leave you, but she couldn't do what she wanted here."

"Make movies," Joey said. "I know. And it's better for me to stay here and go to school and all that stuff. I like it when Mom comes back to visit, or when I get to stay with her in the summer, but..."

But Max knew he couldn't remember a time when she'd lived with them—and he couldn't remember a time when Sara hadn't. Until recently.

"What about Sara, Dad?"

"Yeah." Max started walking, relieved when Joey fell into step with him. "I asked her to come back, but...she said not yet."

"Why not?" Joey latched on to his dad's coat sleeve, putting him to a halt halfway across the empty parking lot. "She used to like it at the ranch."

Sure, she'd liked it just fine before he'd told her she should leave.

"Don't you want her to come back?"

"Of course—"

"Then do something, Dad!"

Max had to clamp his jaw shut before he yelled at his son. To Joey it must look like he wasn't doing anything, but the problem wasn't inaction, it was uncertainty. "I'm doing the best I can, Joey. I'm trying to get Sara to come back, but it's going to take some time. And…" And here came another hard lesson his son was learning much too early, that the man who was supposed to be his hero had feet of clay. "And maybe I won't be able to."

Chapter Thirteen

Sara poked her head in the back door of Max's ranch house, trying not to notice the scorch marks on the wall and counter, the new curtains and the partially melted trash container. She'd spent weeks trying to forget that videotape. Besides, she hadn't driven all the way out to the ranch to deal with Max. This visit was all about Joey.

She didn't have to look far to find him. He sat at the kitchen table, chin resting on his folded arms, staring at the robotic dog she'd given him for Christmas. The dog stared back, silent, eyes blank and empty. The real dogs lay at his feet, one of them with his muzzle resting across the toes of Joey's shoes. They were obviously taking their mood from him.

"Hey, Joey," she said.

He looked up, his expression wary and guarded. Thank heaven she'd changed her mind and decided not to wait until Monday, Sara thought. Staying away from the ranch to prove her point to Max wasn't worth what it was doing to Joey.

"Dad said you weren't coming over tonight," he said.

"I thought I'd surprise you." She stepped inside, ruffling his hair. "Where's your dad?"

"In the barn, unloading the hay he picked up today."

Sara drew her first deep breath since she'd pulled into the

driveway. She needed to set things right between Joey and her. In order to do that, she was going to have to be as honest about her feelings as she could, and that wouldn't be possible with Max around.

She took off her gloves and unwound her scarf, stuffing them into the sleeves of her coat before hanging it on the coat-rack. She knew she was stalling, and she hated it. She'd never had a problem talking to Joey before, but then she'd never had a reason to feel guilty before, and the fact that he was watching her every move as if she might suddenly strike out at him only made it worse.

She sat down in the chair opposite his and pulled the ro-botic dog over to her. It was kind of cute, all silver with shiny black wraparound sunglasses where its eyes should have been. But it wasn't very good company. "Is it broken?"

Joey reached over, flipped a switch, and the thing leaped into frenzied life, demonic red eyes winking on and off.

Sara set it on the table and it began to clomp around on stiff plastic legs, tail wagging with a metallic clatter. Every now and then it halted and gave off a tinny, echoing bark that sent the real dogs racing in and out of the room, barking frenziedly.

"It does some tricks," Joey yelled over the din. "Want to see?"

"Maybe another time."

His eyes brightened, an impish grin curving his mouth.

Sara had no idea why, but she grinned back. "What?"

"You won't let me bring my robodog to school so that means you're going to be here. Right?"

"Well—"

"I don't want you to leave town, Sara."

"I know."

"You said you'd do whatever I wanted."

"But—"

"You promised!"

"When?"

That stopped him. He sat back in his chair, his bottom lip disappearing between his teeth as he racked his brain. "The day you knocked Mr. Delancey off the light pole in town."

"I didn't knock him off the light pole, I only bumped into the ladder," Sara defended automatically. She cast her memory back, but an awful lot had happened that day. Things like being turned into a human Christmas tree. Things like Max almost kissing her, right there in the middle of Main Street. And then not kissing her. The details of her conversation with Joey seemed to have gotten lost in all that uproar. "So what is it you're asking me to do?"

"Move into your house again."

"Whoa." She shoved her chair back, then thought better of leaving the table in case Joey took it as rejection. "I can't do that."

"But you said we'd always be best friends."

Now that she remembered telling him. "And friends don't let each other down," she said, "but a friend doesn't ask another friend to do something that would be bad for her."

"But—"

Sara held up a hand, cutting off his protest as effectively as if they were in the classroom. She'd known it would come to this, but that didn't make it any easier. "I can't live here again, Joey. It would be too painful to see M—your dad every day when things are so confused and...and...messed up between us."

He took it a lot better than she'd expected. "I guess I can understand that, Sara. But why do you have to leave town?"

She sat back in her chair, caught off guard by the simplicity of that question. "I don't know. It just seems...necessary."

"Why? Everyone in town likes you. Don't you like them?"

"Well, yes. Mostly."

"And don't you like teaching at the school?"

"I love teaching at the school, Joey."

"Then why do you have to leave town just because you and my dad don't get along anymore? I mean, as long as you're not living out here, you won't hardly ever have to see him, right?"

"That's true." She loved her job, she had friends here and a career. But she wouldn't be able to move on as long as she stayed in Erskine. There was too much history here, and too many people who knew it. Even if she met another man she liked, she wasn't about to try having a relationship with everyone in town keeping score. Including Max. "You know, Joey, you're right. I don't really want to leave town, but I don't think I can stay here—"

"Why are you giving up so fast?"

"Joey—"

"No." He pushed away the hand she'd reached out to him, jumping up so fast his chair crashed to the floor behind him. "You keep saying you want to stay here, but you're not even *trying* to get along with Dad."

"That's not fair."

He gave her a look, anger and disgust mixed together. "That's so lame. I had one stupid argument with Jason, and Dad made me apologize to practically everybody. You guys have been fighting forever, but all you do is stay away from each other and make excuses."

Sara tried to make her voice calm and reasonable when inside she was shaking. "We talked today." For all the good it had done them. "I'm here now."

"Because I got in trouble and the principal made you."

"Because no matter what else is going on, Joey, we both love you."

"Well, I hate you!" he screamed at her. "I hate you both!"

She caught him as he ran by, caught him and held on tight

until he stopped fighting her and went limp, his little body
racked with sobs. Sara cried too, let the tears she'd been holding back for weeks finally flow. Some of it was heartache,
some self-pity, some guilt—and anger at Max—for what their
stubbornness had done to the one innocent person in this mess.

She didn't know how long they sat like that, but Joey finally pulled away and wiped his cheeks.

"I'm hungry," he said.

Sara felt better, too. "It smells like your dad has something
in the Crock-Pot."

Joey wrinkled his nose.

"That's not a good thing?"

He shrugged. "I like your cooking better."

"He's trying, kiddo."

He gave another shrug, with a sigh thrown in for good measure. "Maybe someday you and Dad will get along again."

"Joey…"

"If he apologized?"

It was Sara's turn to sigh. "An apology doesn't fix everything."

He sat there waiting for an explanation. And she felt compelled to give him one. Better that than have him internalize
everything again.

"There are feelings involved, here, kiddo. If your dad…if
Max doesn't feel the same way about me that I feel about him,
an apology won't really help all that much."

As explanations went, it was pretty cryptic; she'd kept it
that way on purpose. But Joey just digested it for a minute, a
considering little smile on his face.

"You love my dad, right?"

"Yes…"

"And he loves you."

Sara lifted his chin so she could look into his eyes. "I know
you want him to feel that way. So do I—"

"But he said it! I asked him if he loved you and he said he did."

Sara could only stare at Joey, his eyes filled with sincerity, his features set in the same expression of determination she'd seen on Max's face dozens of time. "When?" she managed to croak out, despite the fact that all the breath had left her body at the mere idea that Max might actually love her.

Joey pulled his robodog in front of him, scratching his thumbnail over a rough spot in the plastic.

Obviously he was uncomfortable talking about his feelings, but she had to know. "When did he say it, Joey?"

"On Christmas," he said without looking up. "It was funny not having you here, and I asked him if he loved you and he nodded. Then he said he was trying to fix it, whatever that means."

Her head began to buzz. Sara rubbed her temples, trying to convince herself that Joey couldn't be remembering right. Christmas was more than a month ago.

But it made a weird sort of sense. Max wouldn't have ignored a point-blank question of Joey's, and he would have tried to be as truthful as possible. If he'd loved her as a friend he wouldn't have hesitated to say so, but nodding was just the sort of evasive response she'd expect from a man who was really in love and too uncomfortable with his feelings to say it out loud.

That didn't mean Sara was letting him off the hook. She'd been in hell, waiting for him to figure out that he loved her, and he'd known for weeks! So why hadn't he told her how he felt?

That question was still rocketing around inside her head when Max walked in.

Sara jerked to her feet and stepped back, wrapping her arms around her waist—automatic self-defense maneuvers that did little to stop her heart from battering at her breastbone as if it could break free and escape the whole ordeal altogether. That would be the only way it would get out of there, because her feet seemed to be stuck to the floor.

His eyes flicked from her to Joey—who made a big show of studying a nick in the tabletop—and back to her. "I saw your car parked in the driveway," he said, brushing at the snow coating his shoulders and hair. "You still mad at me?"

Her mouth opened, but she couldn't even answer that question for herself. Was she angry? Yes, a little, but she was also relieved, dazed, amazed. And hurt. Max loved her, but he'd felt no need to tell her on any of the occasions they'd spoken in town.

But he'd been awfully anxious to get her to the ranch tonight. He'd been positively insistent, as a matter of fact, and her heart made such a huge and precipitous leap of faith that her mind had no choice but to follow.

"I made dinner in the Crock-Pot," he said as he peeled off his coat and kicked off his boots. "I had to go out and buy one."

"There's one in the pantry," Sara cut in, seizing on the mundane topic as a way to get her mind off the possibility that Max had lured her out here, away from all the prying eyes and listening ears in town, so he could tell her how he felt in private. It didn't pay to hope when she could see no indication of it in his behavior. "It's on the top shelf in the corner."

"Doesn't hurt to have a spare."

Sara moved around to the opposite side of the table from Max, not the least bit ashamed of needing a physical barrier between them. "I should be going."

"I thought you were staying for supper," Joey said.

"She is, Joey, go wash up." Max watched him race off upstairs, then glanced over at Sara. "You're not going to get far in this snowstorm, anyway."

"What?" Sara raced to the window and saw a solid wall of

white, sometimes falling straight down in big clumps the size of a half-dollar, sometimes whipped against the house by a driving wind that whistled around the eaves and rattled the windowpanes. "How long has it been doing this?"

"Not long," Max said, coming to stand behind her. "But when it's doing this it doesn't take long to make the roads impassable."

Sara could feel the big, solid bulk of him almost but not quite touching her, so close that his breath stirred her hair. She slipped away and took a moment to let her nerves settle. It wasn't nearly long enough, considering that her voice still wavered a little before it steadied. "So, I'm stuck here?"

"You're not driving in this."

She might have argued with him, despite the flat decisiveness of his tone. She should have bristled at being ordered around, but he crossed the room to join her just then, and she couldn't even remember her name, let alone what he'd said or how he'd said it.

"Sit down and have some dinner. I got your wood burner going when I saw your car and realized you wouldn't be able to make it back to town tonight. Your house is small, but it'll take some time to heat up, and there's nothing to eat over there. Then again, maybe this will stop and you'll be able to get back to Janey's after all."

Escape! That was what she should be thinking about. She had to get out of there before she made a complete fool of herself—not that she minded making a fool of herself, but now Max would know why. She glanced dubiously at the window, half-obscured by a blanket of heavy, wet snow. "I think I should go over to my house now, while I can still find it."

Sara was already moving, so when Max took her arm she stumbled.

He caught her around the waist, pulled her against him and held her there for a long moment. His breath was warm at her temple, the feel of his body a sweet fire she didn't want to extinguish. His hands flexed once, then gentled to smooth along her rib cage, inching higher as he lowered his head to nuzzle the side of her neck—

"I'm hungry, Dad. When're we gonna eat?"

Sara was grateful there was a chair handy. Max was gone before Joey's compact little body followed his voice into the room, before her legs were steady enough to hold her. Thankfully Joey didn't seem to notice that she was laboring for breath, that her face was flushed and her hands were shaking.

Max didn't either, but then he was working too hard at hiding his own upheaval to notice hers. He went to the cupboard and got out three bowls, retrieved some cutlery and a stack of napkins and put them on the table, careful not to look at her. By the time he'd dumped the contents of the Crock-Pot into a serving bowl, the tremors racking his body had settled into infrequent spasms of need that screamed along his nerve endings with something too close to pleasure for him to wish them away.

He wrapped both hands around the serving bowl and took a deep breath, carrying it from the counter to the table. He turned back, grabbed the bread and butter and sat down, silently thanking whatever power had helped get him into his seat without dropping supper, falling on his face or making a fool of himself.

He took a deep, cleansing breath and turned his attention to the hunger he could satisfy now. There would be time for the other one later, he promised himself. "Who's hungry?"

An expectant quiet descended over the kitchen, the three of them studying the contents of the serving bowl with varying degrees of skepticism. Max couldn't blame Joey for being cautious; not all his collaborations with Betty Crocker could be called successful. This one was compliments of Campbell's, though, and he was reasonably sure it wouldn't poison them.

"It smells good," Sara said, though her expression while she watched him fill her bowl was less than optimistic.

Max had to admit it was a little on the gray and lumpy side, but looks didn't mean everything. He passed Sara's bowl back across the table, filled Joey's and his own, then passed around the bread and butter. A lot of buttering happened, some drinking went on, and the salt and pepper made the rounds. Nobody ate.

Max scooped up a heaping spoonful, took a deep breath and stuck it in his mouth. He had to suck in air while he chewed because it was piping hot. Joey and Sara were watching him closely, so he crossed his eyes and wrapped both hands around his throat, sliding down in his chair while he made gagging sounds.

Joey started laughing immediately and by the time Max sat upright, even Sara was smiling a little. She took a bite, chewed hesitantly then swallowed, her smile widening. "It's good. Or maybe I'm just starving," she amended when she noticed his self-satisfied grin. "I can't remember what I had for lunch—or if I even had lunch. What is it?"

Max shrugged. "The recipe came off the back of a soup can."

Joey took a cautious bite, then began shoveling it in at record speed. While Max finished up his first helping, Joey was scraping his bowl clean for a second time and asking to be excused.

When Max let him go, Joey raced into the living room to choose a video.

"You should be proud of yourself," Sara said to Max before the silence could become awkward. "It can't be easy juggling all the responsibilities you have *and* managing to get a hot meal on the table."

Max shrugged off the praise, though he felt himself flushing with pleasure. "You should know—you used to do it every day."

"I didn't have to get up before dawn and do chores, then work outside all day."

"No, but you have to deal with a classroom of eight-year-olds."

"But I love teaching."

"And I love ranching."

"Then I guess we're both pretty lucky." But she didn't feel lucky, Sara thought, staring down at her tightly folded hands. She felt empty and lonely and so aware of Max she called herself a fool for ever believing she could resist him when the temptation to surrender had been inside her all along.

They'd sat like this hundreds of evenings after some meal she'd cooked, Joey making a racket in the other room as they talked about the events of the day and their plans for the weekend to come. She'd always wanted more, wished she truly belonged instead of feeling she haunted the edges of their lives. Now she was the one being haunted, beset every waking moment of every day by the ghost of loving Max.

She had only to look at him and she was in his arms again, surrounded by his scent and heat, the harsh sound of his breathing mingling with the thunder of her own pulse. Her lips remembered the feel of his mouth, her skin the callused, gentle touch of his hands. Her body knew how it felt to be joined with his, to take the breathless, spiraling climb that left rational thought behind and filled her with pleasure—

"Sara," Max said, the word a rasp that throbbed along her raw nerve endings.

She tore her eyes off him and sprang out of her chair. "I'll do the dishes."

"Sara, I—"

"It's only fair," she said. "You cooked, I'll clean." She turned on the water, almost jumping out of her skin when she heard the scrape of his chair sliding back.

She kept her back turned, her nerves stretching tighter with each step he took until he was right beside her. She shoved her hands under the water to hide their shaking—she was trembling from head to toe, afraid he would touch her.

He stood there for what felt like an eternity, and she could feel his gaze on her. And then he walked away and she realized that the only thing worse than his touching her was his not touching her.

He began clearing the table, stacking the dishes next to the sink. Aside from the three bowls, three spoons and three glasses they'd used, there were only a few other things, but it seemed to take him forever to transport it all from table to counter. And whenever he brought something over, he managed to brush against her.

After the first two times, Sara moved aside so he had plenty of room.

Max felt a sudden need to put the dishes directly in the sinkful of water, his wet, soapy hand sliding over hers. And then he decided to put the next load of dishes into the sink from the other side so that when she thought she was moving completely away from him, she ran into him instead.

He steadied her, one hand on her upper arm, the other curled around her waist so they were face-to-face, almost embracing.

She shook him off and stepped back, glaring through her screaming need to throw herself across that narrow margin of overcharged, superheated air between them and into his arms. What would be the harm in letting him have his way when it would give her exactly what she wanted…?

Letting him have his way—*that* would be the harm in it. Having her own weaknesses used against her so that she wound up exactly where she'd promised herself she wouldn't—not until he told her how he felt.

She'd intended to hold her ground the next time he came

over, but she found herself leaning into the contact. Actually let a little purr rumble around in the back of her throat. Torturing him as much as he'd tortured her.

Max fled across the polished linoleum floor so fast his stocking feet almost slid out from under him. "You came here to see Joey," he said, his voice low and strained. "Why don't you go see him?"

Sara let out her breath. It didn't diminish her tension one notch, but at least she didn't have to worry about Max crowding her anymore. "He must still be picking out a movie or he'd be out here telling us to hurry up."

Except for the sounds of water trickling and cutlery clinking, it grew quiet. Sara began to relax. It almost felt like old times, she and Max cleaning up from supper while Joey chose a movie.

"I haven't thanked you yet for coming out here tonight," Max said, a hint of huskiness in his voice. "I don't know what you said to Joey, but it's good to see him acting like his old self again."

"Yes, it is," she said. And too bad, she added silently, that they couldn't do the same. "Maybe it's time we put this all behind us and became friends again."

"That's not what you want," Max said.

"Sometimes you have to settle."

He took her by the shoulders and spun her around. "I don't ever want to hear you say that again. Sara—"

"What movie do you want to watch?" Joey asked from the doorway.

Max stared at her for a second and then his hands fell away from her shoulders. "I'd better go help him before we end up watching *Star Wars* for the zillionth time."

She watched him go, speechless, heart pounding and head spinning. He got her all worked up, physically and emotionally, and then, just when he was about to make some sort of declaration, he walked out and left her hanging.

It was exactly what she'd done to him, she realized. Not once, not twice, but at least three times in the past couple of months, and that was if she didn't count that day at the Ersk Inn. They hadn't actually spoken then, but there'd been enough of the unspoken going on between them to fill a Greek tragedy.

Sara wondered how he'd stood it, being brought to this kind of emotional fever pitch all those times and then dropped cold. But the answer was there, in the pit of her heaving stomach. He'd dealt with it the same way he'd dealt with Julia walking out on him: complete and utter retreat into that emotional black hole she hated so much.

And it was her own fault. All this time, she'd been waiting for Max to tell her how he felt, hoping and praying he'd find the strength and the courage to risk loving again, and here she'd been—showing him every chance she got that she couldn't be trusted with it.

But she was done letting fear motivate her, done running like a hamster on a wheel and getting nowhere. By the time she'd dried the dishes and put them away, and made a bowl of popcorn, she knew exactly what she wanted to say to Max and exactly how she was going to say it.

As usual, it was her timing that stank. She could hardly speak her piece with Joey sitting on the sofa between them and *Twister* wreaking havoc on the television screen. As movies went, it was a good choice: flying cows, exploding oil tankers and mass destruction for Joey. And for her, two main characters who obviously loved each other but couldn't find the right words to fix what had gone wrong between them. She'd seen the movie at least a dozen times, and she'd never understood what kept them apart. She did now; she couldn't put it into words, but she understood it.

She stared at the television screen, thinking about how those two people had been dancing around the truth, just as she and Max had been dancing around it. And when the hero finally told the heroine how he felt, the words apparently torn from his very soul, she could feel Max's gaze. She didn't dare return it, not while she was wondering if there was a reason he'd chosen this particular movie.

"Joey's asleep."

Sara jumped, slapping one hand over her pounding heart. Max didn't seem to notice, already on his feet and bending to gather the warm, limp weight of his son into his arms.

"Kid weighs a ton," he said, giving a little groan as he straightened. "I'll take him upstairs."

"Max..."

He turned back, shifting Joey to a more comfortable position.

Sara's voice deserted her. The picture of the two of them, Joey's head nestled in the crook of his father's shoulder, brought tears to her eyes. Max was a gentle, loving man, and if he couldn't always get that across in words, he certainly managed to say it with his actions. She needed to remember that.

"If you're not too tired, maybe we could talk," he said, his voice soft and sincere. "Let me get Joey into bed and I'll be right down."

"No, maybe it would be better talking at my house—in case there's yelling."

"There might be yelling?"

Sara shrugged. This time she was getting things settled once and for all, and she didn't want to worry about waking Joey up. "You never know."

Chapter Fourteen

Max lifted his hand to knock on Sara's door, then dropped it instead. What if she didn't answer? What if she told him to go away or, worse yet, what if she told him to come in? It wasn't that he didn't want to see her. He just couldn't get that comment about yelling out of his head. Especially since she had every right to yell.

He hadn't exactly behaved himself tonight, touching her every chance he got, but it had been hard not to when she looked so damned sexy. She'd changed from the skirt and sweater that had driven him crazy in her classroom into a pair of faded jeans and a different sweater—one that didn't require snowflakes to draw his attention. He'd seen her wear those jeans and that sweater dozens of times before and never been incited to touch her. He'd seen her wash dishes before, too, and never noticed the way her hips shimmied when she scrubbed a pot, but just the memory of it made him feel he was on fire, even in the subzero Montana night air. If that gave her a reason to yell at him, he might as well get it over with.

He opened the door without knocking and walked inside, almost swallowing his tongue at the sight that met his eyes. Sara was nowhere to be seen, but just about every flat surface in the small main room held a lit candle. An open bottle of wine sat on the kitchen table, two glasses beside it, and when Sara walked out of the bedroom…

Max frowned. The scene was set for seduction, but if he'd been expecting sexy lingerie, he would have been sadly disappointed. Not to mention delusional. She wore a heavy flannel shirt, one of his that hit her midthigh. Underneath was a pair of sweatpants, bagged at the ankle over thick white socks. His pulse took a little jump when he noticed that her hands were busy at the buttons of the shirt. And then he realized she was putting them through the holes, not taking them out.

She glanced up, saw the look in his eyes and gathered the shirt together in both fists.

Max could've told her it was no use. If he wanted in that shirt, he could get her to let him in. What he couldn't figure out was why she had it on in the first place. "What are the candles for?"

"It smelled musty in here after being closed up so long."

"And the wine?"

Her hands clamped even tighter on the flannel. "I…I'm a little nervous."

"Me, too," Max muttered. He walked over and poured two glasses, chugging one of them and refilling it before handing the other one to Sara. He was careful not to touch her.

"Thank you," she said softly.

"You're welcome."

"Sooo…" She twirled her glass, watching the candlelight dance in the pale pink wine. "You wanted to talk?" she asked, sliding her gaze up to him without lifting her head.

"Uh…" Max took a sip of wine. "Hmm." He sipped again, but one-syllable noises seemed to be the extent of his vocabulary at the moment.

Sara wasn't as verbally challenged. "You love me, don't you?" she said, and although she seemed to have thought long and hard before she decided to say it, her face turned a shade of red Max had never seen before.

For the life of him he had no idea what to say—or do, for that matter. Every coherent thought seemed to have run screaming from his brain, scared off by the notion of being in love, let alone admitting it out loud.

Sara stalked over and poked him in the chest. "Joey told me you said you love me. On Christmas."

"I really hate it when you do that," he said, catching her wrist before she could poke him again. "Joey told you?"

"Yes."

A lot had happened on Christmas, but he was fairly certain he would've remembered telling Joey he was in love with Sara. He looked into her eyes and saw that she suspected Joey was trying to help things along, but she wanted to believe it, and she was asking him to make it true.

His hand loosened to a gentler grip on her wrist, but he didn't let her go. "I thought you said if you have to put the words in my mouth, they don't mean anything."

"Only if there's no feeling behind them." She raised her chin and looked him square in the eyes. "Is that what you're saying? You don't feel it?"

Max might have been able to protect himself with anger; he didn't like being manipulated, even by his own son for his own good. But her lower lip trembled and he couldn't bear to hurt her, just to make a point. "No, that's not what I'm saying."

"So?"

"So if I say it now, you'll think I said it to get you into bed."

She tried to walk away, but he still had his hand around her wrist. He reeled her in, brought her close enough so their bodies brushed and she had to tilt her head back to look up at him.

Sara's last coherent thought was that she never should have let him touch her. And then his mouth crashed down over hers and she was straining up onto her toes, throwing herself right into the heart of the flames.

His lips left a trail of heated skin and short-circuited nerve endings down her neck and along the edge of the flannel as he undid the buttons she'd so prudently and carefully fastened because—

He gave a strangled groan and her eyes flew open. She tried to gather the sides of the flannel shirt together again, but he tore the rest of the buttons open, spreading the edges wide.

He opened his mouth but nothing came òut. His eyes were on her breasts, or rather what she was wearing over her breasts. Black satin and red lace.

"All my clothes are at Janey's," she said before he ran his finger along the lace, then back down to the V of bare skin between her breasts.

His other hand joined the first, skimming lace and skin to her shoulders, pulling off the shirt. As it fell to the floor in a pool of flannel, his hands moved to the waistband of the pants. He tugged them down, sinking to his knees. She steadied her hands on his shoulders as he lifted one foot, then the other, peeling off the pants and thick white socks.

His hands skimmed up her legs, stopping abruptly when he reached her backside. He looked at her, a mischievous smile on his face.

"I couldn't find the panties," she said, remembering where they were right about the time his grin widened.

"You won't be needing them, anyway." He stood but his hands stayed put, cupping her backside and drawing her against him.

"Max, I—"

"Shh." He pulled her into his arms. "Trust me," he whispered. He knew he didn't have any right to ask it of her, not after what he'd put her through. But when he felt her relax

against him, felt her face lift, her mouth hot on his neck, there
was such a rush of gratitude and love inside him....

Love.

Of course, he thought as he gathered her up in his arms and
carried her into the bedroom, he loved Sara. He hadn't been
sure before; too much of the past had still obscured his feelings, like a film of dirt on a window that kept him from seeing the full glory of the sunrise.

Now he realized that with Sara in his life it didn't matter
if the sun never rose again, because he was warmed and illu-
minated from within. There was a center to his life, around
which everything else revolved in its proper place and time.
And Sara was that center. He belonged to her just as completely as she belonged to him, heart and soul.

And body.

He placed her on the bed and she came into his arms at the
first touch, warm and soft and willing. Her mouth nuzzled into
his neck, her hands moved over his body, lingering at all the
sensitive spots she'd discovered during that one incredible
night all those weeks ago.

Max forced himself to take it slow, to savor the way she shivered when he ran his fingers down her spine and laughed when
he danced them back up across her ribs. His body screamed for
release, his mind for the sweet oblivion of it, but his heart re-
belled at the idea of physical satisfaction without a purer, deeper
joining. He wasn't just loving Sara, he was in love with her.

She noticed the change in him, felt him holding back and
wondered if she'd pushed him too hard too soon for the commitment she wanted so desperately. Then she discovered the
gentleness in his touch and the reverence in his eyes. He
swept his hands over her, lingering at her breasts but not to
tease, tensing at her waist and slipping over her hips as if each
inch of her was too precious to overlook.

He kissed her, deep and long, before his mouth traveled the path of his hands to taste and savor the essence of her. He took her to that first peak, urged her over with a loving insistence she couldn't resist, then joined his body to hers, taking her to a place where there was nothing but color and light and beauty, pleasure so intense it couldn't be described at all. Afterward, he cradled her in his strong, safe arms.

He leaned his forehead on hers, careful to spare her his full weight, and said, with his chest still heaving, "I love you, Sara."

I know, Sara thought. She'd known even before she heard the words because he'd already given her everything he was.

Max moved aside and gathered her close, wiping away the first tear with his fingertips. "You keep crying every time we make love, and I might think my technique needs work."

His voice held a teasing note, but she could see in his eyes that he needed some reassurance from her. She threaded her fingers into his hair, rubbing her thumb across his cheek. "You did everything exactly right, Max. Absolutely everything."

He closed his eyes, exhaling in relief.

"And as for your technique…" She pulled him back down to her. "Maybe I can give you some pointers."

"When you put it like that," he said after a kiss that began with exquisite tenderness and ended with a sizzle, "all I can say is you're the teacher."

IF ANYONE HAD TOLD MAX one of his own flannel shirts would acquire the ability to send him into paroxysms of lust, he'd have suggested hospitalization for the poor deluded soul, psychoanalysis at the very least. But when he walked in his own back door and saw Sara wearing the very flannel shirt he'd peeled her out of last night, he got a sudden flash of black silk and red lace. All he could think was that he had to get his hands on her. But somehow his feet got all tangled up; he took one step and went down on the second. Joey was just coming in behind him and tripped over his dad.

Max caught a muddy boot on the chin, but he was too busy sucking in air and trying to roll into a fetal position to notice, all thoughts of lace and silk destroyed by an eight-year-old's elbow. The next thing Max knew, Joey was gone and Sara was kneeling next to him, cool hands cupping his face.

"Max! Are you all right?" She yanked open his coat and ran her hands over his chest to check for broken ribs. "Where does it hurt? What can I do?"

Stop touching me, he wanted to say, but all he managed was a groan as his body tried to respond to her nearness in a valiant and manly way. "My ribs are fine. I'm fine."

"No, you're not."

He didn't blame her for not believing him, considering that he sounded like Joey did when he talked through the back of a running fan. She tried to resume her injury-finding explorations, but he fended off her hands, rolling away and sitting up in one quick movement that made his eyes cross with pain.

By the time the agony subsided enough for him to get to his feet and into a chair, Sara had her back to him, pulling platters from the warmer at the back of the stove. When she joined him there was barely enough room for their plates between platters of eggs and toast, hot cakes and sausage, syrup, butter, jelly, pitchers of orange juice and milk, and a carafe of coffee.

Joey dug in as if he hadn't eaten in a month. After three hours of chores on an empty stomach, Max could sympathize. He filled his plate, moaning in delight as the first bite of hot cakes melted on his tongue.

"It's been so long I almost forgot what a great cook you are," he said without glancing up. Food was a lot safer than flannel in mixed company. "I can't tell you how nice it is to have a hot breakfast on the table after chores."

A mutter that was obviously agreement came from Joey's side of the table.

"Don't talk with your mouth full," Max said from habit.

Joey made a big show of chewing and swallowing, then wiped his face with his napkin. "Can I be excused?"

"Sure, as long as you're going upstairs to clean your room."

"Da-aa-aa-ad."

"That was our deal, kiddo. You keep your room clean or the sleepovers at Jason's stop."

Joey groaned, sliding reluctantly out of his chair.

"And don't come back down here till it's clean enough to pass inspection," Max warned.

He was about to remind Joey to clear his place, but Sara had already done it, piling the first load of dishes next to the sink as Joey went upstairs, dragging his feet the whole way.

When Sara came back to the table, Max grabbed her around the waist and pulled her onto his lap, kissing her until she relaxed against him and he was on the verge of completely forgetting where they were.

He pulled away, lifting her arm to lay it across the back of his neck and resting his cheek against her collarbone. "You don't know how hard it is to see you in that shirt and not touch you."

"You didn't have any trouble stopping a few minutes ago," she said, getting up from his lap.

Max could have kept her there, but something in her expression made him let her go.

"Joey was here," he pointed out. "It's not like you have to go back to town tonight. The roads are probably clear, but there's no school until Monday."

"I can't wear your clothes the rest of the weekend, Max."

"I'm not complaining. In fact, you can leave all your sweaters at Janey's—as long as you bring back all the things you wear underneath."

She stopped at the sink and turned to look at him. "I'm not moving back here, Max."

"Okay."

"You're not angry?"

"Your mind is made up—I finally get that, Sara, and you were right. You can't live here until after we're married."

She sort of sagged back against the counter, putting both hands on it as though she needed the support. "Are you asking me to marry you?"

"Yes." Max grinned so wide his cheeks hurt. "I'd be an idiot if I didn't realize how much I'd missed you, Sara. As soon as you're ready, I thought we could go to Plains City and have a nice, quiet wedding."

"Why Plains City?"

"It doesn't have to be there," Max said, feeling a stirring of unease in the pit of his stomach. "We'll get married anywhere you want."

"How about Erskine?"

"The whole town will expect to be invited."

"What's wrong with that?" she asked, turning to confront him.

"Nothing. I just didn't think you'd want all those people teasing and making comments."

"Maybe not, but I won't be married in a hush-hush ceremony somewhere like we're ashamed of how we feel about each other."

"I'm not ashamed, Sara, but I've been married before. I just don't feel the need for a big ceremony."

"Then we'll have a small one here in town, just a few of our friends and my family."

"Why don't we go to Las Vegas, or maybe Hawaii?" Max suggested, if only to block the horror of an Erskine wedding from his mind. "It'll be just the two of us, Sara. Tom Hartfield and I always trade chores, and I'm sure Jason would jump at the chance to have Joey stay over there for a few days."

"Now you don't even want Joey at our wedding?"

"Of course I want him there. I'm just trying to find a way to make us both happy. A compromise."

"Compromise!" Sara spun on her heel, pacing across the kitchen. "After all the concessions I've made because of your pigheaded, stubborn…" She threw up her hands, rounding on him. "And now *you're* willing to compromise?"

"You've made all the concessions! What about last night?"

Her eyes narrowed. "What about last night?"

"You wanted me to say I love you and I did…" Max trailed off as soon as he realized how that sounded, but it was too late. Her anger had drained away, but the hurt that took its place was even worse.

"So you only said that because I made you. Are you only asking me to marry you because you think that's what I want?"

"Of course not. I love you, Sara." He crossed the kitchen and tried to take her in his arms, but she wouldn't let him.

"Then why did I have to drag it out of you?"

"Because every time I tried to talk to you, you walked away before I could get it out."

"Say it, Max."

"Say what?"

"*Just like Julia.* Isn't that what you were thinking?"

Max wanted to deny it, but she was right. They both knew it. He had compared her with Julia, and not just when she walked away. Every time he thought about a relationship with a woman, any woman, the failure of his first marriage was there in the back of his mind, like a dark cloud that cast a shadow on everything—only he'd lived under that shadow for so long he'd stopped noticing it. Until Sara made the sun come out again.

"That's been the problem all along," she said, folding her arms over her chest and rubbing at her breastbone with the heel of one hand. "I've spent so much time trying to figure out what I was doing wrong, why you couldn't love me, and all the time it's been you, hasn't it? You don't trust me. No, it's deeper than that—you don't trust love."

It was Max's turn to pace, to try to outrun the mirror she was holding in front of his face. "I loved Julia," he said, but instead of shattering the reflection of what he'd allowed the past to do to him, those words only threw the image into stark, blinding clarity. Sara was almost right. He didn't trust love, but it went deeper than that. He didn't trust his own heart.

"I fell in love with Julia when we were both in the eighth grade," he said, glancing at Sara, then quickly away. In all the years he'd known her, he'd never really told her about his life with Julia, but he needed to now, for her own good. "She said she loved me, too, but how far did that get us?"

He pulled out a chair and sat down, suddenly tired. Instead of lifting the weight from his heart, confession seemed to resurrect the sadness and pain he'd refused to acknowledge all those years ago, made so much heavier this time by doubt and guilt. And fear. "I love you, Sara, and you love me, but we can't seem to go twenty-four hours without getting into an argument."

Sara shook her head, a bittersweet smile tilting up the corners of her mouth. "Loving someone doesn't guarantee a happy ending, Max. We're living proof of that. But I'm not happy this way, and neither are you. That's not your fault— at least not entirely. It's not like I've been the poster girl for taking chances. It took me six years to realize that living on the edge of your life was worse than the possibility that I'd have to let go completely.

"But I've come too far to go back to the way things were. I want it all, your friendship and your love, and I'm willing to risk everything to have what I want. But marrying you would be a mistake if you don't trust the strength of your love—and mine—to see us through the hard times."

She went to the coatrack and put on her coat and hat. "If you're ever willing to take a real chance on us," she said as she opened the door, "then you know where to find me."

"Until you leave town," he said, not caring that he sounded sulky.

"It's four months until the school year is over," she said, half turning to face him while she kept her hand on the doorknob. "If it takes you that long to make up your mind, it won't matter if I'm still in town or not."

Chapter Fifteen

"You spent the night out at Max's ranch?" Janey peeked over her shoulder, assuring herself that Jessie was tuned in to Saturday-morning cartoons on the television, then lowered her voice anyway, just in case SpongeBob SquarePants didn't hold her complete attention. "You slept with him again, didn't you?"

"Yes." Sara hunched farther down on the window seat, hugging her knees to her chest. She felt Janey sit on the other end of the cushion, but she kept her eyes trained out the window. A stiff wind blew last night's fresh snow into a whimsically sculpted landscape of curves and angles that blurred with each fresh gust, settling into new and different shapes that were just as quickly whipped away. Montana's version of the tide, she thought, and just as soothing. She could have watched it for hours, preferably in silence.

Unfortunately, ignoring Janey only made her more persistent. "So what are you doing here when there's so much weekend left to burn? And how come you don't look like a woman who's just had multiple orgasms? Not that I remember how that is," she said, sounding decidedly gloomy about it, "but Max doesn't strike me as a once-a-night kinda guy, especially considering the way he looks at you. I'd think you'd be a little more relaxed and a hell of a lot happier."

Sara sighed, resting her cheek on her drawn-up knees.

"That was definitely not an I've-just-spent-the-night-in-paradise kind of sigh. What happened?"

"If I tell you, will you go away?"

Janey shrugged. "Eventually I'll have to eat."

"I went out to the ranch last night," Sara said. "Max and I slept together, he told me he loves me, and we broke up. End of story."

"Whoa." Janey tapped her on the top of the head when she tried to go back to her snow-gazing. "That may be the *end* of the story, but if you don't come up with a whole lot more detail in the middle, there's going to be violence."

Sara just looked at her.

"Fine," Janey said, "then I'll call Max and get it out of him."

Sara jumped off the window seat and grabbed her by the shirt.

Janey kept going, dragging Sara behind her, sock feet sliding along the polished wood floor. "I outweigh you by at least twenty pounds that I'll admit to," she said, scooping up the phone, index finger poised. "Either you start talking or I start dialing."

"Fine." Sara let go of her shirt and dropped into a chair at the kitchen table. She'd known she would have to tell her best friend the truth. It might actually be good for her, too, but she didn't intend to go into any more detail than necessary. Living through it once was bad enough. "I went out to the ranch to talk to Joey last night. I was worried about him."

"I know that part," Janey said over the clatter of the fridge being opened and closed, a milk bottle being set on the counter next to the stove. "Is he okay at least?"

"I don't know. He seemed okay after we talked, but with me leaving again…" She shook her head. "I don't think this is going to do him much good."

Janey banged the can of cocoa in her hand onto the counter.

"You have to stop worrying about Joey, Sara—no, let me finish. He has a mother, and he has a father, and if he's lucky, he'll have you for a stepmother, but that's up to Max. What you need to think about now is what's right for you, not Max and not Joey."

"But Joey was so angry, Janey. He said he hated us."

"And don't think he didn't know what it would do to you to hear him say that." She shook her head. "You've spent as much time around kids as I have. You know what natural little manipulators they are."

Sara thought about that for a minute, replaying her conversation with Joey. "Jeez," she said, smacking herself on the forehead when she realized how he'd played her. "Joey told me Max loved me and I fell for it."

"Man, he's even better than I figured."

Sara shook her head, smiling reluctantly. She felt like a fool, but she had to give Joey credit. "I should've known what he was up to, but I wanted to believe it so badly that I just did, and then I confronted Max with it."

"And he denied it?"

"No, he admitted it."

"And you spent the night together. So what's all the upheaval about?"

Sara spread her hands. "Everything sort of fell apart this morning."

Janey slewed half around to glare at her, one hand on her hip, the other stirring the cocoa she'd concocted while they were talking. "Sara, look how long it's taken him to get this far. If you were expecting him to propose—"

"He did propose."

"What?" Janey cut the gas to the burner, all but wrenching the knob off. She stalked across the kitchen and slapped both hands on the table, glaring mad. "He said he loves you *and*

he asked you to marry him, and you're not celebrating? You'd
better have a damned good reason or you'll be getting a hard
time from everyone in town, starting with me. And don't give
me that confused, innocent look."

She straightened, retrieving two cups from the cupboard
and slamming them on the table. "The way my life is going,
I'll probably never get married. I've been living vicariously
through you for months. So has half the town, and we're all
expecting a wedding at the end of this. If we don't get one,
there's going to be hell to pay."

"Tell that to Max."

"Wait a minute, back up. It sounds like you're the one
who's putting a stop to the happy event." Janey brought the
hot chocolate over to the table and sat down, her eyes narrowing. "What did Max do?"

Sara poured out the cocoa, concentrating very hard on that
simple task as a way to hold some of the pain at bay while
she told her best friend about Max's suggested wedding plans.

"Hawaii I could almost go for, but Las Vegas?"

"Can you believe it? Why is it that men think there's anything the least bit romantic about Las Vegas?"

"Let's see, mostly naked showgirls, gambling, cheap food,"
Janey ticked off on her fingers. "Playing poker with a bunch
of guys while scantily clad women serve you free drinks.
What surprises me is that men live anywhere else."

"I said romantic."

"That's where the wife comes in—especially if she's still
on a honeymoon high."

"Not in my lifetime."

"I can understand why you'd be angry," Janey said, "but
why didn't you stick around and have it out with him, change
his mind?"

Sara had promised herself she'd stop sighing, but another

one slipped out before she could prevent it. "Everything was perfect last night. Joey and I got some things cleared up, we all had dinner—Max cooked and it was actually good. Joey fell asleep and before Max took him upstairs, he said he wanted to talk. It made more sense to talk at my house so we wouldn't wake Joey, but when I got there it smelled all musty so I lit some candles, and then all my winter pj's were here, so I was wearing one of my summer nighties—"

Janey smirked. "And you didn't plan any of that?"

"I can see how you'd be skeptical, but I was so worried about what Max was going to say that I really didn't think about anything else. It all just sort of…fell into place."

"I should be so lucky."

"Besides," Sara continued, "I wasn't slinking around in a negligee. I had on sweatpants and one of Max's flannel shirts that was there to be mended."

"Oh, yeah, men just hate it when a woman parades around in one of their shirts. And finding black silk underneath— don't give me that look, I go shopping with you. I know what kind of depraved taste you have in lingerie, although from what I hear, Max seems to like your taste. Half the town is staring at his backside when he walks by, and not because he has a cute butt. We're all wondering what's in his back pocket."

A man who was carrying around your underwear really ought to understand you better, Sara thought to herself and sighed again.

"Don't stop now, " Janey prompted. "You were just getting to the good part."

"Like I said, everything went fine last night."

"More than fine, judging by the color in your face. You know, since I'm getting all the bad news, the least you could do is give me the juicy details."

"No."

"C'mon, just tell me how long—"

"Janey!"

"I was just going to ask how long the candles were burning before you blew them out." The grin completely ruined her wide-eyed innocent act.

"We never did blow them out."

Janey whistled through her teeth and fanned herself. "So what happened this morning?"

Sara snorted. "He wouldn't even touch me with Joey in the room, let alone talk about anything important."

"And when Joey was gone Max sprung the travel plans on you and you left."

"Give me a little more credit than that. I didn't leave until I realized that it's not *me* he doesn't trust, it's himself. He's always waiting to be hurt again, and all the love in the world can't change that until he's ready to change it himself."

"If it was me," Janey muttered, "I'd marry him anyway."

"No, you wouldn't." Sara pushed her chair back, suddenly restless. "If he'd asked me a year ago, or even three months ago, I'd have been so ecstatic I never would have stopped to wonder if he was ready or not, but with everything that's happened…" She spread her hands. "He's had so many opportunities to tell me how he feels over the last few months, and he could never get the words out until I forced the issue."

"He didn't have to say it at all," Janey pointed out.

"No, he didn't," Sara said, remembering how he'd made such tender, incredible love to her that she couldn't doubt the strength of his feelings. "I believe Max loves me, but I can't marry him, knowing he's waiting for it all to fall apart. He'll always be holding a part of himself back from me, and I won't live like that."

"Yeah, living with me is so much more fun."

"If you can stand to have me around a little while," Sara said, swallowing her tears. "I'm hoping it won't be too long."

"And what are you going to do if Max doesn't get a clue?"

"I'll go on with my life." Sara took her cup to the sink and emptied it, watching the brown dregs trickle down the drain. Silence settled over the kitchen, broken only by the old cuckoo clock measuring out the seconds. The quiet space between each ticktock seemed impossibly long and empty. "Janey?" she said, as the reality of what she might be facing finally hit her.

Like the best of best friends, Janey answered the question Sara hadn't asked. "I'm not going anywhere."

Chapter Sixteen

When Max heard the knock at the back door, his first thought was Sara. She was always his first thought—except at night when she was his last thought. She didn't usually knock, but considering the way they left things the week before, she wouldn't walk in uninvited. And even though he tried to tell himself it wasn't Sara because it hurt too much to hope, he was through the house and had his hand on the doorknob before it registered that the face peering between the curtains covering the back window was Joey's, back from his sleepover with Jason Hartfield.

Unless Tom Hartfield had suddenly developed a penchant for cross-dressing, though, he wasn't the one who'd brought Joey home. Max could only see a woman's hand, where it rested on Joey's shoulder, but it wasn't Jason's mother, and it wasn't Sara, either. Not with those manicured, inch-long nails that looked as if they'd gotten their color directly from some poor soul's jugular. Sara kept her nails short and neat, and she rarely used anything but clear nail polish. And even if her skin hadn't been dusted with freckles, more often than not there was finger paint she hadn't quite gotten off at school.

And it definitely wasn't Sara's coat, trimmed with some sort of fur that didn't look fake. It looked expensive, just like the manicure, just like the pampered, smooth white skin.

Max wrenched open the door, then wondered why he was standing there, staring stupidly at his ex-wife when he'd already figured out it must be her. The disappointment he had no trouble understanding.

"Julia."

"Max." She stepped inside, her arm still around Joey's shoulders.

Max looked at Joey, who wouldn't meet his eyes, then back at Julia. "I thought you weren't coming until your movie was done shooting. May, wasn't it?"

"March," she corrected, "but you're right. I wasn't coming for a visit until after the wrap. However…" She looked down at their son, an expression on her face Max couldn't figure out until she said to Joey, "I'm sorry, but I'll have to tell him." She looked up at Max again. "Joey called me in the middle of the night."

Max forgot all about the fact that he couldn't remember Julia ever apologizing for anything. "You called her from the Hartfields' in the middle of the night?" he asked Joey.

"Don't be angry with him." Julia walked past Max, pausing to look around the kitchen, her expression less than enthusiastic. But then, she hadn't liked it six years ago, and not much had changed. "And if you're planning to be angry with me, I'd rather you save it for later. I traveled all night and all morning to get here, then I went straight to the Hartfields' to pick up Joey. I'm exhausted."

She headed out of the kitchen, removing her coat as she went. Her demeanor was brisk, all-business, a let's-get-this-situation-handled-and-get-back-to-our-own-separate-lives kind of attitude. Never mind that the "situation" was their son, whose world was falling apart for the second time in his short life.

"I'm not mad," Max said, Joey trailing along behind him

as he followed Julia into the large front room. "I just want somebody to tell me what's going on."

Julia looked at Joey. Joey looked at his father, then down at the floor. Max waited for one of them to answer his question, and when neither of them came through, he said to Julia, "Well?"

"Joey wants to know…" she began, uncharacteristically hesitant "…he called to ask—"

"I want to go live with Mom," Joey announced, his eyes meeting his father's.

Max stared at the defiance on his son's face, saw the determination in his eyes and still couldn't believe what he'd heard, even with those terrible words ringing in his ears. He slumped into a chair, stunned, sick, hurt. The only other time he'd felt this level of betrayal had been when he'd asked Sara to marry him, and instead she'd walked out of his life.

He rubbed his face. He'd always thought he was destined to be alone, had always felt alone, what with his determination never to marry again, and the certainty that Joey would grow up and move away someday. But suddenly he couldn't imagine the house without other people in it, without Joey and his friends and animals making noise. He still hadn't gotten used to Sara's being gone, and now this?

"Is that coffee I smell?" Julia asked. "I could really use a cup, Joey."

Max watched his son walk from the room before he moved his attention to his ex-wife. He'd forgotten how stunning she was: willowy, blond, with the purest skin, like fresh milk. She had all the beauty of a movie star, and as for talent, even before she'd headed for Hollywood it had been difficult to separate what was Julia and what was celluloid. Like the way she was looking at him now, soft green eyes filled with understanding and sympathy. If he didn't know better he'd think she really cared—that maybe, just maybe, there'd been more to the end of their marriage than Julia's drive for fame. Oh, he knew there were always two sides to any divorce, but this life had been good enough when she married him, right? He hadn't changed, so didn't that mean she had? Wasn't she the one who'd woken up one day and decided she couldn't live like this anymore?

Or maybe, like Sara, she'd been hoping he would change, Max realized. Maybe he had more to answer for than he'd ever allowed himself to admit. Blaming Julia all these years had allowed him to ignore his part of what had gone wrong in their marriage. And it had allowed him to repeat the same mistakes with Sara.

"Max? Did you hear me? What's going on here?"

He lost that promising train of thought, but at least he didn't have to answer Julia's question because Joey came back into the room just then, walking slowly, his eyes on the brimming cup of coffee in his hands.

Julia took the cup from him, sipped and made a face. "Your dad's coffee hasn't improved," she said to Joey. "I'll need cream and sugar. A lot of sugar." She watched him walk from the room, then said softly, "I miss him, Max. If it comes down to it, I'll take him with me."

"It's not quite that simple, Julia."

"It is that simple if he's truly unhappy."

"He hardly knows you."

She sucked in a breath. "He knows me well enough. He's spent time with me every summer and we talk on the phone at least once a month."

"Once a *month?*" Max thought of the illnesses, all minor thankfully, that he'd suffered through with Joey, the childhood scrapes, even the day-to-day tasks of clothing and feeding him that Max had handled while Julia was off having a glamorous life in Hollywood. And now she assumed she could just walk in and take Joey away with her? "I thought your career didn't have room for kids."

Julia went…not just quiet, although she didn't reply right away. But there was a stillness to her, a turning inward that made him think of the first seconds of hurt, when you just had to close yourself off and absorb it so you could breathe again. It was a side of Julia he'd never seen before, that vulnerability. Or maybe he'd forgotten it while he was busy blaming her for the way their marriage had ended.

"You want to hurt me," Julia said at last, "and maybe I deserve it, but I'm not the only one in pain. You sound so bitter." He tried to reply but she waved it off. "I didn't come here to fight with you.

"Six years ago we decided Joey would be better off here, Max. Both of us. He was so little and I didn't know where I was even going to stay when I left here. No, that's not entirely true. I could have taken him with me. Somehow I would have found a way to look after him, but I…I was selfish enough to know I'd never achieve my dream if I did."

"I would never have let you take him, Julia."

She glanced up from her tightly interlaced fingers, managing a slight smile. "I know that, but thank you for reminding me. The bottom line is, we both got what we wanted. You had Joey with you and I got my freedom. That doesn't mean I don't love him, and if he's no longer happy here, you can bet I'll do whatever it takes to make room in my life for him."

Max looked away from the determination on her face, tired of feeling angry and on edge, tired of having the life he'd always wanted and no one to share it with. Julia had left because she wasn't happy. So had Sara. And now Joey was unhappy. If that was the criterion for leaving, then he might as well pack up, too, Max thought sullenly. He started to say as much, but

Julia gave a slight shake of her head, her gaze going to the door leading from the kitchen.

Joey appeared again, cream and sugar in his hands, the handle of a spoon protruding from his mouth.

Julia laughed softly, thanking him as she took the cream-filled ceramic cow she'd bought when she and Max were first married, and the mismatched sugar bowl, and set them aside. She plucked the spoon from Joey's mouth and wrapped her arms around him, hugging him hard for a moment before she put him at arm's length again and studied his face with eyes that shone suspiciously. "Now what's this about you coming to live with me? I'd love it—" her voice cracked, but she had herself under control almost immediately. "But do you really want to leave your friends, all your animals? Who's going to take care of Spielberg?"

Joey shrugged.

"C'mon," she coaxed. "No, don't look at your dad. You tell me."

He stuffed his hands in his pockets, worrying at a ragged spot on the rug with the toe of his boot. When he ventured a glance, Julia crossed her arms and raised perfectly manicured eyebrows.

Joey looked down again. "I heard Dad and Sara talking—" his eyes flitted to his Dad again "—about you."

"About me?" Julia turned to Max.

He didn't say anything.

"Dad wanted Sara to move back to the ranch," Joey continued, "and when she said no…"

"Your father accused her of walking out on him," Julia finished, "just like I did."

"Sara said it," Max said, giving in to the urge to defend himself.

"And you weren't thinking it? Sara just decided to move out overnight? C'mon, Max, there was more to it than that."

Max lifted his eyes in silent appeal, but there was no intercession from the powers that be, no crack of thunder or horde of locusts. He saw no way out of this conversation—not without going through all the sorry details of the past three months. Julia would settle for nothing less. "Sara told me she was unhappy, that she needed time…"

"Sounds familiar," Julia said.

"Then her parents came for Thanksgiving—"

"And you were instantly convinced she was going to leave you, so you pulled away."

"And then she told me how she felt about me," he corrected, "and I, we…" He glanced at Joey and spread his hands.

"Sara told you she's in love with you," Julia said.

Max nodded.

"And you love her."

"C'mon, Dad," Joey said, "you told me you did on Christmas."

Max hunched his shoulders. "This isn't exactly the kind of conversation I want to have with my ex-wife and eight-year-old son," he muttered.

Julia snorted. "This isn't the kind of conversation you want to have with anyone, Max, including yourself, but you're not going to solve anything by ignoring Sara's feelings. Or yours."

"Fine," he bit out, giving a brief—and sanitized—rundown of what had gone wrong between him and Sara since Halloween, ending with, "I asked her to marry me and she—"

"She did walk out on you," Julia said. "Good for her."

"I might have known you'd take her side."

"What else could I do? She's holding out for what she wants, Max, which is more than I can say for myself."

Max saw the regret on her face when she looked over at Joey. For the first time since their divorce, he got an inkling of what it must have cost Julia to leave. He wasn't sure he wanted her to speak freely, but he figured he owed it to her. "Go do your chores, Joey."

Joey studied his parents, first one, then the other. Whatever he saw in their faces, he obviously decided it wasn't worth objecting. He headed out of the room, mumbling something about missing all the good stuff.

His parents shared a smile, but it was a short-lived one.

"If I'd done what Sara's doing," Julia said as soon as she heard the back door close, "we would never have gotten married in the first place, let alone divorced."

"We got divorced because you wanted a career."

"We got divorced because you kept a part of yourself closed off, Max, and whenever I tried to talk to you about it, you shut down more."

"You wanted things I couldn't give you, Julia."

"But Sara doesn't." She waited for him to deny it and when he didn't, she went on. "Look, Max, there were two of us in that marriage, and two of us in the divorce. But what you're doing to Sara—"

"You should stay out of that."

"Fine, but I won't stay silent when it comes to Joey. If you want to push Sara away, you'll have to live with that, but if you push Joey away, we all live with it."

"I'm not pushing Joey away."

"He's unhappy—"

"Because Sara left—"

Julia threw up her hands and got to her feet. "Here we go," she said, pacing across the room and back to confront him. "You tell yourself everything is fine, ignore all the signs until everything blows up. Then you wander around with a dazed expression on your face, wondering why this kind of thing always happens to you and blaming everyone else for it. Sara's been here for six years, and she doesn't even have a wedding ring on her finger. How much more faith do you expect her to have?"

"How come you're such an authority on what Sara wants?" Max asked. "You've never even met her."

"Everyone in town knows how she feels, Max. When's the last time you really looked at her?"

He didn't want to think of the last time. She'd been leaving then. But Max remembered the *first* time he'd really looked at her, really seen what she was feeling. When she'd told him she was in love with him, he'd gazed into her eyes and realized how hard it must have been for her to be on the fringes of his life when she wanted so much more. He saw now the courage it must have taken for her to speak, to know that in revealing her feelings she was risking the destruction of her hopes and dreams.

"I won't presume to tell you what to do about Sara," Julia said quietly. "But while I think you have a lot of admirable traits, Max, I won't let you turn Joey into a man who closes himself off from everyone because he's afraid of being hurt. He'll end up alone and miserable, just like you. Because you ultimately push away everyone who loves you."

Of course Joey came in just in time to hear that last bit. Julia held her arms out for a hug, but he squared off against his dad.

"Is that true? Did you push Sara away?"

"Joey—"

He turned around, and for a moment, the belligerent expression on his face gave way to uncertainty.

"It's all right," Julia said quickly. "Sara's been here and I haven't. I understand how you feel about her and so does your dad. He's trying—"

"He's not trying hard enough." Joey turned around to look at his dad again. "Mom left and now Sara's leaving, too."

"Joey—"

"I want to go with Mom. Nobody stays here because it's sad here, and I don't want to be sad anymore."

Max dropped his head into his hands. Julia was right. Their son was eight years old and already he was trying to run away from his problems. And it was his fault, Max knew. There wasn't anyone else he could blame this on.

"I think you should stay here and work things out with your dad," Julia said.

Max lifted his head and saw that she'd crouched down in front of Joey.

"If you leave with bad feelings, you'll regret it." She looked over his head at Max. "Trust me, I know."

"But, Mom—"

Julia got to her feet, half turning so Joey wouldn't see her wipe her cheeks. "I'll stay in town for a couple of days, and if you still want to go with me, we'll work it out." She sent one last look at Max so he'd know she meant exactly what she said, and then she was gone.

MAX SENT JOEY OFF to deal with the indoor animals and straighten his room while he made dinner. He knew it was hardly helping the situation, but he needed some time to organize his thoughts.

He could deal with all this, he kept telling himself, just as soon as he got past his feelings, compartmentalized them so he could think and reason. It didn't take him long to figure out what was wrong with that kind of logic.

Locking his feelings away was what had gotten him here in the first place. Blaming fate or bad luck for depriving him of everyone he'd loved was naive, believing he was always destined to be alone was foolish, and letting that belief color every relationship in his life was self-destructive.

He'd married Julia, but, just as she'd said, he'd held a part of himself back from her. She'd left him, that was true, but he saw now that, as terrible a time as it had been, there'd been a sense of relief as well. He'd always known she would go, and when she did, he didn't have to fight anymore, didn't have to work at something he'd always believed was doomed to failure anyway.

What he'd done to Sara was even worse, though. He'd let her take up residence in every part of his life, let her put down roots in the community and be, in all but name, Joey's mother. But the minute she asked for more than he was prepared to give, he put limits on their relationship that he knew she wouldn't accept. And when he feared he was really going to lose her, he'd even asked her to marry him—out of town, without their friends or even Joey in attendance, so that if she came back it would be on his terms, and if she didn't he could blame her for leaving. Even as he told himself he was making concessions to her, he'd done his best to drive her away.

And now he was doing the same to his own son. Even if Joey stayed, Max knew he'd be teaching him how to live just as lonely and unhappy a life as he was living, not because of fate or bad luck or someone else's failures. It was his fault, his choice that made it so.

"Joey," he called out at the top of his lungs, which, considering how quickly the kid appeared, was probably unnecessary.

"I'm not really hungry."

"Me neither," Max said, although he didn't regret the time spent. Cooking, he'd found, was an oddly calming thing to do. "Let's give it a try anyway, huh?"

Joey shrugged and slid into his seat at the table.

Max took his chair, put food on both their plates and figured there was no time like the present. "I'm sorry for…all this."

"It looks okay, Dad." Joey bent and stuck his nose over his plate. "Smells okay, too. I'm just not hungry."

Max laughed, glad to see a smile on Joey's face as well, even if it wouldn't last. "I'm not talking about dinner. I'm talking about Mom, you, Sara."

"Oh." And there went the smile. "What about Sara?"

"Well, I'm getting to that, but there's something I want to say to you first." Max laid his hands flat on the table, hoping to hell he could get this right; judging by his son's face, he was only going to get one shot at it. "I want you to stay here, Joey, but you have to understand that whether you stay with me or go to live with your mom, it won't make any difference to what happens between me and Sara—she'll decide to stay or go on her own, just like you will."

"But you *want* her to stay, right?"

"Yes, and I know what it will take to get her back, but…" He didn't want to think about it, let alone say it, but avoiding his feelings hadn't really spared him any pain. And it sure hadn't spared Joey. "Maybe she doesn't want to come back anymore. Maybe I've blown it with her completely. I don't know what's going to happen, but I don't want to lose you, too."

Joey mulled that over.

"I know I don't deserve a second chance, but I'd be grateful if you'd give me one."

"Okay, sure."

Hardly the rousing agreement he'd wanted, but Max took it. Now all he had to do was convince Sara to make the same deal.

"Dad?"

"Yeah."

"Do you think Mom will be hurt if I don't go to live with her?"

Max remembered the tears in Julia's eyes. "I think she'll be sad, Joey, but we could probably work it out so you could spend more time with her from now on, maybe a holiday or two."

"Really? Do you think that would be okay with her?"

"I think she'd like that. We'll go talk to her tomorrow and work it all out."

Joey picked up his fork and buried it in the mashed potatoes on his plate. "Dad?"

"Yeah."

"I don't really want to live anywhere else, at least not now, but when I'm older..."

"I know, Joey. When you grow up, you'll move away. That's how it should be, but I hope you'll always think of this as home."

Joey smiled and started to eat.

Max smiled, too, but he couldn't eat around the lump in his throat. It wasn't all right yet, not totally, but Joey had made his point in the only way he knew how. Max had promised to do his best to fix things, and Joey had no reason to distrust his father's word.

Sara did. He'd said he loved her, he'd asked her to marry him, but he hadn't really been ready to give her his heart, and after everything he'd put her through, it was going to take something bigger than mere words to win back her trust.

Max didn't have a clue what would do the trick, but there was one thing he did have. Hope.

Chapter Seventeen

A frigid wind rattled street signs, skittered around corners and whistled through every crevice in every eave on Main Street. It scoured the tops off the waist-high drifts lining the street, flinging snow against the sides of the buildings hard enough to peel paint and sting any patch of skin foolishly left exposed. It felt to Sara as if the skies hovered just overhead, heavy and gray, threatening to bury the world under an avalanche of snow.

She hunched inside her coat, trying not to equate the miserable climate with her miserable mood, but the day she'd broken up with Max, bad weather had crept through the mountain passes and stalled over Erskine.

As one day passed into one week and one week became two, the town seemed to hunker down into the landscape, like a homeless vagabond huddled with his back to the wind. Hardly anyone ventured out—in person or in spirit. Shutters were closed, shades drawn, miserly stripes of golden light leaking out from around them, hinting at the warmth being hoarded inside.

Even if she hadn't been on her way to school, Sara wouldn't have been tempted to go into any of the shops or stores she passed. She felt more like an outsider than when she'd first come to Erskine.

When Julia showed up out of the blue, news of it ran through town like wildfire, and Sara wasn't the only one who understood what it meant. She might as well make her airline reservations now; with proof of his past folly right under his nose, any hope she'd had that Max would risk his heart was gone. Everyone in town knew it as well as she did. Those who would even make eye contact anymore looked at her with such pity she couldn't bear to see it. In that sense, the weather was a blessing. It gave her a reason to keep her head down when she walked through town each morning on her way to school and each afternoon as she went home. She could've driven the half mile or so, but she refused to hide, even though it felt as if she was wearing a sign: Loser. Reject. Spinster. Any of them would do. Or all of them.

It had been two weeks since she'd all but challenged Max to vanquish his demons and come after her. Whenever she crossed paths with him, though, he moved to the other side of the street or turned around and headed in the opposite direction. The one time she'd gotten a good look at his face, there'd been no heat, no anger, nothing. His face had been blank, almost stiff, the face of a stranger—or a man who wanted to be one, at least where she was concerned. He couldn't have made his feelings any clearer if he'd taken out a full-page ad in the *Erskine Examiner*. It was officially over between them. There wouldn't even be a friendship anymore, let alone a marriage. She'd backed Max into a corner, challenged him to really deal with his feelings, and he'd turned tail and run.

In time the weather would blow over and so would her notoriety. Someone else would grab the town's attention; people would stop staring and whispering whenever she walked by. But her life would never be the same again.

Sara stopped at the corner, lifted her face out of her collar to check for cars, but all she saw was Max. And he saw her. His eyes locked on hers and even from a half block away she could see how haggard he looked. There were bags under his eyes and he hadn't shaved in at least two days.

They both stood there for what felt like forever, and then Max took a step forward. Toward her. It wasn't even a full step, really, more of a shifting of his feet, but it was enough to have her heart cartwheeling in her chest, her mind whirling with all the possibilities.

Someone called Max's name, and for a second reality snapped out of focus and she thought it had come from her, the deepest yearning of her soul given a voice of its own. Then Max half turned, sort of slow motion, and glanced behind him. Sara followed his line of sight and saw Tom Hartfield standing not far from him. She didn't know where he'd come from, but the scene jerked back to full-speed reality right then and she realized it had been Tom's voice she'd heard.

Max walked over and talked to him. They spoke too quietly for her to hear, but she could tell from the look on Tom's face that the conversation went from earnest to heated before he took Max by the arm and the two of them walked away.

Sara felt the sting of tears as she crossed the street. The edges of her vision began to blur and waver, but she could still see well enough to know there weren't any cars coming, just a bunch of faces peering at her out of store windows.

By the time she got to the bakery, the urge to cry was reduced to an occasional sniffle she blamed on the cold weather as she plucked a tissue from the box next to the cash register.

"Here's your order," Mr. Tilford, the town's baker, said, setting a big box on the counter and flipping back the top.

Inside were two dozen cupcakes she'd ordered for the Valentine's Day party at school, each one slathered in pink frosting and decorated with a variety of sayings, many of which substituted the word *love* with a little heart.

"They look great," Sara murmured, slipping off her gloves and fishing an envelope out of her bag.

"I noticed you didn't order one for yourself," Mr. Tilford said, "so I put an extra one in there for you."

Sara pulled the envelope back and reached for her wallet.

"No, it was my pleasure, Sara. I know things seem grim right now, but—"

"Earl," Mrs. Tilford called, poking her head out the doorway that led into the kitchen. Her face was bright red from the heat of the ovens, her mouth pursed as if she'd been testing the lemon filling for the doughnuts. "The deep fryer is on the blink again," she said, sending Sara one last glare before she disappeared.

"She never quite got over seeing her cat hanging from the top of the belltower," Mr. Tilford said with a shrug.

There didn't seem to be anything she could say to that, so Sara just set the envelope on the counter and shut the top of the bakery box.

As she turned to go, Mr. Tilford reached out and laid a hand on her arm. "Are you sure you don't want me to deliver them later?"

"No, I can handle it." There'd been a time, she thought as she walked back out into the frigid winter, that she wouldn't have dared carry a box of cupcakes around while Max was in the vicinity.

But after what she'd just been through, she knew she was strong enough to handle anything. She had to be.

"MISS LEWIS, can we have recess outside today?"

Sara started, realizing that once again she'd been staring out the window, lost in her own sorry musings. She swiveled

her chair around and found Jason Hartfield standing beside
her desk.

His brows were drawn down into a pleading expression and
he fidgeted from foot to foot. "Ple-e-e-ase?"

"We're having a party this afternoon, remember? It's Valentine's Day."

"Can't we go outside now?"

She almost said yes. The weather had been so atrocious
lately that the children had been cooped up, both at home and
at school, for most of the past two weeks. She would have
loved to take them outside for some fresh air and sunshine,
but Mrs. Erskine-Lippert was a stickler for schedules. "It's not
recess time yet," she said, then added by way of compensa-
tion, "I'm sure your mom will let you play outside after
school." It didn't seem to help much.

Jason sighed heavily, gave her one last hangdog look and
headed for his desk, feet dragging the whole way. "We can't
go outside because we got a party today," Sara heard him re-
port back to Joey.

Oddly enough, Joey didn't commiserate. He glanced up,
saw her watching and then glanced over at the bakery box sitting on top of a file cabinet, out of the reach of curious third-
graders. "I'll bet we get candy and stuff."

Mystery solved, Sara thought. Not much could compete
with Joey's stomach, not even the possibility of playing outside in the snow with his best friend.

But when Jason muttered, "Dumb old Valentine's Day," she
couldn't help agreeing with him.

The regular days were bad enough, but being single on yet
another Valentine's Day... That thought had her sighing and
staring absently again, wishing there was something she could
take for the pain lodged just behind her breastbone. But the
sorry fact was that time was the only cure, the sad truth that

it was going to take a lot more than two weeks for her to start getting on with her life. This morning had proved that beyond the shadow of a doubt.

One look at Max and her entire day was upended. She'd caught herself staring out the window every few minutes, her heart throbbing dully at the memory of how he'd turned around and walked away without a backward glance. Even when the weather finally began to break around noon, the patches of blue sky only reminded her of his eyes, the tattered remnants of clouds like the shadows she'd seen in his gaze. She'd put those shadows there with her ultimatum; an apology would make them go away. But then she'd always wonder what might have happened if she'd stuck to her convictions.

The door opened and she jumped again, spinning around to see Mrs. Erskine-Lippert standing just inside the room. Sara noticed that the principal was wearing her coat and boots, but that didn't seem very important next to the state of her classroom. She hadn't realized how high the noise level had gotten until the room fell quiet enough to hear Joey's stomach rumbling.

The principal gave him a look that even his digestive tract obeyed. "I've decided to take your class on a field trip," Mrs. Erskine-Lippert said. "The children have been indoors far too long."

"But…" Sara made a vague gesture toward the bakery box, the bottles of red soda pop and the gaily decorated "mailboxes" the children had made earlier in the week. "We're having a Valentine's Day party."

"We'll have the party in town. The sun has come out and it has warmed up at least fifteen degrees since this morning."

Which put the temperature at a toasty thirty degrees—before the windchill factor the weathermen were so fond of mentioning. Her students didn't seem to care about frostbite, though, or chapped lips or red, runny noses. At the principal's signal they raced out into the hallway to shimmy into snow pants and jam their feet into boots. Then came down-filled coats, mittens or gloves and heavy hand-knit caps with matching scarves. Erskine mothers took their winter wear seriously.

It was a wonder the children could get their backpacks on after all the bundling up, but amazingly quickly they were assembled into an orderly line. Mrs. Erskine-Lippert had them load their gift bags into their backpacks and gave the pop bottles to a couple of the larger boys to carry. She held out the bakery box, then frowned at Sara. "Why aren't you ready? The children are getting overheated."

"Let's leave the cupcakes here," Sara said while she threw on her coat and hat. "I'll wrap them up and send them home with the children later."

Mrs. Erskine-Lippert didn't say a word; she didn't have to. One jet-black eyebrow disappeared beneath her hairline and Sara gave in to the inevitable. She took the awkward box and followed her students out of the room and into an eerie silence. Her classroom sat in the middle of the long hallway, which meant they had to pass about half of the classrooms in the school before they got to the front door. Every one of them was empty. That didn't really surprise her; she wouldn't have noticed if the building had collapsed around her, as preoccupied as she'd been all day.

It did surprise her that the playground was completely unoccupied, as was the street leading into town. Shades were up in the houses they passed, but they felt uninhabited, dark windows seeming to stare at them like empty eye sockets.

The children began to run, spooked, she supposed, by the strange stillness. Mrs. Erskine-Lippert looked back at her, laden down with the unwieldy box, and broke into a surprisingly nimble trot. In seconds they had all disappeared around the last corner before Main Street, leaving her to straggle after them.

She breathed a sigh of relief when she rounded that final corner and saw the children joining a large crowd of people. It looked like everyone in town had turned out for the impromptu celebration, complete with a Valentine's Day banner that must have been strung across Main Street since she'd walked through town that morning. Her eyes were on the crowd, though, making sure all her students were present and accounted for. The principal might have arranged the field trip, but Sara was still responsible for her kids.

As she mentally ticked off the last couple of students against the class list in her head, she noticed that everyone was staring at her. Not exactly a unique event, but it was a little disconcerting to be stared at by everyone in town at the same time. And they were all so silent, probably still mad at her for turning down Max's proposal.

Just thinking of him made her heart heavy. She veered off toward the sidewalk in front of the Five-and-Dime. She didn't want to ruin anyone's mood, and anyway she wasn't there to have fun. Plus, it would be a good vantage point to keep an eye on her class—the fact that it let her stay on the outskirts of the crowd was strictly a bonus.

Before she got there, Joey appeared out of the crush of people and raced toward her.

"Just let me put this down," Sara said, bobbling the big pink box because he'd caught hold of her sleeve and was trying to drag her back out into the center of the street.

Joey refused to be sidetracked, saying, "You have to see the banner first."

She automatically glanced up, the objection she'd been about to voice lodging in her throat as she struggled to make sense of what she saw. "I Love You," the banner read in big, misshapen letters that looked like they'd been created by grade-school kids rather than the town's decorating committee, of which Max was…a member…

Her steps slowed. "I Love You," was an odd way to word a banner for a town celebration. She would have expected it to say, "Happy Valentine's Day," or maybe even "Be My Valentine," but "I Love You" sounded as if it was meant for a specific person….

Her feet had stopped moving but that didn't prevent her from jumping to a conclusion—one she was afraid to believe. And then the crowd parted and she saw Max, with Joey coming to stand by his side. Right above their heads was a shorter swatch of banner, hanging low enough to have been hidden by the crowd. There was one word blazoned across it in huge letters. *Sara.*

She read the whole thing, then read it again, but the words didn't waver and disappear like so many of the daydreams she'd had before. *I love you, Sara.* That was what it said— what Max was saying—in front of the entire town!

His huge, lopsided grin dimmed, fading into a frown when she didn't smile, or scream or laugh. Or faint.

He came over and took the bakery box, handing it off to someone she couldn't see for the tears in her eyes. She felt Max take her hand and she tried to talk, but there were those damned tears again, closing off her throat. She'd been waiting for this moment forever and when it finally came she was completely incapacitated.

"That's okay," he said as he tucked her hand in the crook of his arm and led her through the crowd. "You don't have to talk, Sara. Neither of us has to talk." He took her by the shoulders and turned her around to face the way he'd just brought her.

She dashed the heels of her hands across her eyes, her mouth dropping wide as she read the other side of the banner. She spun around to find Max down on one knee, the words she'd seen on the other side of the banner coming out of his mouth. "Sara Lewis, will you marry me?"

She looked at the ring he held up, a simple circle of gold set with diamonds, and felt her heart ache with love.

"They called it an anniversary band at the store," Max said, his mouth curved into the crooked smile she loved so much. "There are six stones, one for every year you should've been an official member of the family."

"Oh." Her hand crept up to cover her mouth as a fresh wave of tears spilled down her cheeks.

"Say yes," someone yelled out, others joining in until the entire crowd was chanting it.

"Say yes," Max echoed.

Sara opened her mouth, then closed it again, walking past Max and stopping a few feet away. When she looked back he was still kneeling in the snow, peering over his shoulder with a puzzled frown on his face. She beckoned him toward her with a wave of her mittened hand.

He snapped the ring box shut and stuffed it in his pocket as he got to his feet, making a huge production of brushing the snow off his knees. Apparently he didn't like being beckoned, any more than the townspeople liked being made to wait for their happy ending—or wonder if there'd even be one. Tough, was all Sara could think. She'd been waiting for this day a long time and she was going to make damn sure all that suffering was worth it.

"There are a couple of things we need to clear up," she said, once Max had sauntered over.

He scanned the crowd, once again silent and straining to hear their hushed conversation. "This isn't exactly the time—"

"This is the only time," Sara said. "Otherwise the answer will have to be no."

"You'd turn me down? In front of the whole town, after…after…" He threw his hands up in the air and started to walk away.

She caught his sleeve and he came to a halt with a heavy exhalation. "I don't know what you want from me anymore, Sara."

"I just want to know you're sure, Max."

"How can you doubt that?" he asked, looking up at the banner. "You wanted a declaration, I gave you a declaration."

"Why?"

So she was going to make him bare his heart. Deep down he'd known it would come to this, that the splashy proposal would only go so far in righting the wrongs he'd done them both. That she would need to know he understood what he was really offering her and, in understanding, embraced the risk.

"You were right, Sara," he said. "When Julia walked out of my life I stopped trusting my own feelings. I convinced myself for years that I didn't love you because I didn't want to lose your friendship. I guess I never believed I could have both, so I told myself I was happy the way things were. The truth is, I was scared to put my heart on the line, and when I proposed and you turned me down, I told myself I'd done everything I could. That you'd made your choice.

"Then Joey decided to go live with his mom—"

She turned immediately to find Joey, but Max brought her back around to face him.

"He's not—we worked all that out. And I know what you're thinking, but this isn't about Joey. It's about me. I pushed you away because I didn't want to risk my heart, but when I thought about living without you, really thought about it, I realized I was a lot more afraid of not having you in my life than of living every day with the possibility that something might go wrong."

He could have stopped there, but he wanted to get it all off his chest because she was right. They'd have to be honest with each other, and themselves, if they wanted their love to last. And he wasn't going to settle for less than a lifetime with Sara. "What I feel for you, Sara… If you go away there won't be any point in staying here because my heart will be wherever you are. So if you're leaving, you'd better buy three tickets, because you're not going anywhere without Joey and me."

"Oh, Max," she said, tears filling her soft brown eyes. "You're my home, you and Joey, and the ranch and this crazy town." She looked behind her, at the crowd of people who were willing to brave a cold Montana afternoon to make her dream come true— and have a front-row seat to any mayhem that might ensue. "I'm not sure I really want to admit this, but I belong here."

He took off his gloves and wiped at the tears streaming down her face. "Is that a yes?"

"It's a maybe," she said, holding him off when he tried to take her in his arms. "I know how hard it was for you to admit all of that to yourself, let alone say it out loud, but there's one other thing we have to settle. I mean…you're a private person, and, well, I do have a tendency to make a spectacle of myself. And damage personal property. And sometimes cause minor injuries to people and animals. I guess what I'm saying is, I can't guarantee I'll never embarrass you."

"And I can't promise not to cringe when you do," he said. "I'm not going to develop a sudden fondness for being the center of attention, but if the worst thing we ever have to face is a little embarrassment, I think I can handle it. I can handle anything, as long as we're together.

"So, how about it? Will you marry me?"

He flipped the ring box open and held it out to her, but she wasn't about to let herself get cheated out of the full-proposal scenario. She grabbed his free hand and led him back to the middle of the street. "Go on," she urged when all she got from him was a puzzled frown. "We're doing this right. You have to kneel again."

Max shrugged, but he dropped to one knee and held up the box again and said, very solemnly, "Sara Lewis, will you marry me?"

"Yes!" she said, and kissed him so hard Max wound up on his backside in the street, the slushy snow soaking into the seat of his pants, to the delight of the crowd.

He didn't care that everyone was laughing. He jumped to his feet and shoved the ring on her finger, then threw his arms around her. "You can't change your mind now," he said in her ear. "I've got witnesses."

"Neither can you," she replied, leaning back to look up at the banner. "I've got it in writing."

They both laughed and the crowd cheered in the background, calling for a kiss. Max was only too happy to oblige them this once, but just as he leaned in, sixty-five pounds of eight-year-old barreled into them.

"Congratulations, Dad and Mom!" Joey shouted, trying to stretch his arms around them both at once.

"Mom," Sara repeated, her heart lurching. She would have thought she was all cried out, but more tears brimmed over.

"Hey, why is she crying, Dad?" Joey asked. "You said if we made the banner she would be happy again."

"I am happy." Sara yanked a tissue from the supply she always kept in her coat pocket and mopped at her face. "You couldn't have come up with a more perfect way to propose, Max, considering it was the Open House banner that started this whole thing. But how—"

"Meet my secret weapon," Max said, smiling at someone over her shoulder.

Sara turned around just in time to be engulfed in a huge, hard hug from her best friend.

"Congratulations," Janey said, sniffling herself.

Sara pretended not to notice that her friend's eyes were misty, too. "So this is what my kids have been doing in art class for the last week."

Janey shrugged. "I guess I must have a romantic streak after all. But I want you to know, Sara, that I only suggested the banner after Max came to me."

"I wanted to do something big," he said, stepping forward to slide his arm around her waist. "I owed you something big." He squeezed her close. "I'm sorry it took me so long to figure it out."

"I'd say we put each other through a lot, Max."

"Not to mention this town," Janey added. "They were all in on it, you know. You can't imagine how hard it was for everyone to keep a secret for an entire week. Heck, Max had the most riding on it and he almost blew it this morning."

"So that's why Tom Hartfield dragged you in the opposite direction," Sara said. "And that's why no one would meet my eyes." She stepped around Janey and confronted the crowd, hands on hips. "You know what this means," she said in her best disappointed-teacher voice. She almost laughed when one or two people actually hung their heads. "It means you're all invited to the wedding."

"That includes us, I hope."

Sara heard it, but she couldn't quite believe it. She looked at Max, who was grinning like a fool, then turned around, and there were her parents.

"Max called us," her mom said as Sara went into her open arms. "He wanted to be sure it was okay with us."

Sara pulled back and searched both their faces, but she already knew the answer before her father gave it.

"Your happiness is all that matters to us, Sara."

None of them realized the crowd had been holding its collective breath until a ragged cheer rose up, and everyone surged forward. There were hugs and pats, kisses on the cheek and handshakes. They all streamed into the town hall, Sara and Max bringing up the rear. By the time they got their coats and boots off, the First Annual Erskine Valentine's Day/Engagement Party was in full swing, but when they exited the coatroom, the crowd split, leaving an aisle down the middle.

Mr. Tilford appeared at the end of it, wheeling a low table holding a large, square cake. On the cake it read, "Sara and Max." Underneath there was an arrow-pierced heart outlined in red frosting, and in the heart was written "Accidentally Yours."

Sara absolutely refused to cry again, but she did brave Mrs. Tilford's wrath by giving Mr. Tilford a big hug. "It's perfect," she said, laughing at the chagrin on Max's face.

"I was kind of hoping to put all that behind us," Max muttered, but he was smiling when he took the bottle of champagne the mayor handed him. He peeled off the gold foil and wrapped his hands around the ice-cold bottle, both thumbs prying at the plastic cork, which refused to cooperate.

"I hope you can open your own jars, Sara," a woman called out from the crowd.

"Maybe he's trying to save his strength for the wedding night," someone else said.

"That might not be a bad idea. If he can't get a little cork out of a bottle, she'll probably have to carry him over the threshold."

Max applied more pressure, eager to get the thing opened, but not to spare himself the laughter and commentary. He didn't really mind being the center of attention for once, as long as it got him Sara. But he had no intention of waiting for their wedding to get her in his arms again, to slip off her floaty black skirt and that sweater decorated with all sizes and shapes of hearts, to discover what kind of lingerie she was wearing—

The plastic cork shot across the room suddenly, champagne fizzing onto his shoes. He barely noticed as the cork hit the blade of an antique plow, pinging off to the right and up, then ricocheting off the edge of the wagon wheel chandelier. The crowd gasped as the cork whizzed past the American flag and thunked into the stained-glass window depicting Jim "Mountain Man" Erskine's rescue of the Indian maidens, which the mayor had finally had repaired after Sara's speech at the Ersk Inn.

It went deathly still, and everyone watched for the first crack to appear, waited for the glass to fall in chunks onto the empty street outside, wondered which pane would bite the dust and what interesting configuration might be left behind.

Thirty seconds crawled by, one minute, a minute and a half. Nothing happened.

"Well, it looks like the Max Devlin Pool is over," Max said into the silence.

Sara laughed, wrapping an arm around his waist. "I love you, Max," she said for his ears alone.

He kissed her long enough to have the room filled with whistles and hollers of appreciation. "I love you, too," he whispered in her ear.

She looked up at him, her eyes sparkling, that sweet smile he loved so much on her lips. "You know," she teased, "you're putting your heart into the hands of the town klutz."

"I trust you, Sara."

She pressed her hand over her mouth, touched beyond words.

"I've always trusted you. And I trust myself, too. It just took me a while to figure it out, so you'd better stick around and make sure I don't forget it."

Sara cradled his cheek in one hand and laid the other over his heart. "Just try to get rid of me now.

Welcome to the world of American Romance!
Turn the page for excerpts from our May 2005 titles.

THE RICH BOY by Leah Vale

HIS FAMILY by Muriel Jensen

THE SERGEANT'S BABY by Bonnie Gardner

HOMETOWN HONEY by Kara Lennox

We're sure you'll enjoy every one of these books!

The Rich Boy (#1065) is the fourth and final book in Leah Vale's popular series THE LOST MILLIONAIRES. The previous titles are *The Bad Boy, The Cowboy* and *The Marine*. In this book, you'll read about Alexander McCoy. He's just found out that the mighty McCoy family, one of the richest in the nation, has a skeleton in its closet. When reporter Madeline Monroe discovers the secret, she will do anything she can to prove that she's more than just a pretty face. This is a story about two people from very different walks of life, who both want to be loved for *who* they are—not *what* they are.

I, Marcus Malcolm McCoy, being of sound mind, yadda yadda yadda, do hereby acknowledge as my biological progeny the firstborn to Helen Metzger, Ann Branigan, Bonnie Larson and Nadine Anders et al, who were paid a million dollars each for their silence. Upon my death and subsequent reading of this addendum to my last will and testament, their children shall inherit equal portions of my estate and, excepting Helen's child, Alexander, who already has the privilege, shall immediately take their rightful places in the family and family business, whatever it may be at that time.
Marcus M. McCoy

Tuning out the chatter from the party going on the other side of the study's locked doors, Alexander McCoy slumped back in the big desk chair. Staring at the scrawled signature at the bottom of the hand-written page, he tugged loose his black tuxedo's traditional bow tie. If only he could tune out the burn of betrayal as easily.

For what seemed to be the hundredth time, he had to admit to himself that he was definitely looking at the signature of the man he'd spent his life believing to be his brother. The brother he'd initially admired, then set out to be as different from as possible. And only Marcus would have had the nerve to belittle legalities by actually writing *yadda, yadda, yadda,* especially on something as important as an addendum to his last will and testament.

Even if Alex could harbor any doubts, he would have had a hard time dismissing the word of David Weidman. The McCoys' longtime family lawyer had witnessed Marcus writing the addendum—though David claimed to have not read the document before sealing it in the heavy cream envelope that bore his signature and noting the existence of the unorthodox addendum in the actual will.

A will that had been read nearly a month ago. Four days after Marcus had been killed on June 8 while fly-fishing in Alaska by a grizzly bear that hadn't appreciated the competition. Before the reading of the will, Alex had grieved for the relationship he'd hoped to one day finally develop with his much older brother. Now...

Muriel Jensen's *His Family* (#1066) is the third book in her series THE ABBOTTS, about three brothers whose sister was kidnapped when she was fourteen months old. At the end of the second book, *His Wife*, we met China Grant, a woman who thought that she might have been that kidnapped daughter, but as it turns out, she's not. No one is happier about that than Campbell Abbott—who never believed she could be a relation.

Campbell Abbott put an arm around China Grant's shoulders and walked her away from the fairground's picnic table and into the trees. She was sobbing and he didn't know what to do. He wasn't good with women. Well, he was, but not when they were crying.

"I was so *sure!*" she said in a fractured voice.

He squeezed her shoulders. "I know. I'm sorry."

She sobbed, sniffed, then speculated. "I don't suppose DNA tests are ever wrong?"

"I'm certain that's possible," he replied, "but I'm also fairly certain they were particularly careful with this case. Everyone on Long Island is aware that the Abbotts' little girl was kidnapped as a toddler. That you might be her returned after twenty-five years had everyone hoping the test would be positive."

"Except you." She'd said it without rancor, and that surprised him. In the month since she'd turned up at Shepherd's Knoll, looking for her family, he'd done his best to make things difficult for her. In the beginning he'd simply doubted her claims, certain any enterprising young woman could buy a toddler's blue corduroy rompers at a used-clothing store and claim she was an Abbott Mills heiress because she had an outfit similar to what the child was wearing when she'd been taken. As he'd told his elder brothers repeatedly, Abbott Mills had made thousands, possibly millions, of those corduroy rompers.

Campbell had wanted her to submit to a DNA test then and there. If she was Abigail, he was her full sibling, and therefore would be a match.

But Chloe, his mother, had been in Paris at the time, caring for a sick aunt, and Killian, his eldest brother, hadn't wanted to upset her further. He'd suggested they wait until Chloe returned home.

Sawyer, his second brother, had agreed. Accustomed to being outvoted by them most of his life, Campbell had accepted his fate when Killian further suggested that China stay on to help Campbell manage the Abbotts' estate until Chloe came home. Killian was CEO of Abbott Mills, and Sawyer headed the Abbott Mills Foundation.

Killian and Sawyer were the products of their father's first marriage to a Texas oil heiress. Campbell and the missing Abigail were born to his second wife, Chloe, a former designer for Abbott Mills.

When Chloe had come back from Paris two weeks ago, the test had been taken immediately. The results had been couriered to the house that afternoon. China had been there alone while everyone else had been preparing for the hospital fund-raiser that had just taken place this afternoon and evening. She'd brought the sealed envelope with her and opened it just moments ago, when the family had been all together at the picnic table.

They'd all expected a very different result.

After spending most of her life as either an army brat or a military wife, Bonnie Gardner knows about men in uniform, and knows their wives, their girlfriends and their mothers. She's been all of them! In her latest book, *The Sergeant's Baby* (#1067), Air Force Technical Sergeant Danny Murphey is in for a big surprise—Allison Raneea Carter is pregnant. With more than a little past history together, Danny has to wonder—is the woman who refused to marry him because she wanted her independence carrying his child? Find out what it's going to take for her to change her mind about marrying him *this* time!

Danny Murphey lay quietly in bed in the darkened hotel room and listened to the soft, rhythmic breathing of the woman beside him. He reached over and caressed the velvety smooth, olive skin of her cheek and was rewarded with a sleepy smile and a soft moan of pleasure. It was music to him after two endless years apart.

He found it hard to believe, after so much time, but Allison Raneea Carter was really here, lying beside him, in this bed. She had responded to him—they had responded to each other as if they were designed to be the other's perfect match. It seemed almost as if the past two years had never happened.

Technical Sergeant Daniel Murphey had dedicated that time to emptying out the dating pools of Hurlburt Field, Eglin

Air Force Base, Fort Walton Beach and Okaloosa County, and had been ready to start working on the rest of northern Florida, when Allison had suddenly reappeared in his life.

He might have told his buddies back on Silver Team of Hurlburt Field's elite special operations combat control squadron that he liked playing the field, but he knew better. He had been trying to forget. Now that he and Allison had reconnected, Danny was ready to chuck it all and do the church and the little redbrick-house-and-white-picket-fence thing.

He'd been certain that he was ready to settle down two years ago, but Allison hadn't been. She'd wanted a career, and he, as a special ops combat control operator, could not envision his wife working. Men were supposed to provide for their families, and their wives were supposed to care for the home and their children. What better way to demonstrate his love than by wanting to provide for the woman he loved.

Allison hadn't seen it that way then, and it had caused a rift they had been unable to close.

They had never been able to compromise, and that one thing, for Allison, had been a deal breaker. She'd walked out on him, accepted a transfer and a promotion, and had not looked back.

Danny was sure that now, after two years apart, two years where he'd sown all the wild oats he'd wanted to and gained the reputation of ladies' man extraordinaire among the other members of his squadron, he and Allison would be able to compromise. He was okay with her working until the kids came along, and maybe when the kids were older and in school, she could go back. What woman wouldn't agree to that?

Allison shifted positions, giving Danny a tantalizing view of her ripe, full breasts. He could imagine his child, his son, suckling at her breasts, and the thought made his heart swell, as well as another part of his anatomy. He brushed a strand of her long, jet-black hair away from her face so he could gaze at her beauty. God, he could watch her all night and never be bored.

He'd always known that Allison was THE ONE. And this time, he was certain that she knew it, too.

As much as he wanted to wake her, to get down on bended knees right now to propose, he'd wait. He wanted everything to be perfect.

He'd ask her first thing in the morning.

This time he was going to do it right. And this time he was certain she'd say yes. "Allison Carter, I want you so much," Danny whispered into the darkness. "I know you're gonna give in and let me take care of you."

He leaned over and dropped a light kiss on her soft, full lips, then he lay back against the pillows and drifted off into contented sleep to dream of what would be.

But, when he woke up…he was alone.

With *Hometown Honey* (#1068), Kara Lennox launches a new three-book series called BLOND JUSTICE about three women who were duped by the same con man and vow to get even. But many things can get in the way of a woman's revenge, and for Cindy Lefler, it's a gorgeous sheriff's deputy named Luke Rheems—a man who's more than willing to help her get back on her feet again. Watch for the other books in the series, *Downtown Debutante* (coming September 2005) and *Out of Town Bride* (December 2005). We know you're going to love these fast-paced, humorous stories!

"Only twelve thousand biscuits left to bake," Cindy Lefler said cheerfully as she popped a baking sheet into the industrial oven at the Miracle Café. Though she loved the smell of fresh-baked biscuits, she had grown weary of the actual baking. One time, she'd tried to figure out how many biscuits she'd baked in her twenty-eight years. It had numbered well into the millions.

"I wish you'd stop counting them down," grumbled Tonya Dewhurst, who was folding silverware into paper napkins. She was the café's newest waitress, but Cindy had grown to depend on her very quickly. "You're the only one who's happy you're leaving."

"I'll come back to visit."

"You'll be too busy being Mrs. Dex Shalimar, lady of leisure," Tonya said dreamily. "You sure know how to pick husbands." Then she straightened. "Oh, gosh, I didn't mean that the way it sounded."

Cindy patted Tonya's shoulder. "It's okay, I know what you mean."

She still felt a pang over losing Jim, which was only natural, she told herself. The disagreement between her husband's truck and a freight train had happened only a year ago. But she *had* picked a good one when she'd married him. And she'd gotten just plain lucky finding Dex.

"It's almost six," Cindy said. "Would you unlock the front door and turn on the Open sign, please?" A couple of the other waitresses, Iris and Kate, had arrived and were going through their morning routines. Iris had worked at the café for more than twenty years, Kate almost as long.

Tonya smiled. "Sure. Um, Cindy, do you have a buyer for the café yet?"

"Dex says he has some serious nibbles."

"I just hope the new owner will let me bring Micton to work with me."

Cindy cringed every time she heard that name. Tonya had thought it was so cute, naming her baby with a combination of hers and her husband's names—Mick and Tonya. Micton. Yikes! It was the type of back-woods logic that made Cindy want to leave Cottonwood.

Customers were actually waiting in line when Tonya opened the door—farmers and ranchers, mostly, in jeans and overalls, Stetsons and gimme hats, here to get a hearty breakfast and exchange gossip. Cindy went to work on the Daily Specials chalkboard that was suspended high above the cash register.

"Morning, Ms. Cindy."

She very nearly fell off her stepladder. Still, she managed

to very pleasantly say, "Morning, Luke." The handsome sheriff's deputy always unnerved her. He showed up at 6:10, like clockwork, five days a week, and ordered the same thing—one biscuit with honey and black coffee. But every single time she saw him sitting there at the counter, that knowing grin on his face, she felt a flutter of surprise.

Kate rushed over from clearing a table to pour Luke his coffee and take his order. The woman was in her sixties at least, but Cindy could swear Kate blushed as she served Luke. He just had that effect on women, herself included. Even now, when she was engaged—hell, even when she'd been *married* to a man she'd loved fiercely—just looking at Luke made her pulse quicken and her face warm.

HARLEQUIN®

AMERICAN *Romance*®

THE ABBOTTS

A Dynasty in the Making

A series by
Muriel Jensen

The Abbotts of Losthampton, Long Island, first settled in New York back in the days of the *Mayflower*.

Now they're a power family, owning one of the largest business conglomerates in the country.

But…appearances can be deceiving.

HIS FAMILY
May 2005

Campbell Abbott should have been thrilled when his little sister, abducted at the age of fourteen months, returns to the Abbott family home. Instead, he finds her…annoying. After a DNA test proves she isn't his long-lost sister, he suddenly realizes where his prickly attitude toward her comes from—and admits he'll do anything to ensure she stays in his family now.

Read about the Abbotts:

HIS BABY (May 2004)
HIS WIFE (August 2004)
HIS FAMILY (May 2005)
HIS WEDDING (September 2005)

Available wherever Harlequin books are sold.

If you enjoyed what you just read,
then we've got an offer you can't resist!

Take 2 bestselling love stories FREE!

Plus get a FREE surprise gift!

HARLEQUIN®

AMERICAN *Romance*®

THE LOST MILLIONAIRES

A new miniseries from

Leah Vale

The McCoys of Dependable, Missouri, have built
an astounding fortune and national reputation of
trustworthiness for their chain of general retail stores
with the corporate motto, "Don't Trust It If It's Not
The Real McCoy." Only problem is, the lone son and
heir to the corporate dynasty has never been trustworthy
where the ladies are concerned.

After he's killed by a grizzly bear while fly-fishing in Alaska
and his will is read, the truth comes out: Marcus McCoy
loved 'em and left 'em wherever he went. And now he's
acknowledging the offspring of his illicit liaisons!

THE BAD BOY (July 2004)
THE COWBOY (September 2004)
THE MARINE (March 2005)
THE RICH BOY (May 2005)

The only way to do the right thing and quell any
scandal that would destroy the McCoy empire is to
bring these lost millionaires into the fold....

Available wherever Harlequin Books are sold.